FRANCINE PASCAL'S
SWEET VALLEY High ®

JESSICA'S SECRET DIARY

Volume II

Private! Keep out! — Jessica

W9-CDZ-749

I just got off the phone with Todd Wilkins. At one point Elizabeth actually picked up! When she heard my voice on the line—thank goodness Todd wasn't talking!—she apologized and hung up, but I still almost had a stroke. I feel so guilty I want to die. But I'm aching to see Todd, and he really wants to visit—in SECRET! He'd stay in a motel, and we'd have to meet on the sly, and it would be horrible and wonderful and I just don't know what to do. I still love A.J. . . . don't I?

SWEET VALLEY High.

JESSICA'S SECRET DIARY

VOLUME II

Written by
Kate William

Created by
FRANCINE PASCAL

BANTAM BOOKS
NEW YORK · TORONTO · LONDON · SYDNEY · AUCKLAND

To Elaine Anastasi Pepple

RL 6, age 12 and up

JESSICA'S SECRET DIARY VOLUME II

A Bantam Book / August 1996

Sweet Valley High® is a registered trademark of Francine Pascal
Conceived by Francine Pascal
Produced by Daniel Weiss Associates, Inc.
33 West 17th Street
New York, NY 10011
Cover art by Bruce Emmett

All rights reserved.
Copyright © 1996 by Francine Pascal.
Cover art copyright © 1996 by Daniel Weiss Associates, Inc.
No part of this book may be reproduced or transmitted
in any form or by any means, electronic or mechanical,
including photocopying, recording, or by any information
storage and retrieval system, without permission in
writing from the publisher.
For information address: Bantam Books

If you purchased this book without a cover you should be aware
that this book is stolen property. It was reported as "unsold and
destroyed" to the publisher and neither the author nor the publisher has received any payment for this "stripped book."

ISBN: 0-553-57004-8

Published simultaneously in the United States and Canada

Bantam Books are published by Bantam Books, a division of Bantam
Doubleday Dell Publishing Group, Inc. Its trademark, consisting of the
words "Bantam Books" and the portrayal of a rooster, is Registered in
U.S. Patent and Trademark Office and in other countries. Marca
Registrada. Bantam Books, 1540 Broadway, New York, New York 10036.

PRINTED IN THE UNITED STATES OF AMERICA

OPM   0 9 8 7 6 5 4 3 2 1

Prologue

"Which should I wear to Amy's party tonight?" Lila Fowler asked me, holding up first a tiny black dress and then an equally tiny red one.

Lila and I had just spent the afternoon prowling through our favorite boutiques at the Sweet Valley Mall, checking out the new shipments from Europe and hunting for special bargains. Well, *I* was hunting for bargains. Lila's father makes like a trillion dollars a year in the computer chip industry. He's one of the richest men in California, and Lila's his only child and he spoils her rotten. And I mean *rotten*—she has a walletful of her own credit cards that she charges to the limit every month. It's sickening, really. Take today, for example. She left the mall with two humongous shopping bags stuffed with dresses, shoes, makeup, and lingerie, all of which was now spread out on my bed, while I bought one measly skirt, on sale, naturally. Where's the justice on this earth?

I'd momentarily tuned her out, so Lila repeated her question as if it was the most burning issue in the history of civilization. "Black or red, Jess? Give me some help here!"

She held up the black dress again, and I squinted critically. "To be honest, Li, it's not your color. Your hair sort of blends into it and you look like one big dark blob. It would look great on me, though!"

I reached playfully for the dress. Lila snatched it away, tossing her long wavy brown hair. "Nice try, Wakefield," she said dryly. "Black looks totally hot on me—you're just jealous because you'll show up wearing something we've all seen ninety-seven times before."

"You know very well it doesn't *matter* what I wear," I countered. "I could wrap myself in a plastic garbage bag and still be gorgeous. Hmm." I tapped my index finger on my cheek, pretending to consider the possibilities. "A plastic bag. With the right belt and shoes . . ."

Lila giggled. I danced across the room to my stereo, planning to crank up the volume—my favorite song on the new Jamie Peters CD was playing. Just then we both heard something from the next room that made us prick up our ears. "Trouble in paradise for the perfect couple?" Lila wondered.

I turned off the stereo. The voices drifting through the bathroom that separates my room

2

from my twin sister's were pretty loud. "Liz and Todd," I confirmed. "Sounds like a major fight."

Eavesdropping isn't against the law in California, at least as far as I know. Not wanting to miss a word, Lila and I tiptoed into the bathroom and put our ears close to the door of Elizabeth's room.

This might be a good time to tell you a little about me and my sister. We're sixteen, and we're identical twins, and we live in Sweet Valley, a beautiful town on the beautiful Southern California coast between Los Angeles and Santa Barbara. One time the local paper profiled a bunch of kids at Sweet Valley High, and the reporter described me and Elizabeth as classic California dream girls. I won't argue with the description! We're both medium height and slim, with decent figures. What am I saying, *decent?* I have a *great* body— there's no point in denying it! Not that I can take any credit for my stunning good looks. I mean, I was born this way. I'm just lucky. But it's excellent!

As for the rest of me, I have long blond hair that looks almost white in the sun, blue-green eyes, and a dimple in my left cheek. Elizabeth is my mirror image. Which isn't to say that people can't tell us apart. I dress much more stylishly than Elizabeth does, and she usually doesn't bother with makeup. I wear my hair loose, and she prefers barrettes and ponytails. She's the one you'll find curled up in a chair with her nose in a book—I'm the one who's at the beach even when it's cloudy.

Her room is neat as a pin, and it revolves around her desk, where she does all her writing. My room looks like a tornado just hit it, and it revolves around my stereo, which I usually play as loud as possible. Elizabeth has a steady boyfriend—I like to play the field. We're as unalike in personality as any twins could possibly be!

We have a great family. My dad, Ned, is a lawyer, and my mom, Alice, has her own interior design firm. So I probably shouldn't have been whining a little while ago about how much money Lila has. My family's definitely comfortable. We have a really nice split-level stucco ranch house with a pool in the backyard, and my parents give me everything I need (though not always everything I want!). They're pretty cool parents in general. My mom's beautiful—blond and slender and young looking. Strangers always think she's Elizabeth's and my older sister. And Dad could be a movie star. He's tall, rugged, handsome—all my friends have crushes on him!

My friends also swoon over my eighteen-year-old brother, Steven. I'm so glad Elizabeth and I aren't the only kids in our family—it's great having a big brother. The best is when we get to visit Steven at Sweet Valley University, where he's a freshman, . . . and meet all his cute college friends! He takes us to parties, which is a blast, but he's pretty protective—he jumps on anybody who even *thinks* of offering us a beer. He's almost too mature

4

and serious that way, but in general he's cool. He really loves us and takes care of us. Not that I don't fight with him occasionally!

So, as I said, my sister is the one with the steady boyfriend, Todd Wilkins, a tall, good-looking junior at SVH and captain of the basketball team. They've been together forever, except when Todd's family moved to Vermont and Elizabeth started dating Jeffrey French. When Todd moved back to Sweet Valley, Elizabeth broke up with Jeffrey and started seeing Todd again. I'd always thought they'd get married someday. But at the moment, from the sound of this fight, the wedding was off, at least temporarily.

"I can't believe you're getting so worked up about this," Elizabeth was saying.

"You don't think I should be a little upset about the fact that you're seeing your old boyfriend behind my back?" Todd shot back.

Lila and I exchanged wide-eyed glances. This was getting juicy!

"I'm not *seeing* him," Elizabeth protested. "Jeffrey and I went to a movie, that's all. It didn't mean anything!"

"If it didn't mean anything, then why didn't you tell me about it?" Todd asked. "The first thing I know about it, I'm running into the two of you outside the movie theater."

"It was on the spur of the moment," Elizabeth explained. "Jeffrey called me about the French assignment, and we started to talk about new movies

5

we want to see, and then we just decided to take a study break and go."

"When I talked to you yesterday, you were too busy studying to go to the Dairi Burger with me," Todd pointed out, his tone angry and hurt. "But you had time for Jeffrey."

"Why are you making such a big deal out of this?" Elizabeth demanded. "Jeffrey's my friend. I'm not going to apologize for that."

"Right on, Liz," I whispered. "You tell him what's what." Lila nudged me to hush.

"I'm not asking you to apologize," said Todd. "I just want to know why you picked him over me."

"I didn't!" Elizabeth cried. "Listen to yourself, Todd. You're making a huge scene about something completely innocent." Now she was the one who sounded hurt. "After all we've been through, I'd think you'd trust me a little more than that."

"I did trust you," Todd said hoarsely, "but that was before I found out your old boyfriend was calling and asking you out again. And it looks like he's getting plenty of encouragement!"

"I'll say this for the last time." Elizabeth's voice shook, and I could tell she was close to tears. "Jeffrey and I are *just friends*. All we did was go to a movie together."

"If you'll promise it won't happen again . . ."

There was a long pause. Tension crackled right through the door. Lila and I both waited breathlessly for Elizabeth's response.

"Promise *what* won't happen again?" she asked, her tone ominously cool.

"You and Jeffrey."

"You can't tell me not to spend time with him. He's one of my friends!" Elizabeth declared. "I'll talk to him all I want and I'll go to the movies with him all I want!"

"He's *not* just one of your friends, like Enid or Penny or Olivia," Todd argued. "He's your old boyfriend. You used to be in love with him!"

"Just because you and I are dating doesn't mean you can tell me who I can and can't spend time with," exclaimed Elizabeth.

"Then maybe we shouldn't be dating."

"Maybe we shouldn't!"

Footsteps thundered across my sister's room. Her door slammed. Someone stormed down the hall and downstairs. Another door slammed, shaking the whole house, and a moment later a car started in the driveway.

Lila and I watched out my window as Todd roared off in his black BMW. "Wow," murmured Lila.

"I've never heard them fight like that," I commented, shaking my head. "That was intense."

"You're not kidding," agreed Lila, gathering up her shopping bags. A gleeful smile curved her lips. "What excellent gossip. Mr. and Ms. Sweet Valley High just bit the dust and I'm the first to know! It's about time, wouldn't you say? They've been too happy for too long."

7

I helped Lila carry her loot out to her car, a lime green Triumph. As she drove off down Calico Drive, I headed back inside. Lila had a point—Elizabeth and Todd's perfect couple act was definitely nauseating. But unlike Lila, I couldn't see this latest development as just another bit of gossip—even if it *was* superjuicy. My sister's feelings were involved.

Upstairs, Elizabeth's door was closed. I knocked lightly. "Liz?"

There was no answer. I knocked again, and when she still didn't say anything, I turned the knob and pushed open the door.

My twin sister lay facedown on her bed, her hair a wild blond tangle. When she heard me enter the room, she sat up, hugging her pillow the way a man overboard would hug a life preserver. Tears spilled down her face. "Go away, Jess," she croaked.

Ignoring this suggestion, I sat down on the edge of her bed and put an arm around her shoulders. "It sounded like you and Todd had a fight," I said. "Is there anything I can do?"

Elizabeth shrugged off my arm, still sobbing. "I just want to be alone."

I leaned back on my elbows on the bed. "I won't budge until you tell me what happened," I said cheerfully. "You'll feel better if you talk about it."

"What's the point?" Elizabeth cried. "It's over between me and Todd. We'll never get past this."

"Don't be so sure," I replied. "I bet you just need time to cool off. Tomorrow things will look a lot better."

Elizabeth grabbed a handful of tissues from the box next to her bed and blotted her eyes. "What do *you* know?" she snapped.

"I have a little experience in this department," I reminded her. "If I were you, I'd just—"

"Maybe you've dated every guy in Sweet Valley, but you don't know anything about *real* love," Elizabeth interrupted, throwing the tissues on the floor. "So why don't you take your expert advice and get out of here!"

I stared at her, my cheeks flaming. She began sobbing brokenheartedly again, her face in her hands, but this time I didn't reach out to her. "Fine," I fumed. "If that's the way you feel about it!"

I stomped back into my own room, slamming the door behind me. *She didn't really mean it,* I told myself, tuning the radio to a hard-rock station and cranking the volume. *She's just upset.* But Elizabeth's words had cut deep. *What do* you *know about real love?*

"I know more than you think, Elizabeth," I said out loud. "A lot more."

I was drifting off to sleep that night, exhausted from hours of dancing at Amy's party, when the telephone rang. I fumbled for the phone, knocking a pile of fashion magazines off my night table. "Darn," I mumbled as I located the receiver. "Hello?"

"Jessica?" a deep male voice said.

"Yep," I replied, still groggy. "Who's this?"

9

"It's Todd."

He'd left three messages on the answering machine while Elizabeth and I were out earlier, and I knew she hadn't called him back. *Gotta give him an A for effort,* I thought. *Here comes the big apology.* "I'll get Liz," I told him, ready to drop the phone.

"Actually . . ." Todd cleared his throat. "I was calling to talk to you."

I sat up in bed, my eyes wide in the darkness. "Me? How come?"

"I was just thinking about—" He cut the sentence short. "Did you go to Amy's tonight?" he asked instead.

"I wouldn't miss one of her parties for the world."

"Was . . . Liz there?"

"Yes," I replied.

"Was Jeffrey there?"

"Yes, but Todd—"

"They were probably all over each other," said Todd, his voice gloomy.

"Not exactly," I assured him. "They danced together a few times, but she danced with Aaron and Bill and Bruce too."

Todd was silent for a long moment. When he spoke again, there was a new note in his voice. "Jessica . . . I need to talk to you."

I laughed. "This isn't talking?"

"In person."

"Well, I'll be at the beach tomorrow with Lila and Amy."

"I need to talk to you now. *Alone*."

For some reason I felt myself blush. "It's after midnight," I said weakly.

"I'm wide awake. You are, too, aren't you?"

I couldn't deny that my whole body was suddenly tingling with electricity. "Umm . . ."

"Can I come over?" Todd asked.

I opened my mouth to say no. This wasn't a good idea, and we both knew it. Instead of saying no, though, I heard myself whisper, "OK. But be really, really quiet."

The moment I hung up the phone, I started having second thoughts. I shouldn't have said yes. What if Elizabeth found out? *I'm doing it for her,* I tried to tell myself. *I'll talk some sense into Todd and help the two of them patch things up.* But deep inside, I knew that wasn't the real reason I was letting Todd come over in the middle of the night.

My heart pounding, I crossed the room and stood in front of the full-length mirror on my closet door. I could see my reflection in the moonlight—my eyes were luminous, their expression a little bit wild.

I continued to study my reflection. As usual I'd worn nothing but a football jersey to bed, and it was definitely on the short side. I was about to pull on a pair of shorts and a sweatshirt when I stopped myself. On the one hand, Todd Wilkins had been dating my sister forever and was almost like a brother to me. On the other hand . . .

I stripped off the football jersey and rummaged in my dresser for the silk nightgown my cousin Kelly gave me last Christmas. The nightgown was pale blue and flimsy, with delicate spaghetti straps and lots of lace. I'd never actually worn it, but now, as the cool, sensuous fabric touched my bare skin, I shivered pleasurably. I threw on my bathrobe, leaving it unbelted, and then fluffed my hair with my fingers. I looked sleepy, but sexy.

All around me the house was dark and quiet. Stepping into the bathroom, I checked Elizabeth's door. No light showed around the edges, so I felt safe easing it open. Sure enough, she was sound asleep— maybe she hadn't even heard the phone ring. I closed the door again and returned to my room.

At the window I pushed the curtain aside and peered out at the empty street. For a few minutes I watched, my pulse racing with anticipation. *Maybe he changed his mind,* I thought as I waited for his car to appear.

Then I saw the sweep of headlights turning onto Calico Drive. The car parked halfway down the block, in the shadows between two streetlights. The driver got out and walked quickly down the sidewalk toward my house. As he drew nearer I could tell who it was. Todd.

He cut across the lawn, swift and silent, stopping directly beneath my window. I pushed up the screen and for a long, supercharged moment we just stared at each other. Then he began

12

climbing the trellis on the side of the house.

I held my breath, praying our golden retriever, Prince Albert, wouldn't start barking and wake up the whole family. How would I talk my way out of this one? But Todd made it to the top without a hitch. Grasping the windowsill, he swung one long leg over and jumped lightly into my bedroom.

Our eyes met, and suddenly the situation struck me as hilarious. I clapped my hand over my mouth to keep from laughing, and Todd grinned. "What's the joke, Wakefield?" he whispered.

I shook my head. "I got all dressed up for this," I whispered back, gesturing to my fancy nightgown. "Can you believe it?"

Todd looked me up and down, his eyes shining. "You look gorgeous."

I dropped my eyes. "Yeah, well . . ."

I stepped away from him, suddenly unsure of myself. Sitting down on the edge of my bed, I crossed my arms primly. I wanted him to keep his distance—it seemed safer that way—but since my desk chair was buried by a pile of clothes, there was no place for him to sit but right on the bed next to me.

For a couple of minutes neither of us spoke. Then Todd said, "It looks like Elizabeth and I are through."

I nodded. It *did* look that way.

"The fight we had this afternoon . . ." He sighed. "It didn't come out of nowhere. We've been disagreeing about everything lately. Has she said anything about it?"

I shook my head.

"I don't know whose fault it is," he went on. "Both of ours, I guess. I never thought we'd drift apart like this."

"I'm sorry," I mumbled, not because I really was, but because it seemed like the right thing to say.

Todd looked me straight in the eye. "Are you?" he asked quietly.

I blushed. Was I that transparent?

"Because maybe it's for the best." Todd put a hand on my arm. "Jess, do you remember . . . ?"

He didn't need to finish the question. *Our secret,* I thought. No one else—especially not Elizabeth—not a soul, knew about the relationship Todd and I had once shared. "How could I forget?" I whispered.

"I've been thinking about it a lot lately," Todd confessed. "Thinking about you. And how different things might have been for us."

"It would have been impossible," I reminded him.

"Back then," he agreed. "But now . . ." He took my hand. "I'm free, Jess, and so are you. Will you give me a second chance?"

As I looked searchingly into Todd's warm brown eyes, a wave of remembered emotions cascaded over me. A second chance. Could we? Should we? My body trembled like the palm fronds outside my window.

Todd leaned forward, and I could smell the warm, spicy scent of his aftershave. His lips brushed

14

mine with a light, tantalizing kiss, a kiss that promised passion, devotion, and more. "Just think about it, Jess," he whispered.

He rose to his feet and crossed silently to the window. Then he was gone.

I sat on the bed for a long moment, my hands clenched tightly. I couldn't believe what had just happened. *Maybe I'm dreaming,* I thought. But the curtains billowed at my open window, and in the distance a car's engine started with a low rumble. I could still smell Todd's aftershave and hear his deep, husky voice. My lips tingled from his kiss.

I checked the clock on my night table: two A.M. I lay back on the bed and closed my eyes, but it didn't work—I was wide awake. *I'll never get back to sleep,* I realized, sitting up and reaching for the light switch.

With the lamp on and the moonlight chased away, it was hard to imagine Todd climbing into my room. But our conversation had been real—my head was still spinning from it. "A second chance," I whispered out loud to myself. What would that be like?

I climbed out of bed and padded over to my closet. Hidden at the bottom of a big cardboard box filled with keepsakes, I found a fat, slightly tattered spiral notebook, which I carried back to bed with me.

My journal.

.

I'm not sure what inspired me to start keeping a journal. Maybe it was Elizabeth's influence. She's a serious writer, with her own column in the school newspaper. *Her* diary is probably twenty volumes long by now, and she also writes poems and short stories. People would probably be surprised to discover that I like to write too. I'm not supposed to be reflective and poetic—I usually like more active things: cheerleading, the beach, shopping, parties, boys. But sometimes it feels really good to write things down in my journal. It helps me sort through stuff, figure out how I feel. I can be totally confused about something, but then I start writing and pretty soon I start to see problems more clearly.

Anyway, I hope no one—my twin sister in particular—ever finds this diary. It's not *all* top secret, of course, but some of it . . . ! Especially the stuff about Todd.

Back then, writing in my journal helped me deal with what was going on between me and Todd, I recalled, opening the notebook. *Maybe reading it now will help me decide what to do next.*

Part 1

Tuesday night

Dear Diary,
    I haven't written in here for a while because I've been too depressed about what happened to Regina Morrow. I still can't believe she's gone. There, see what I wrote? "Gone." It's really hard to face reality. She's not gone; she's dead. We'll never see her again—she won't grow up to go to college, get married, have a career and kids, be a grandparent. I mean, it's not like she was my best friend or anything. But Sweet Valley's a small town. Everyone knew Regina because she was so unusual and sweet and beautiful, and it was so incredible how she was born partially deaf but

17

then went to Switzerland for an operation that restored her hearing.

Anyway, I'm not sure what kind of lesson to learn from Regina's death. "Say no to drugs," that's one. She tried cocaine at Molly Hecht's party and her body had a rare reaction. It sent her into cardiac arrest, and when the ambulance came, they couldn't revive her. But she wouldn't have been at the party with Justin Belson in the first place if she hadn't been totally bummed because Bruce Patman blew her off to go out with Amy Sutton. I'm not sure why Regina was so wild about Bruce, but she was. Maybe because he actually acted like a nice guy when he was around her. For a while, anyway. It was inevitable that at some point he'd revert to his true arrogant, impossible self. He usually dates a bunch of girls at once because he thinks it's a crime not to spread his charms around. Blech! Poor Regina. Was she trying to prove something to Bruce by going to that party and doing drugs? The idiotic things people do when they're in love! I hope I never get that crazy. Heavy-duty romance just gets people into trouble, if you ask me.

So, understandably, things have been pretty grim at Sweet Valley High. But I think we're all ready to get on with living.

Which is what Regina would want—she was so fun loving and vibrant, she'd hate to have us mope and mourn. To that end, I've come up with a brilliant plan to create a little intrigue and excitement. A surprise birthday party for Lila! Of course, Li's expecting a surprise party, so this will require tons of scheming, but I'm sure I'm up to the challenge. . . .

Lunch is definitely the high point of the day at Sweet Valley High. We all look forward to that hour in the cafeteria more than anything. I've often thought it would be fun if it was the opposite, and we had lunch all day long with just an hour of class in the middle—that would be my kind of school!

Not that eating is the primary activity during lunch period. The cafeteria is an excellent place to see and be seen. For prime visibility we cheerleaders—I'm cocaptain of the varsity squad—prefer the big table by the window. But sometimes I sit with the football players, and sometimes if I'm in a *really* charitable mood, I'll even sit with my sister and her nerdy newspaper friends.

On this day Lila and I had decided to work on our tans during lunch period. We were lying out in the grassy courtyard with our heads pillowed on our book bags, faces to the sun. Elizabeth had joined us and was sitting in the shade a few yards away with her back against a tree trunk, scribbling on the legal pad that rested against her knee.

"It can't really be true what they say," Lila murmured, stretching her body luxuriously. "All that skin cancer stuff. I simply refuse to believe something that feels this good can be bad for me."

"You'll believe it in thirty years when your face is as wrinkled as a prune," I told her, reaching into my bag for a tube of suntan lotion.

Lila shrugged. "Why do you think they invented plastic surgery?"

It was a valid point. I'm sure someday Lila will be known as the Plastic Surgery Queen of Southern California. In the meantime she's absolutely right about one thing: lying in the sun feels great, and a suntan is sexy too. My skin is golden brown all year long because the weather in Sweet Valley is always warm and beautiful and I spend as much time as possible outdoors.

"Did I tell you my dad's in Italy on business?" Lila asked.

"Umm," I mumbled.

"Well, he'll be home in a few days. And he's promised to bring me a planeload of clothes from Milan. The hottest new fashions—he goes straight to the designers and basically takes the dresses right off the models. I'll be wearing things that aren't even in the stores yet!"

I yawned. "So what's new? George *always* buys you stuff when he's in Europe."

"Yeah, but this is a special occasion." Lila flashed me a brilliant smile. "It's my birthday a week from Saturday, remember?"

I yawned again, not commenting. Lila's smile turned upside down into a scowl. "Did you hear me, Wakefield?"

"Yeah, sure. Your birthday."

"You don't sound very excited," Lila remarked, piqued.

"It's not like it's a national holiday," I pointed out.

"Well, it should be," said Lila. "*Someone* could make it really special for me, you know."

The hint couldn't have been much broader, but I played dumb. "Like who?" I wondered.

Lila sniffed. "Like my best friend. That's you, and it's a pretty enormous honor. And with honor comes responsibility."

"Responsibility for what?"

"My birthday party."

"You're giving yourself a birthday party?"

"I'm not giving the party," Lila spluttered. "My *friends* are supposed to—"

"That's a great idea," I cut in. "Throwing your own birthday party. Your servants'll take care of everything, and that way the rest of us won't have to do any work."

"Heaven forbid you should break a sweat over something as insignificant as your best friend's birthday," Lila snapped. She hopped to her feet,

21

still glaring at me. "I think I've had enough sun. See you later."

As she stomped off I bit my lip to keep from laughing. Over by the tree Elizabeth looked up from what she was writing. "I didn't think Lila Fowler had feelings, but she seemed really hurt that you didn't offer to give a party for her," my sister observed.

I sat up, hugging my knees and grinning. "Good. She fell for it, then."

"Fell for what?"

"My I-couldn't-care-less act. I *am* going to give her a party, but I want it to be a genuine surprise," I explained. "So it'll be on Sunday instead of Saturday. The day *after* her birthday."

Elizabeth shook her head. "You really think you can pull it off?"

"Sure," I said breezily. "And Lila will be even happier about the party because I'll make her so miserable in the meantime pretending I don't care about her birthday."

Elizabeth groaned. "Lucky Lila. With a friend like you, who needs enemies?"

I smiled. "Exactly!"

Wednesday afternoon

Lila was pretty ticked off at lunch today. I have to admit it's kind of fun to have an excuse to give her a hard time.

*She's played some pretty mean tricks on
me in the past. Like the time she talked me
into getting a bad haircut, telling me it was
the latest look when really she just wanted
me to be hideous so she'd look better in
contrast. And practically every time a guy
at school gets interested in me, she tries to
steal him away. (Not that I don't do the
same when Lila meets somebody!) I'll prove
once and for all that Jessica Wakefield is the
true mistress of deceit. I'll also prove that
I'm the best friend she could ever hope to
have. This will be a birthday she'll remember forever.*

*And Lila deserves that, you know? She's
so spoiled and bratty, I sometimes forget
how lonely she is inside. It must be really
hard not having a mother—Lila's mom ran
off when Lila was a little girl, and now she
lives somewhere in Europe and Lila never
sees her or hears from her. I'd be lost without my mom. We don't always see eye to
eye—about curfew, for example!—but she's
always there for me. She's the backbone of
our family, my hero, my role model. Lila
pretends that everything's fine, that she's
totally mature and independent and way
too cool to need nurturing, but sometimes
when she's over at my house, I catch her
looking at my mother with this kind of*

wistful expression on her face. Her dad showers her with money and gifts, but all the clothes in Italy can't make up for not having a mother. Love isn't for sale.

Excuse me for getting so philosophical for a minute there! The important thing is, Lila's surprise birthday party is going to be awesome.

Thursday afternoon

As usual, Diary, I have incredible gossip practically before it happens. Sandra Bacon from the cheerleading squad finally has a boyfriend! Manuel Lopez is in our class and he runs track, and after practice today I caught the two of them behind the bleachers in a major clinch. Can you believe this is the first guy Sandy's ever gone out with? I mean, I don't think she'd ever even been kissed! How a girl could reach age sixteen without once falling in love is beyond me, but she's finally catching up with the rest of us. And I've got to admire her taste—Manuel is hot. Great bod, gorgeous curly hair, sexy dark eyes. What I can't figure out is why Sandy's trying to keep her relationship with Manuel a secret. That won't be easy when there are people like me around!

Thursday night

Dear Diary,
Normally I'd never write in you twice in one day. Unlike Elizabeth, my journal isn't my life—doing things is more fun than writing about them! But I'm bursting with excitement about Lila's surprise party. It's shaping up even better than I expected— it'll definitely be the social event of the season. I just hope Li doesn't have a heart attack when she walks in and realizes that her friends do care about her after all. We're faking her out pretty bad. . . .

Amy Sutton and Cara Walker met me at the Valley Mall after dinner. Amy wanted to go to the record store and buy some new CDs, but our first stop as usual was Casey's Ice Cream Parlor.

Cara studied the list of flavors, a tormented look on her face. "I know I should get nonfat frozen yogurt," she said, "but I'm dying for a hot fudge sundae."

"Have the sundae—Steven likes you curvy," I teased. Cara goes out with my older brother.

Cara stuck out her tongue at me. "I'll have a double-dip mocha chip cone," she told the kid behind the counter. "No, better make that a single dip," she amended with a sigh.

When we had gotten our ice cream, we sat down at a wrought-iron table and I whipped a sheet of paper out of my purse. "Here's the list of people I want to invite to Lila's surprise party," I announced, tearing the page into thirds. "If we split up the phone calls, it won't take long at all."

Amy and Cara pocketed their parts of the list. "So the party's a week from Saturday?" asked Cara.

I shook my head. "No, *Sunday,* the day *after* her birthday. We have to tell everyone to pretend to be incredibly bored and disinterested by the topic of Lila's birthday, which she's bound to bring up every five minutes. We also need to come up with something else to do on Saturday so we can say we have other plans and can't be with her."

Amy's gray eyes twinkled. "Boy, will she be steamed!"

Cara frowned. "I don't know. It sounds kind of mean. Why can't we have the party on Saturday?"

"Because that's what she expects," I reasoned. "I want her to go to sleep on her birthday thinking we totally blew her off. That way the party will come as a complete shock. And no gifts until Sunday, too."

Cara licked her ice cream cone, still looking dubious, but Amy was on my wavelength. "We don't have a choice," Amy agreed, tossing her silky blond hair for emphasis. "We have to go to extremes because she's used to getting everything she wants even before she knows she wants it."

"Sometimes you have to be cruel to be kind," I concluded.

Finally Cara nodded. "Well, OK. I guess in this case the end justifies the means. But if this backfires and Lila ends up hating us, don't blame me."

"I've thought it all through and it won't backfire," I said smugly, polishing off my ice cream. "Not in a million years."

Monday evening

Mission accomplished. Well, almost. Everyone's invited to the surprise party, Amy's making an excellent dance tape, and Cara and Elizabeth are going to help me with the food and decorations. I still don't know what I'm going to buy her—she already has everything a girl could possibly want—but I'm sure I'll think of something. Now we just have to keep Lila from getting wind of any of this. So far my scheme is working. She's about to lose her mind—we've really got her convinced we're not planning anything for her. . . .

"Good, now you're all here," Lila said briskly as I deposited my tray on the table in the cafeteria. Amy, Sandy, Cara, and Jean West were already eating their lunches. "I just want to find out what's really going on Saturday night so I can tell my dad. He wants to take me out to dinner at Jacques'

Bistro in San Mirabel," Lila explained, "but I told him you guys were doing something for me, so maybe he should take me out for lunch instead."

"Doing something for you? Why?" asked Amy, her expression innocently perplexed. I stifled a giggle.

"Because it's my birthday!" Lila shrieked. "Jeez, how many times do I have to remind you? Your brain must be made out of mesh!"

Amy shrugged. "Sorry, Li. I guess I don't see why you want anyone to make a fuss. I mean, we're not eight years old anymore. Birthdays are for little kids."

"Not true," Lila argued, pushing her lower lip out in a pout. "You don't have to be a kid to want a birthday party."

"A party?" I echoed. "You weren't expecting a *party*, were you? We were thinking about maybe taking you out for pizza. And it'll have to be Sunday."

"*Pizza?*" exclaimed Lila, stunned. "*Sunday?* You're joking!"

"Nope," Amy replied. "Steven's getting tickets for a concert at Westwood Stadium on Saturday. The Boys, that hot new British rock band. Right, Cara?"

We all turned to Cara, who twisted the stem off her apple, looking distinctly unhappy. "Well, he was going to *try* to get tickets, but for all I know it won't work out and—"

"He *did* get tickets," I interrupted, kicking Cara under the table. "He called last night and told me."

"A concert." Lila wrinkled her nose. "It could be fun to do that before the party, I suppose."

"But Li," I said, sounding surprised. "Steven only reserved four tickets, for him and Cara and me and Amy. We assumed you wouldn't want to go. You *hate* British rock!"

"But it's my birthday!" cried Lila. Her voice trembled slightly. "W-what about you?" she asked Sandy and Jean.

"Sorry, Li," Sandy answered. "I have a date."

"I'm going on a camping trip with my family," said Jean.

"Wait a minute." Lila grinned broadly. "This is a joke, right?"

I shook my head. "We really didn't think you'd want to go to Westwood, Li."

Lila stared at me for a full minute, obviously hoping I'd change my story. When I didn't, her face crumpled. "I can't believe you guys are going to a concert on my birthday and you didn't even invite me." She jumped to her feet, yanking the strap of her leather book bag over her shoulder. "I thought you were my best friends. I guess I thought wrong!"

I got a good look at her face before she flounced off with half the tables in the cafeteria gawking at her. I'd never seen Lila look so close to tears.

"Li, wait!" Cara called. Lila didn't turn back.

"Maybe we were too hard on her," Sandy worried.

"No way," I declared. "This is good for her. She won't take us for granted after this."

"We're really going to go through with it?" asked

29

Cara. "Go to the concert on Saturday without her—ruin her birthday on purpose?"

"You bet!" I replied.

Monday night

I've got an update on Sweet Valley High's newest couple. You know the gossip column Elizabeth writes for the Oracle, *"Eyes and Ears"? Well, she was going to include some stuff about Sandy and Manuel in this week's column, but when she mentioned it to Sandy—you know, thinking Sandy would get a kick out of it—Sandy practically fainted and begged Elizabeth to take that part out. Elizabeth told me Sandy's still trying to keep the relationship a secret from her parents. Apparently Mr. and Mrs. Bacon are incredibly snotty and Sandy's worried that they'd bum out because Manuel is Hispanic. Is that stupid or what? Manuel's family is absolutely the nicest, and he is a complete gentleman—thoughtful, responsible, sweet. Elizabeth remembers that Mr. Bacon once wrote a letter to the editor of the* Sweet Valley News, *though, complaining that Mexican immigrants were ruining our community. I guess if that's Sandy's parents' attitude, if they're just going to judge Manuel without even getting to know him, then I don't blame her for hiding him from them.*

Anyway, I spotted the not-so-happy couple in the Dairi Burger this afternoon. It's like Romeo and Juliet, the way they have to sneak around. They were having a pretty intense discussion, but despite my best efforts at eavesdropping (I walked by their table twenty times to put quarters in the jukebox), I couldn't hear a thing. I wonder what they were saying?

Tuesday night, late

Dear Diary,

You won't believe what happened today. My heart is still pounding like a hard-rock drum solo. Elizabeth went boating today after school at Secca Lake with Sandra and Manuel and the boat EXPLODED. Elizabeth could have been killed!!! When she told me what happened, my own life flashed before my eyes. I don't need to tell you what she means to me. Being twins is really freaky in a way—it's like we're one person split in half and walking around in two bodies. I mean, we have our share of differences and we fight like all sisters do, but inside there's this un-breakable bond that nothing could ever sever. Not even death, maybe. I can't even stand to think about it! Thank goodness she's OK. But that's not the end of the story—get this!

31

Sandra lied to everybody, including the police. When the explosion knocked her unconscious, Manuel pulled her out of the burning boat and swam to shore with her, but she's pretending that she and Elizabeth were alone. She's still trying to keep her parents from finding out about Manuel. . . .

"It was awful," Elizabeth said, taking another sip of hot lemon-flavored tea. "Manuel had just saved Sandy's life. And she told him to get lost!"

We were all sitting around the kitchen table, listening to Elizabeth's account of the accident at Secca Lake: me, my parents, and Elizabeth's boyfriend, Jeffrey French.

"Didn't anyone on the shore see the explosion?" my father asked in lawyerly fashion. The attorney side of him comes out at moments like this, and he always sounds like he's cross-examining a witness.

"There were a couple of people there, but they were too far away to have a clear view," Elizabeth answered. "One man was ready to swear he saw a third person swim to shore, but Sandy flatly denied it, so after a while he admitted that maybe he'd been mistaken."

Jeffrey whistled. "I can't believe Sandy did that to Manuel. He's such a great guy. He deserves to be treated better than that."

"You should have seen his face," Elizabeth

agreed glumly. "He'd just risked his life for her—he loves her so much."

"I thought she loved him too," I put in.

"Not enough to tell her parents she's dating him," Elizabeth replied. "She promised Manuel she'd tell them, but she kept putting it off. Now I think it's too late."

"So what did you do, honey?" my mother asked Elizabeth.

"I didn't know what to do," Elizabeth confessed. "Sandy was telling everybody—the lifeguards, the park rangers, the reporter from the *Sweet Valley News*—that *I* was the hero, I was the one who pulled her from the burning boat. She seemed so desperate—I couldn't contradict her. What if her parents found out about Manuel and she got in trouble?"

"They're bound to find out sooner or later," I remarked.

"Maybe. Maybe not," Elizabeth said, her eyes clouding. "Not if Manuel never talks to Sandy again because of what happened at the lake!"

I think it's crazy that Sandy is so worried about how her parents might react to Manuel, who's probably the nicest boy at Sweet Valley High. Who wouldn't want their daughter to date a hero? But I guess Sandy knows her parents better than I do, and she thinks they're just too prejudiced to give Manuel a chance. I'm sure glad I'd never

33

have to worry about something like that with my mom and dad. They're totally tolerant—too tolerant, sometimes. Of course it's wrong to dislike people because of something they can't control, like the color of their skin or their religion or being poor. But my mom doesn't get that it's OK to be snobby about some things, like if a person has absolutely awful taste in clothes or a really bad haircut or too much eye makeup. Sometimes when we're at the mall together, I'll play fashion police and point out some complete glamour faux-pas and she won't even crack a smile!

I don't know. Maybe I shouldn't be so quick to judge Sandy and her parents, to claim that I'd do things differently. The fact is, I don't know how I'd act in that situation because I've never gone out with a guy of a different race or ethnicity. I guess I can see how it might get complicated. But it shouldn't. People should just accept each other for who they are.

Wednesday afternoon

Dear Diary,
I think it's time for a twin switch. Elizabeth's picture was on the front page of the newspaper with a huge headline, "Local Girl Saves Friend in Boating Accident." And

Sandy's parents gave Elizabeth this beautiful gold bracelet, and the head of the PTA just called to say that she's going to get a special award from the school board. Elizabeth is the talk of the town. But she isn't even enjoying the attention! Instead of having fun, my holier-than-thou sister feels guilty taking credit for something she didn't do. Isn't that just like her? Moments like these are completely wasted on her. I wish I'd been on the boat with Sandy and Manuel. That bracelet would look pretty nice on my wrist. And when the PTA gave me a medal, instead of hemming and hawing about how I don't deserve it, I'd just say "Thank you"!

Saturday afternoon

Today is Lila's birthday. My fingers are itching to dial her number, but I haven't even called her. I can't admit this to anyone, Diary, but I'm not so sure anymore that I'm doing the right thing. What if Lila gets so depressed that she jumps out a third-floor window at Fowler Crest or packs up and moves to New York or something? I finally went to the trouble to put myself in her shoes and I realized that if she were doing this to me, I'd be incredibly hurt (as well as furious). Maybe I'll call her and just say *happy birthday. No, I can't do that—it would ruin the surprise. I'll just have to cross my fingers and hope for the best!*

By the way, everything worked out for Sandra and Manuel. There was a total crisis—Manuel was accused of tampering with the Bacons' motorboat and causing the explosion! When Sandy found out that he was about to be arrested, she finally came forward and told the truth. Elizabeth was there, and she said Mr. and Mrs. Bacon were pretty surprised at first, but they ended up being really grateful to Manuel and respecting Sandy's right to think differently than they do. All's well that ends well, as Shakespeare would say. (See? Elizabeth isn't the only literary one in this family!) Sandy's bringing Manuel to the surprise party tomorrow night. If there's a surprise party—if Lila ever forgives us for being so mean to her!

Sunday, midnight

Watch out world, here comes Jessica Wakefield. I really should make a career out of giving great parties—I'd be a millionaire before I'm twenty! You should have seen Lila's face when she walked into the house tonight. Although it was touch-and-go for a while. I almost thought we weren't going to pull it off. . . .

"What do you mean, she won't come?" I hollered over the telephone on Sunday evening.

For half an hour Elizabeth had been helping me blow up balloons that said Happy Birthday, Lila—we were both red in the face. But the hard work was worth it. The living room of our house had been transformed, with colorful streamers and birthday banners and a big bulletin board plastered with photos of Lila from babyhood on. We'd baked cakes in the shape of the letters in Lila's name, and there was about a ton of Million Dollar Mocha ice cream, Lila's favorite flavor, in the freezer. And now Cara and Amy were telling me they couldn't get Lila in the car?

"We didn't know what to say," Amy confessed. "We told her we wanted to take her out for a birthday ice cream cone, and she said she was on a diet and slammed down the phone."

"Well, call her back," I instructed, knotting a red balloon with a snap. I rubbed it on my T-shirt so it would get static and stick to the wall. "You've got to have a game plan, though. She's mad, right? Play up to that. Blame it on me. Tell her going to the concert last night without her was my idea. Say you're really, really sorry and suggest getting together so you can help her plan her revenge against me."

Amy laughed. "Jess, you're a genius."

"So they tell me."

I hung up the balloon and grabbed my sister's wrist, twisting it to look at her watch—I don't wear one myself. "It'll take them, oh, say an hour and fifteen minutes to go over to Lila's, talk to her, take her to the mall for ice cream, and then bring her here," I calculated. "Which will make it seven-thirty on the dot. Which is exactly when the party was supposed to start anyway! No problem."

Sure enough, at seven-thirty I peeked through the curtains in the living room and saw a car pull up to the curb. "Here they are!" I hissed. "I'm turning off the light. Everybody hide!"

I flicked the light switch and the room sank into darkness. There were thumps and giggles as thirty people—Elizabeth and Jeffrey, Sandy and Manuel, Jean, Enid Rollins, Bill Chase and DeeDee Gordon, Winston Egbert and Maria Santelli, Annie Whitman, Ken Matthews, Bruce Patman, and more—scrambled to hide behind furniture and in closets. Meanwhile I hurried to the front door.

In the stillness Lila's voice carried clearly up the front walk. "I can't believe you dragged me over here," she fumed to Cara and Amy. "I have absolutely nothing to say to that girl!"

"Maybe she has something to say to you," said Cara.

"I doubt it," replied Lila. "Unless it's 'Lila who?' In case you haven't noticed, we're not friends anymore. I always go all out for her birthday, and she didn't even buy me a card."

"I bet she'll apologize when she sees how mad you are," Amy cajoled Lila. "C'mon, let's ring the bell. If nothing else, you can tell her to her face what a jerk you think she is!"

There was a scuffle outside. I swallowed a giggle. It sounded as if Cara and Amy were literally dragging Lila up the steps!

The doorbell chimed. "No one's answering," Lila said after a few seconds. "Let's get out of here."

"Jess probably has the stereo blasting and didn't hear the bell. Look, the door's open," Cara observed, turning the knob. "Let's tiptoe upstairs and surprise her."

"OK," Lila reluctantly agreed. "But I'm not going to pull any punches, you two. I'm going to tell her exactly how I feel!"

"You do that," Amy encouraged.

I pressed myself against the wall behind the door as Lila, Amy, and Cara stepped into the shadowy hallway. "Hello?" Cara called. "Anybody home?"

That was our signal. I pointed a finger at Elizabeth, who was manning the living room light switch, and at the exact same moment I flipped on the hall lights. "Surprise!" thirty voices boomed.

I wish we'd thought to have somebody videotaping the scene—Lila's expression was classic. Her jaw dropped and her knees buckled—Amy had to grab her arm to keep her from falling. "W-what?" Lila squeaked, her wide eyes taking in the party decorations and the laughing faces of her friends.

"Happy birthday, Lila," I sang, rushing forward to give her a big hug.

"J-J-Jess, did you d-do this?" she stammered.

I nodded happily. Everybody started chanting Lila's name. Elizabeth ran around sticking plastic champagne glasses in people's hands, and Winston, who had three psychedelic birthday hats strapped to his head, followed on her heels, filling the glasses with soda.

I took advantage of the fact that Lila was still basically speechless and lifted my glass for a toast. "I know you thought we forgot about you, Li, but we wanted to really and truly surprise you. It's hard to top the awesome bashes you throw at Fowler Crest, but this party's special because it's in honor of the beautiful, talented, one-in-a-million Lila Fowler, my best friend."

Lila's golden brown eyes filled with tears. I'll admit mine were a bit damp too. "I can't believe this," she said, sniffling. "I really thought you didn't care about my birthday. I thought you didn't care about *me*. I should've known you'd come through, Jess. You're the best friend ever!"

We hugged again, both of us bursting out laughing when Lila knocked my glass of soda all over the floor. Then the music started, and everyone else pushed forward to kiss and hug her and pile her arms high with presents. I watched, a huge smile on my face. I know what Elizabeth would say about a moment like this—something nerdy like, "It's better to give than to receive." But you know what? She'd be right. I'd never felt happier.

It really was the best party ever, Diary. Even though it was a school night, everybody stayed pretty late—my parents didn't mind. Best of all, Lila had a blast. She danced nonstop, got tons of excellent gifts, laughed at the pictures on the bulletin board, and ate three pieces of birthday cake. So much for that diet!

Amy's party tape was great except for a couple of slow songs she snuck in. There's nobody I'm into right now, so I sat those out. A good opportunity to paw through Lila's presents and see if there were any clothes or CDs or jewelry I might want to borrow (there were!). Speaking of slow dancing, Sandy and Manuel were out of control. We're talking hands all over each other, making out in the corner, everyone else might as well be invisible stuff—a hundred times worse even than Elizabeth and Jeffrey. Why can't people have any self-restraint? Listen to me, Diary. Do you detect a hint of sour grapes? OK, I'll admit it. I never thought Sandy was particularly good looking, but tonight—you should have seen the way her eyes were glowing. Sometimes I wonder what it would be like to feel that way. . . .

Part 2

Friday evening

Dear Diary,

How's this for a blast from the past? I got a letter from Todd "Boring but Cute" Wilkins today. You haven't seen that name in these pages for a while, have you? Not that I ever wrote about him all that much. True, when he first moved to town, I thought he was pretty hot—we all did. But he fell in love with Elizabeth, of all people— that pretty much says it all. I get sick of Elizabeth and Jeffrey mooning over each other, but if I remember correctly, she was even worse with Todd. Those two actually used to read poetry to each other! A hot date for them was a trip to the library.

Dullsville. Anyway, they were much too se-
rious, so it was almost a relief when Todd's
dad got transferred and his family moved to
Vermont. Elizabeth was brokenhearted, but
eventually she got over it as I knew she
would and now she's with Jeffrey. With any
luck he'll move and she'll finally realize that
it's much more fun to play the field. Life is
too short to spend it with only one guy!

Back to Todd. You should see this letter!
Three pages of tiny handwriting—I mean,
the guy spent some time on this! Doesn't he
have better things to do? I guess girls in
Vermont don't compare to us Californians—
he asked me to write back and send some
pictures. Of course, it's pretty obvious that
he only wrote to me because he misses
Elizabeth. He asked like a million questions
about what she's up to these days. Officially
they're still friends, but you know how it is.
He probably doesn't feel like he can write to
her anymore because of Jeffrey. So I
showed Elizabeth the letter, and she got this
really funny look on her face. . . .

"Hey, Liz," I shouted, pushing open the sliding
glass door to the patio. "Look what I got!"

My sister was sitting on the edge of the pool in
our backyard, her feet dangling in the cool, turquoise water. She had on a royal blue tank suit,

43

with goggles pushed up on her forehead—getting ready to swim laps.

"What?" she said, squinting in the bright sun to see what I was holding.

I waved the envelope in front of her eyes. "A letter. From your old boyfriend."

Elizabeth's cheeks flushed pink. She reached for the envelope. "Wow, I haven't heard from him in a long—"

"Not so fast," I said, snatching the envelope away from her. "I didn't say it was for you, did I?"

Elizabeth blinked. "You mean . . . Todd wrote to *you?*"

"Sure. Why not?" I sat down next to her and slipped the pages out of the envelope. "He was my friend too. And he must know that if he's homesick for Sweet Valley gossip, I'm the one to contact."

I could tell Elizabeth was dying to see the letter. I held it at an angle so she couldn't read over my shoulder. "'Dear Jessica.' That's how it starts," I informed her. "'You probably thought I dropped off the face of the earth. Burlington does feel about a million miles away from California. What's new?'"

I paused. Elizabeth waited, a little bit breathless. "Well?" she said.

I lowered the letter. "Todd's old news to you—you probably aren't interested," I remarked.

"No, um, go ahead," Elizabeth said, trying to sound nonchalant.

I smothered a grin and read on. "'I'm keeping

44

busy with the usual stuff,' Todd says. 'The basketball coach is tough—practices are grueling. The guys on the team are cool, though, and we have a good time. One of my friends, Mike, had a party last weekend and—'" I put the letter down again. "I shouldn't bore you with this," I said to Elizabeth.

"No, it's OK." She dabbled her feet in the pool, pretending to be incredibly interested in the water dripping off her toes. "I don't mind hearing what he's doing."

No kidding! I thought. Nothing like an appreciative audience—I cleared my throat in theatrical fashion. "Ahem. So then he writes, 'The party was pretty wild. These New Englanders know how to have a good time, maybe because they're snowbound half the year. I thought of you because there's this girl on the cheerleading squad who's sort of chasing me around.' Hear that?" I gave Elizabeth a playful smile. "He thought of *me*. OK, where was I. . . . 'Her name is Cybil, and she's gorgeous. But here's where she doesn't remind me of you—there's not a whole lot going on upstairs, if you know what I mean. It's kind of hard to have a conversation with someone who only has about ten words in her vocabulary.'"

I laughed loudly. Elizabeth scowled. "Are you sure you want to hear this?" I asked my sister solicitously.

She nodded, her expression grim. I flipped the page to read the other side. "'So what's happening in Sweet Valley? I'd love to see a copy of the *Oracle*, find out how the sports teams are doing. Is Elizabeth still writing her column?'" I dug my elbow into Elizabeth's ribs. "Sweet of him to ask after you."

Elizabeth grunted.

"Hmm, let's see." I skimmed the rest of the letter. "Dum de dum, no, this wouldn't interest you. . . ." I could tell it was killing her not to know what Todd had written, even though in actuality it *was* really boring stuff about his teachers, the weather in Vermont, and a recent family trip to Boston. "Here's the last part," I said. "'If you're ever out this way, I'll teach you how to ski moguls. Miss ya, Jess. Love, Todd.'"

Of course, everybody knows that when someone says "ya" instead of "you"—"miss ya," "love ya," that sort of thing—they don't really mean it. But even though she was trying to hide it, Elizabeth was clearly bummed by the fact that Todd had written this cheerful, affectionate letter to me and not her.

"Good ol' Todd," I said, hopping to my feet. "I kind of miss him too, you know? When I write back, should I tell him you say hi?"

Elizabeth pulled the swim goggles down over her eyes. "Sure," she muttered before diving into the pool.

I walked back inside, laughing.

It's always fun to yank Elizabeth's chain a little. Maybe I will write back to Todd . . .

if I can find the time in between tanning and shopping!

Saturday evening

Went to the beach today with Lila, Sandy, and Jean. As usual it was sunny and warm—paradise. I can't imagine living anyplace else—what if it was cold and rainy all the time and I turned fat and pale from never getting any sun or exercise? Anyhow, I wore my new flowered bikini. I wonder if having a tan as good as mine is even legal! Sometimes I worry that the life-guards won't be able to keep their eyes on the ocean with me around!

Elizabeth roped me into helping her make this video documentary about Sweet Valley. It sounded too stupid, but then she told me that it's for a junior filmmaker showcase sponsored by Susan Stewart's father, Jackson Croft, a famous Hollywood director. Elizabeth's idea is pretty boring, but with me as narrator, who knows what might happen? I could end up on TV or in the movies. Watch out, Madonna!

Elizabeth is going to write the script and I'll read it. Naturally Jeffrey will do the filming (he's a photographer for the school newspaper—that's how those two got to-

47

gether). Maybe I'll tell Todd about all this if I ever get around to writing him back.

Monday night

    Elizabeth dragged me over to Enid's today. Kicking and screaming, I might add. Did you know that if you look up the word "dull" in the dictionary, the definition is "Enid Rollins"? Seriously. Whenever I talk to her, I always end up yawning and dying for a nap. She's a really pretty girl, but she wears the most boring clothes and no makeup, and she always has her nose stuck in a book, just like Elizabeth. They deserve each other, those two. Actually Enid's not all bad. She'd do anything for Elizabeth. I wish I could say that about my girlfriends, but if truth be told, our loyalty to each other is only skin deep. For example, if a cute new boy moves to town, it's every girl for herself!
    So we went to Enid's because she's helping with Elizabeth's documentary. (Enid's mom's boyfriend, Richard, is the program director at Sweet Valley TV and he's going to show Elizabeth and Jeffrey how to edit the video.) The newest development Chez Rollins is that Enid's grandmother, who's a widow, just moved in with them. Three generations of women under one roof sounds like a recipe

for disaster to me, but Enid seemed thrilled to jump up every two minutes to make tea for Nana, bring her the newspaper, fluff up her pillows, etc. What a Girl Scout.

Tuesday afternoon

Observation of the day: Mr. Collins is a god. In English, when he was reading aloud from the Shakespeare play that was assigned for today (I didn't read it—I don't even remember the title!), I almost swooned. His voice is so incredibly sexy. And that strawberry blond hair, and those bright blue eyes, and that fantastic body. . . . He's too good looking to be a teacher, I'm telling you. I guess I'm glad I don't write for the Oracle like Elizabeth. He's the adviser, and she's always in the newspaper office alone with him, and I just wouldn't trust myself. I'd probably lose control and jump him! I can't tell Elizabeth because she looks at him kind of like a father figure. She's nuts!

Anyway, I just thought you'd like to know for the record. Roger Collins is the cutest teacher at SVH. And if he ever marries Ms. Dalton, they'll be the cutest couple. But I hope he stays single so I'll have a chance at him when I'm older!

Wednesday, late

Dear Diary,
We started shooting the documentary today. The more I think about it, the more I think the film would be much *more interesting if I were the* subject, *not just the narrator. I suggested this to Elizabeth, but my twin doesn't know an award-winning idea when she hears it. . . .*

"How do I look?" I asked Elizabeth, pirouetting.

I was wearing my sister's white linen suit, a pale blue silk blouse, pearl earrings, and high heels. I knew I looked fabulous, but it's always nice to get confirmation.

Elizabeth gave me a quick once-over. "Great," she said, smiling. "You're ready to meet the mayor!"

We were standing on the sidewalk in front of Town Hall. Enid was double-checking the list of questions I'd be asking the mayor while Jeffrey loaded a new tape into the video camera.

So far, it had been a good morning. I'd memorized my lines with no problem, and I couldn't wait to see the footage of me strolling through downtown Sweet Valley, chatting about what a unique, interesting, close-knit community it is. There'd only been one small glitch.

I narrowed my eyes at Jeffrey. "Are you *sure* you erased Winston?" I asked.

Jeffrey shot a glance at Elizabeth before turning to me with a grin. "You mean the part where he comes out of the novelty shop with the plastic arrow through his head and starts following you, and you keep saying your lines and it's like three blocks before you realize he's there? I erased it, Jess. I swear."

I relaxed and mustered a smile myself. "Good. Because I don't want that clown ruining my video debut!"

Elizabeth looked at her watch. "It's eleven. The mayor's expecting us."

The four of us trooped into Town Hall and took the elevator up to the top floor. At the reception desk Elizabeth said politely, "I'm Elizabeth Wakefield— we're filming a documentary about Sweet Valley. We have an appointment with the mayor."

The receptionist picked up the phone and murmured a few words, then buzzed us through the glass door. As we walked down the hall we saw Thomas Finch, the mayor, who's tall and lanky with grayish red hair and freckles, step out of his office to meet us. "Good morning, friends!" he boomed, flashing his trademark grin.

Jeffrey lifted the camera to his shoulder and filmed the mayor giving my hand a vigorous shake. Then Mayor Finch ushered me into his office. Jeffrey was still filming. "Your window looks right down on Main Street," I observed, crossing the room to admire the view . . . and making sure the camera had a good angle on me. My profile is stunning, if I may say so myself. "I guess you don't miss a trick!"

"I like to keep my finger on the pulse of Sweet Valley," Mayor Finch agreed.

We sat down and I fired off my questions. Some were pretty predictable, and they gave the mayor a chance to reel off his standard speech about what a great town Sweet Valley is and all that. But there were a few surprises, and he ended up really having to think about some stuff and saying things that were funny and unexpected.

We wrapped up the interview. "I'd like to see the video when you're done with it," Mayor Finch said as he escorted us downstairs to the lobby and shook hands all around. "Maybe we can show it at the Civic Center for tourists."

Elizabeth could hardly contain her excitement. We hurried back outside into the sunshine. "You were great!" she exclaimed, giving me a hug.

I shrugged modestly, although I knew I deserved heaps of extravagant praise. "What can I say?" I asked my sister. "I was born to be in front of a camera!"

I really am a natural talent, if I may say so myself. The question is: Should I start on TV or go straight to the big screen? I always thought I wanted to be an actress, but this interviewing stuff is pretty fun too. I could have my own syndicated talk show. "The

Jessica Wakefield Hour"—that has a nice ring to it. All the big-name designers would vie to provide my wardrobe, and I'd get someone famous from Hollywood to style my hair and do my makeup. If Elizabeth wants, I'll let her book my celebrity guests!

Anyhow, it was a fun day, but tiring. It's amazing how many hours of video we have to shoot just to end up with one hour of finished product. After the filming we stopped by Enid's house to check on her grandmother. Mrs. Langevin was taking a nap on the couch and we woke her up by accident. Man, is she one cranky old lady! Even Saint Enid appears to be getting a little tense.

Time to get my beauty sleep. Check in with you later.

Sunday night

We filmed at the beach today and I was really in my element, interviewing a bunch of hunky blond surfers and joining in a beach volleyball game. And I created quite a sensation in my French-cut silver maillot, I'm happy to report. I started off the shoot in this prissy pink sundress that Elizabeth picked out for me, but fortunately Prince Albert, our golden retriever, went with us to the beach and jumped all over me with *wet sandy paws (Jeffrey was filming at the time, but he promised to erase that part of the tape). I had to change. What a shame!*

"Hey, guys," I called, strolling over to a bunch of my friends, who were splashing around at the water's edge tossing a football. Jeffrey walked at my side, filming my every move. "You're on Candid Camera!"

Bill Chase tucked the football under his arm and gave me a broad smile. Ken, DeeDee, and Amy also started mugging for the camera. Ken did some bodybuilding moves, bunching up his biceps and tightening his stomach muscles. DeeDee and Amy, meanwhile, dove into the surf and started doing silly synchronized swimming strokes.

"I guess you're the straight man in this crowd," I said to Bill. "Tell us about a typical day at the beach in Sweet Valley."

I held the microphone out to him. "Well, the waves are great." Bill pointed out to sea. "They break out there on the sandbar, which means closer to shore it's nice for swimmers, but the surfers still get lots of action."

"And Bill's a surfer," I said, turning to Jeffrey and smiling into the camera. "A California state-champion surfer! Will you show us your stuff, Bill, and maybe teach us some of that gnarly surfer-dude lingo?"

Bill laughed. "Sure thing. Let me grab my board."

As Bill jogged up to the dunes, I continued

54

walking. I was glad to observe that Jeffrey had taken a few steps back, so he was getting a full-length view of me. I looked so good—it would have been a shame just to get a head shot!

We came up to a couple of guys I didn't know, lounging on the sand with their surfboards, the tops of their wet suits unzipped. "We're making a documentary." I greeted them with an outrageously flirtatious smile. Why not? "Here's your chance. What do you want to say to the world?"

The guys all smiled back at me, frank admiration in their eyes. "Sweet Valley, California," one of them declared, addressing Jeffrey's video camera. "Best waves—and best-looking girls—in the world!"

> *That about says it all, doesn't it, Diary?*
> *Enid was supposed to help out with the documentary today, but she never showed up. Something to do with that grandmonster of hers, I imagine. We did fine without her—she's not adding a whole lot to the project, to be honest. I mean, I could be doing this all by myself! Jeffrey told me he's getting some of his most unforgettable footage ever of me. Those were his exact words: unforgettable. That's me!*
> *Anyhow, I was so charged when we got back that I used my extra energy to write a letter to Todd. . . .*

There's nothing like a long shower after a day at the beach to cool off your sizzling skin. I patted myself dry with a soft towel, ran a comb through my damp hair, then slipped on a tank top and lightweight cotton shorts. Feeling refreshed, I flipped on the radio to a modern-rock station and flopped onto my bed with a pad of paper and a pen. *Dear Todd,* I wrote.

For some reason I was feeling incredibly energized and inspired. In practically no time I'd scribbled a page and a half.

Just as I started a new paragraph, there was a knock on my door. "Can I come in?" Elizabeth called.

"Sure," I answered.

She had an armful of neatly folded clean clothes. "Where should I put these?" she asked.

"Oh, anywhere," I said with a careless wave. It didn't really matter—all my clothes, dirty and clean, end up on the floor sooner or later anyway.

Elizabeth deposited the laundry on my desk, then walked over to the bed. "What are you doing?"

"Don't laugh," I told her. "I'm writing to Todd."

"You're kidding!" she said, her eyebrows lifting.

"He wrote to me first," I reminded her. "It'd be kind of rude not to write back."

"True."

She sat down on the edge of my bed, looking at the pad of paper curiously. I covered the letter with my hand. "Do you mind?" I asked. "This is kind of personal."

"Oh, yeah. Sorry." Elizabeth stood up again, visibly disappointed at not getting to read the letter. She started to say something, then changed her mind and headed for the door. "See ya."

I put my face into the pillow so Elizabeth wouldn't hear me laugh. She really is too funny. She's madly in love with Jeffrey, but I guess she still thinks of Todd as hers!

The letter really wasn't that personal, of course, but I couldn't resist giving her a hard time. As soon as she was gone I read what I'd written, admiring my breezy epistolary style.

"It was a great surprise getting your letter," I'd started. "I'll pretend you didn't just write to me because I'm Elizabeth's sister! She's fine, by the way. Jeffrey treats her really well, so you don't need to worry. You'd better not be pining over her, though! I bet there are plenty of cute girls in Vermont—maybe not as tanned and blond and gorgeous as some of the girls here (particularly one with the initials J. W.!), but still. You didn't say in your letter, but is there anybody special? I'm currently single myself. That doesn't mean I'm sitting home on Saturday nights—I'm not going to sit around waiting for Mr. Right to ring my doorbell!"

I'm really good at this, I thought, uncapping my pen to resume writing. Maybe *I* should be the twin with a newspaper column!

Just finished my letter to Todd. I wonder if Elizabeth has any stamps? Dumb ques-

tion—knowing my sister, Ms. Organization,
she probably has a ten-year supply.

Monday afternoon

Dear Diary,
We're almost done filming the docu-
mentary. It's been a busy couple of days.
We have clips from a town meeting and the
annual Sweet Valley Dance Festival, and
we also did a historical piece on an artist
colony that used to be on the beach here—I
expected that to be boring, but it turned
out to be pretty interesting. Today was the
highlight, though. I had a one-on-one
interview with Jeremy Frank! Judging
from the look in his eyes, he could see im-
mediately that I'm a rising star. . . .

There's no question that I'm destined to have
a career in entertainment—I felt perfectly at
home entering the building of the Sweet Valley
TV station. The visitor pass around my neck
bounced as I stepped up the pace. Jeremy Frank
was waiting for me!

I have a history with Jeremy Frank. A while back
Elizabeth and I volunteered as candy stripers at
Fowler Memorial Hospital. It was one of Elizabeth's
do-good ideas, needless to say—being a candy
striper is the most boring, menial job on the planet.

But as luck would have it, Jeremy Frank was one of my patients! I didn't mind fluffing his pillows, I'll tell you that. He was so incredibly handsome and charismatic, even lying in a hospital bed. I had a huge crush on him, obviously, and later when he was back at work, I managed to charm my way into a guest spot on *Frankly Speaking*! So the two of us go way back. But this interview was something special. Jeremy and I would be meeting as colleagues. It was really important that I impress him—he could really boost my career.

Enid studied the directory, her forehead wrinkling. "Studio nine," she muttered anxiously. "How come I don't see studio nine up here?"

"Because," I said, jabbing an index finger at the directory, "they tape the talk show in studio four!"

Enid looked down at her notes. "I must have written it down wrong," she mumbled.

Elizabeth, Enid, Jeffrey, and I hurried down the crowded corridor. "Wow," gushed Jeffrey as we entered studio four. "It's the set from *Frankly Speaking*!"

"No kidding," I said, my tone worldly wise.

"And there's Jeremy Frank," said Elizabeth, pinching my arm. "More gorgeous than ever!"

I have to admit my knees knocked a little at my first sight of him. Jeremy Frank is tall and dark haired, with commanding features and blue eyes that burn right through you. But I reminded myself that I looked pretty darned good too, in my sage green wrap miniskirt and matching short jacket over an ivory silk tank top. A lot of beautiful people have strolled into this studio, but I'll match my legs against any of theirs!

Jeremy Frank strode over to greet us. He clasped my hand, holding it for a long moment while gazing straight into my eyes. I experienced total nuclear meltdown. "How wonderful to see you again, Jessica," he said, his voice deep and thrilling. "I'm so honored to be included in your documentary."

I flashed a glance at Elizabeth. "It's really my sister's documentary," I had to admit. "But I worked with her to develop the material, and of course as narrator I'm adding my own perspective."

This was sort of an exaggeration of my role, but even as I spoke I realized that I *should* have had a bigger hand in developing the material. I would have written a much more exciting script than Elizabeth and Enid!

Jeremy escorted us over to the talk-show set. "As you know, this is my usual post," he said, waving to a plush armchair. "But why don't you take that seat, Jessica. You're the one asking questions today."

My heart skipped a beat as I lowered myself into the chair. Jeremy's chair!

Jeremy, meanwhile, sat on the other side of the low coffee table, crossing his legs elegantly. While Jeffrey readied the camera, Enid handed me a small notebook with the questions I'd be asking.

Elizabeth handed me a compact mirror and I checked my lipstick. Then Jeffrey gave me the thumbs-up sign. "Camera rolling," he announced.

I sat forward slightly, my back ruler straight, and flashed my most dazzling smile at Jeremy. "We're on the set of *Frankly Speaking*, Sweet Valley's very own talk show," I began, my tone a careful blend of crisp professionalism and conversational warmth. "Jeremy Frank is going to tell us how a local boy got into this business, and why Sweet Valley's the perfect setting for one of the most widely watched programs in Southern California. First, Jeremy . . ."

I dropped my eyes to the notebook resting on my lap. We'd run over some of the questions a few days earlier, and I knew Elizabeth and Enid had refined and added to the list. But the questions staring up at me in Enid's neat, tiny handwriting were completely unfamiliar. *Do you remember what life was like in California in the late nineteenth century? Can you tell me about the first time you saw an automobile? Rode in an automobile? Where were you when you heard about Pearl Harbor?*

Oh, no, I thought. *This is for my interview with Sweet Valley's oldest living resident, the hundred-and-three-year-old man!*

"Cut," I commanded, signaling to Jeffrey. He lowered the camera. Everyone looked at me in surprise. "Enid," I said, standing up and handing the notebook back to her. "These are the wrong questions!"

"Oh." Enid flushed scarlet. "Let me see . . ." She ruffled the pages of the notebook, then fumbled

61

around in her leather portfolio. Pieces of paper fluttered all over the place, but apparently she couldn't find the *right* piece of paper anywhere. "I'm sorry, Jessica," she said with a helpless shrug.

For a split second I panicked. Then Elizabeth placed a hand on my arm. "It's OK," Elizabeth said with an encouraging smile. "Jess can wing it. The interview will be even fresher and more fun that way!"

I took a deep breath and then nodded. Elizabeth was right. Since when was I ever at a loss for words when a good-looking guy was around? I didn't need Enid's stupid notes!

"Let's start again, OK, Jeremy?" I suggested, my poise returning.

"I'm all yours," he replied.

I smiled. That was what I wanted to hear!

My interview with Jeremy ended up going great—but of course, I'm a natural. Enid was a mess from start to finish, though. I think she's having a midlife crisis twenty years early. We ran into Enid's mom's boyfriend, Richard Cernak, at the station and Enid was really rude to him even though the guy's bending over backward to help with the documentary and obviously he's only doing it to butter up Enid. I think we should jettison her from the project before she wrecks it, but Elizabeth won't hear of it. I don't know—maybe I should have more sympathy. Elizabeth says things are really falling apart in the Rollins household. Mrs. Langevin takes up all Enid's free time, and that puts a strain on Enid's relationship with Hugh Grayson, which I guess is tough in the best of times because he lives in Big Mesa and they hardly ever see each other. According to Elizabeth, things aren't going that well these days between Mrs. Rollins and Richard, either. I hate to say I told you so, but I knew there'd be trouble when the grandmonster moved in!

Monday night

Me again. I'm still flying high from my interview with Jeremy Frank, so I just walked down the block with Prince Albert to stick my letter to Todd in the mailbox on the corner. Elizabeth was going to mail it for me this morning, but after dinner I noticed the letter still sitting on her dresser. I guess she forgot. Do you think Wonder Boy will write me back?

Friday, midnight

The Beach Disco was wild tonight—the Droids really rocked. Too bad there wasn't anyone in particular I wanted to dance with.

Sweet Valley guys are fun, but they don't exactly make my heart pound. When do you suppose I'll meet somebody who does?

We taped our very last segment for the documentary at the Beach Disco: a couple of Droids' songs and some interviews with my hard-partying friends. Of course the second we put a microphone in front of Bruce's face, he started yammering about the Patmans being the founding family of Sweet Valley. That boy has an ego the size of L.A. Thanks to the fine art of film editing, we can cut out the parts with Bruce. He'll be so bummed when he sees the finished tape and he's not in it anywhere! It'll serve him right.

Enid and Hugh were at the Beach Disco together, so I guess they haven't broken up yet, although according to Elizabeth they're on the verge. Enid better hold herself together until we wrap up the documentary. I had this brilliant idea to have a Hollywood-style premiere of our movie next weekend. (Actually it was Cara's idea, but who's counting?) Can't you see me in a strapless gown with long white gloves?

Saturday, VERY late

Dear Diary,
Tonight was perfect. I really know how

to give a party! We rented a giant projec-
tion TV for the video premiere and invited
everybody we knew. There I was on the
screen, larger than life. . . .

"Do I look like a movie star or what?" I asked
Cara, twirling to show off the short, strapless red
dress I'd borrowed from Lila.

Cara zipped me up in back. "You look fabulous," she confirmed. "Don't forget lipstick,
though."

I spritzed myself with perfume and puckered
up to apply fire-engine red lipstick. Heels and a
silk scarf completed the picture. "Come on," I said
to Cara. Voices drifted up the stairs. "Sounds like
some people are here already."

Sure enough, Elizabeth and Jeffrey, Aaron
Dallas and his girlfriend, Heather Sanford, and Bill
and DeeDee were milling around the living room.
"Hey, Jessica," Aaron greeted me, reaching into
one of the bowls of popcorn I'd set out. "This place
is really set up for serious movie watching!"

I eyed the living room with approval, glad that
my efforts were appreciated. I'd worked all afternoon to create the feeling of a movie theater—I'd
bought vintage movie posters from a video store in
town and made some posters of my own that said
World Premiere! and Exclusive First Night
Showing! Rows of folding chairs faced the screen,
and my father had helped me install a light switch

dimmer. It would have seemed anticlimactic to watch the documentary on a regular old TV after we worked so hard on it.

"Thanks, Aaron," I said. I was ravenous, but I avoided the popcorn so I wouldn't get grease on Lila's dress. Not that she couldn't just run out and buy another one.

The doorbell rang, and Elizabeth went to answer it. Giving in to temptation, I carefully picked up a single kernel of popcorn.

"So is the video good?" DeeDee asked.

Good? It's great! I wanted to proclaim. Instead I said modestly, "You'd better ask Jeffrey. He and Elizabeth did the editing, and they haven't let anyone else see the finished tape. I'm seeing it for the first time tonight, same as you."

"It's like that for the big stars too," Jeffrey told me. "They shoot hundreds of hours, and then it gets cut down to two, with the film editor shaping the story."

"Well, I don't know how you managed." I tossed my scarf over my shoulder, lending a little drama to the remark. "The documentary could only be one hour long, but we got so much great footage of me!"

Jeffrey smiled. "It was a tough job, but someone had to do it."

A few minutes later Lila, Amy, Ken, Bruce, Maria, Winston, Lynne Henry, Guy Chesney, and a bunch of other people had arrived and everyone was seated. At the last moment, just as my brother, Steven, was about to dim the lights, Enid dashed in. Her eyes were all red and puffy as if she'd been crying, and she was alone. *Where's Hugh?* I wondered. *More problems with the grandmonster?*

When the room was dark, Jeffrey started the tape. Elizabeth's, Jeffrey's, Enid's, and my name flashed on the credits, and everyone whistled and clapped.

Then there I was on the screen, wearing Elizabeth's white linen suit and standing on Main Street. It was so exciting, I lost my professional cool and grabbed Cara's arm. "Look!" I whispered. "It's me!"

I looked and sounded even better than I'd expected—part sophisticated and sexy, part girl next door. Whoever said the camera adds ten pounds was wrong in my case. "Welcome to Sweet Valley, California," I began, the breeze ruffling my hair. "It's a small town, a quiet town, and maybe a lot like your own hometown."

The picture of me faded out and a montage of Sweet Valley faces and scenes followed. A surfer catching a perfect wave, the Droids playing at the Beach Disco, the mayor making a point during the town meeting, the Sunday morning farmers' market, the Sweet Valley High cheerleaders forming a pyramid while Aaron kicked a goal during a soccer game. Then I was back.

"But Sweet Valley has a life and a character all its own," I promised with a winning smile. "Walk with me for a while and I'll show you what I mean."

I sighed with pleasure. *I'm just too good,* I

thought. But the next image on the screen caused the audience to scream with laughter. It was Winston, trailing me down the sidewalk with the arrow through his head!

"Liz!" I shrieked at the exact same instant the video Jessica started hollering at Winston. "You were supposed to erase that part!"

Elizabeth and Jeffrey were clutching each other, laughing. "We just couldn't," Elizabeth gasped, wiping her eyes. "It was too priceless."

I folded my arms, getting ready to fume and sulk. But as I watched Winston mugging on the screen, I had to admit that the moment was funny. "He's so completely ridiculous, he makes me look great in comparison," I muttered.

I felt totally better when I saw myself on the beach in my sexy maillot and heard appreciative whistles from Ken, Bruce, and the rest of the guys—I didn't even mind that Elizabeth and Jeffrey had included the scene of Prince Albert jumping on me with his wet, sandy paws. Everybody laughed, and I had to admit somehow it seemed to work. It made the movie human—it made me and Sweet Valley real.

The hour flew by. When the documentary ended, everybody jumped up and clapped wildly. "You were great, Jess!" Amy cried, throwing her arms around me.

"You—I mean, *we*—should be on TV every night," Winston agreed heartily.

I beamed as the compliments continued to pour in. Elizabeth stepped to my side and slipped an arm around my waist. "You're not mad about the bloopers?" she asked.

I shook my head. "It's a great documentary," I told her. "I wouldn't change a minute of it—you and Jeffrey did a fantastic job."

"Don't forget Enid," said Elizabeth. I shrugged carelessly. It's hardly my fault Enid is so forgettable!

"Speaking of Enid, I need to talk to her," Elizabeth murmured, searching the room for her friend. "She's really upset, and I'm afraid something happened with Hugh."

I was pretty glad that Enid wasn't my problem and that my friends had more consideration than to dampen my premiere by breaking up with their boyfriends!

The music had started—a Droids tape—and people were dancing or checking out the snacks and drinks in the dining room. Jeffrey had rewound the video and it was playing again, without sound. I smiled at myself up on the screen and lifted my glass of soda. "Here's looking at you, kid!"

Sunday, noon

I'm still basking in the glory of my screen debut. If anyone was ever destined for fame and fortune, it's me. On a more boring note, I just heard Elizabeth on the phone. Sounds like Enid finally worked out the problems with her grandmother and Hugh. I guess last night Nana Langevin made Enid break a date with Hugh—Enid was planning on bringing him to the premiere. Hugh was so mad about being blown off (it wasn't the first time) that he dumped her on the spot. Then Enid got mad and yelled at her grandmother and came to the party anyway, leaving Nana home alone. So Elizabeth just gave me the scoop. Enid apologized to Nana, Nana apologized to Enid, Enid apologized to Hugh, and everyone loves everyone else again. And Nana's moving back to Chicago, which must be an incredible relief!

Since Steven came home this weekend to see the documentary, Cara's hanging around today. They've been going out for ages now. It's hard to believe their relationship got off to a rocky start because Steven was still grieving for Tricia Martin (his old girlfriend, who died of leukemia). Now they're like some boring old married couple. I actually heard Steven ask Cara to pass him the sports section of the Sunday paper! I swear, those two are about as exciting as an afternoon with Enid's grandma. Have they forgotten that they're supposed to be young and in love? If I ever have a steady boyfriend, we're going to *stay infatuated with each other. Otherwise what's the point?*

Friday afternoon

Well, Diary, I guess it's true that the more things change, the more they stay the same. Steven's moving home for a week or so—he's developed these horrible allergies and has to have a bunch of outpatient tests at the hospital. So we'll be one big happy family again. I'm psyched to spend some time with him, but to tell you the truth, I'm sick of Cara talking about nothing but Steven, Steven, Steven. He's just a guy, not a god. I'd much rather talk about myself! Maybe I should never have fixed those two up way back when. Cara used to be so much more fun. . . .

When Cara was done talking to Steven, she handed the phone back to me. "See you tomorrow, then," I told him. "Bye."

I hung up the phone and turned the volume back up on the TV. Cara had come over after cheerleading practice so we could work on a science problem set, but then our favorite soap came on—priorities!

Cara grabbed the remote control and turned the volume down again. "Hey, what are you doing?" I protested. "Lania's about to tell her boyfriend she's fallen in love with his best friend!"

"I don't care about Lania's love life—I'm more interested in my own," Cara said. "I'm so excited that Steven's coming home!"

I slumped down on the couch, pouting. I couldn't believe Cara would rather gush about Steven than watch Lania's exploits on the soap. Steven *is* pretty good looking—tall, dark, and handsome, like my dad. And he's a smart guy, and a lot of fun. But maybe I know him too well to think he's hot stuff. I mean, I see him when he's just woken up on Sunday mornings, with his hair sticking up all over the place, walking around in his boxer shorts and drinking orange juice straight out of the carton. Not a pretty sight. "I guess it's nice for you," I conceded grumpily. "I just hope you two don't get tired of each other."

"We could *never* get tired of each other," Cara declared. Just thinking about Steven gave her a glow—her dark eyes sparkled and a blush tinted her olive complexion. "Even if we see each other twenty-four hours a day!"

"Well, I think you two are way too serious," I said.

"You just don't know what it's like," Cara replied in a lofty, mature tone.

I stuck out my lower lip—I *hate* that kind of remark. It's like something Elizabeth would say. "OK, so why don't you tell me? What sort of big plans have you and Steven made for next week when he's in town?"

"We probably won't do anything special," Cara replied. "He has to keep up with his classes, so we'll probably just do our homework together."

"Do homework?" I sat up and gaped at her. "You're joking."

"No. Why?"

I shook my head. "Cara, Cara. Doing homework is OK if it's just a pretense—like, you say you're going to the library, but you really end up at Miller's Point. But if you're *really* doing homework . . ."

"But Steven has a ton of work!" Cara argued. "I don't want him to flunk his classes."

"Would you rather flunk your relationship?" I countered. Cara bit her lip. I pressed my point. "You can't let yourselves get in such a rut," I told her firmly. "You need to keep the romance alive. You need mystery and excitement, like when you first started going out."

"Mystery?" Cara repeated, her eyebrows furrowed.

"Mystery," I confirmed. "You don't want him to take you for granted, do you? He's a college man, remember. There are a lot of temptations waiting for him back at school. Do you want him to start looking around for somebody new?"

I'd finally gotten through to her. Cara twisted a strand of glossy brown hair around her finger nervously. "Mystery, huh?"

I gestured at the TV set. "Take Lania, for instance. She doesn't do homework with her boyfriends. The

73

guys she goes out with never know what to expect!"

"Yeah, and her relationships last all of thirty minutes."

"But she's always in the driver's seat," I reminded Cara. "Men go wild over her and would do anything for her."

Cara sighed. "I don't know. Somehow I don't see myself as the Lania type."

"You don't have to go to extremes," I assured her. "Just try a little harder to keep Steven guessing."

"But I always thought if something wasn't broken, you weren't supposed to fix it," Cara exclaimed. "Things are fine between us!"

"At the moment," I said ominously. "Who knows about tomorrow or next week?"

Cara didn't answer, but she started drumming her fingernails thoughtfully on the cover of her science textbook. I smiled to myself as I turned up the volume on the soap opera. Cara could learn a few lessons from Lania—then she'd thank me!

Personally, Diary, there's no way I'll settle down with just one guy until I reach my golden years. I figure sometime around age thirty.

Sunday afternoon

Cara's relationship with Steven may be as boring as Elizabeth and Jeffrey's,

74

but I have to hand it to the girl—she knows how to entertain. She arranged this incredibly elegant belated birthday luncheon for herself at the Marine House. We had a private room overlooking the harbor, and the guys all wore navy blazers and ties—very classy and nautical. For the record, the guests were Cara, Steven, me, Elizabeth, Jeffrey, Lila, Winston, Maria, Sandy, Manuel, Jean, Tom McKay, Amy, and Bruce.

But even though the food was delicious and the flowers were beautiful and every detail seemed perfect, I'm not sure the birthday girl had a great time. Steven was acting kind of weird. At one point I went to the ladies' room and I saw him in the lobby of the restaurant, holding a letter—pink stationery, very feminine. When Cara went up to him, he shoved it in his pocket. Hmm . . . could Steven have a girl on the side? That would definitely shake things up around here. I'd hate to say I told you so to Cara, but she had to know that if she didn't spice things up fast, Steven's eyes would start to wander.

Speaking of letters, Todd hasn't written me back. Not that I care. At all.

Dear Diary,

    My big brother is up to something, and I intend to find out what it is. All of a sudden he's playing it cool with Cara, and at the same time Abbie Richardson, of all people, has become his new best friend. If you've never seen that name in these pages before, it's not surprising. Abbie and I were actually really tight back in ninth grade, but then she met a guy from Palisades High and she started hanging out with him and his friends. I guess they broke up, though, because all of a sudden Abbie's everywhere I turn. She's a finalist in the Oracle's *humor contest (Amy's the other finalist and she'd better win—she's much funnier!), and she seems to think that makes her Elizabeth's best friend. She's at our house constantly, supposedly working on her comic strip, "Jenny," but she always seems to end up chatting with Steven, who's still home for those allergy tests. . . .*

At the end of the day there's nothing like a refreshing dip in the pool. I'd stripped off the shorts and T-shirt I'd worn to cheerleading practice and changed into one of my plainer swimsuits—no point wasting a sexy one on my next-door neighbors! I grabbed a towel from the linen closet on my way down the hall to the stairs.

On the first floor I detoured through the kitchen to see if any interesting mail had come . . . maybe a letter from Todd. There wasn't a letter, but there were some good catalogs, so I took those outside with me.

I thought I'd have the pool to myself, but there was a regular party going on. Elizabeth, Steven, and Abbie were all sitting on the edge of the pool, splashing their feet and gabbing.

"Hey, Steven," I said to my brother. "What are you doing here? I thought you were meeting Cara at the Dairi Burger after cheerleading practice."

"We changed our plans," Steven said somewhat curtly.

This struck me as a little strange. At practice Cara had seemed really eager to see Steven. *She wouldn't have canceled on him,* I thought, looking suspiciously at Abbie. Abbie had kind of a solemn expression on her face, and she kept darting little glances at Steven out of the corner of her eye. *Hmm.*

Elizabeth got to her feet, wrapping a towel around her waist. "I guess I'll start dinner," she announced.

Abbie started to stand. "I'll do it," she volunteered.

Elizabeth laughed. "No way, Abbie," she said. "You cooked last night when it was Jessica's turn. Once a week is enough. You're not our private chef!"

"If she wants to cook, let her cook," I suggested.

"No, sit back down," Elizabeth ordered Abbie. "Relax and enjoy yourself."

Abbie seemed only too happy to follow these instructions. She sat down again. *A few inches closer to Steven than before?* I wondered, mentally measuring the distance between them. "Gee, it's getting late," I observed pointedly. *Time for you to go!*

Abbie didn't take the hint—neither did Steven. "I'd really like to see your comic strip," he told her. They were both ignoring me—I might as well have been invisible.

"Oh, it's not that good," murmured Abbie, dropping her eyes shyly.

"Elizabeth says it's great," Steven responded. "Give yourself some credit, Abbie."

Yeah, give yourself some credit, Abbie. Her Ms. Modesty routine made me want to gag. *Don't beg too blatantly for compliments and praise from Steven!*

"Well . . . sure," Abbie said at last. "I'd appreciate your feedback, Steven. But you have to promise to be absolutely honest with me. I can handle constructive criticism."

"Let's go inside," Steven suggested. He stood up, then extended a hand to her. As he helped her to her feet Abbie blushed.

I watched them walk into the house together. "What nerve," I grumbled to myself. Abbie and her stupid cartoon. I couldn't believe Steven had blown off Cara for this!

When I asked Steven about Abbie later, he got a little bent out of shape. He said of course she was just a friend, but he kind of was too insistent, you know? In my opinion, Abbie has the words "ulterior motive" written all over her pretty little face. So I took it upon myself to warn Cara. Not that it would be the worst thing in the world if she and Steven broke up, but I think Cara should be in the driver's seat. It's only fair to tell her what she's dealing with. . . .

"That's your third double fault this game!" Lila complained after Cara served into the net, losing the game and the set.

Lila had invited us over to the country club to play some doubles. Now Amy and I lowered our tennis rackets. It had been an easy win—we hadn't even broken a sweat. "How about getting a soda?" I called.

As we walked off the court I couldn't help noticing Cara's dejected posture. "Hey, it's not so bad," I teased her. "You two never beat me and Amy—by now you should be used to it!"

Cara didn't even crack a smile. "That's not why I'm bummed," she said in a small voice.

"What is it, then?" asked Amy as she stuck quarters in the soda machine outside the pro shop.

We carried our icy sodas over to the lawn, sitting on the grass in the shade. Cara stared down at her can. "If you must know, it's Steven," she muttered. She shot a glance at me. "But I guess I'd rather not talk about it."

"Why not?" Lila asked.

"Because he's your brother," Cara said to me. "I feel funny spilling my guts in front of you. I mean, not that you'd tell him what I say, but . . ."

"Don't be ridiculous," I chided. "You should tell me everything because if there's a problem, maybe I can help. I know him better than anybody."

"What's going on?" Lila pressed Cara, popping the top on her soda.

Cara sighed deeply. "*Nothing's* going on—that's what's bothering me. I thought Steven and I would have such a good time this week while he's in town, but instead things are really strange between us. At first I assumed he was just feeling crummy because of his allergies, but it's more than that. He acts really distant and preoccupied, and when I try to talk to him about it, he changes the subject. We used to be so close—we could talk about anything. Now it's like we're strangers."

"That's funny," I commented, sipping my soda. "Steven's been Mr. Congeniality when he's around Abbie Richardson."

"What do you mean?" Cara asked, her eyes shadowed.

"Well, Abbie's come over after school every single day this week," I explained. "She talks to Elizabeth about her cartoon, and then she ends up hanging out for hours. Taking a swim in the pool, staying for dinner—it's like she thinks she's our triplet." I laughed. "I shouldn't knock it—she does my chores for me! And she's a sweet enough girl. But when she's with Steven . . ." I stopped to polish off my soda.

"What *about* when she's with Steven?" Cara pressed.

"It's nothing major," I assured her. "It's just whenever I come across them, either they're laughing like they have some private joke, or they're having a really intense conversation." I shrugged. "I'm sure it's perfectly innocent. It's not like I catch them making out or something."

"Innocent—humph," Lila snorted.

Cara had turned as white as her tennis dress. "I just don't understand," she said, a quiver in her voice. "This week was supposed to bring us closer together. Instead it's driving us apart."

"It sure sounds like Steven's getting interested in somebody else," Lila said with obvious relish.

Cara's chin quivered. I could tell she was about to start bawling. I gave her a hearty thump on the back. "Hey, look on the bright side," I suggested. "If you don't like the way Steven's treating you, then forget him! It's more fun to be single anyway, isn't it, girls?"

Lila and Amy nodded. Cara sniffled. "We'll have a blast, the four of us," I promised Cara. "We'll go to Moon Beach and cruise the cute surfers."

"We'll take you shopping for a new dress to

wear to the Beach Disco," Amy said. "Something that'll have the guys howling at the moon."

"We can have a slumber party at my house," Lila offered. "Stay up all night watching movies and giving each other facials."

Cara still looked sad. "Whatever you do," I told her, "don't let Steven see you like this. Make him think you couldn't care less about him."

"But why?" said Cara, blinking back tears. "I love him!"

"Yeah, but being all clingy and gloomy is only going to drive him into Abbie's arms," I predicted. "Treat him to a taste of his own medicine—play hard to get."

"Why?" Cara said again.

I looked to Lila and Amy for help. "Because it'll make him think about what he's missing," Amy explained.

"And if it doesn't," supplied Lila, "then he doesn't deserve you."

At that moment four totally buff guys who'd been playing tennis on the court next to ours sauntered across the lawn in our direction. I flashed them my warmest, sexiest, most irresistible "come on over" smile, meanwhile murmuring under my breath to Cara, "Think single!"

I don't know exactly what's going on between Steven and Abbie. I don't think he's two-timing Cara yet, but it could be just a matter of time. I have mixed feelings about the whole situation, to tell you the truth. It would be a blast if Cara were single again, but she won't be any fun if she's moping over Steven. If she really does love him, then I hope things work out the way she wants them to. I'll keep you posted on the latest developments, Diary.

Thursday night

Wow! Something major is going on, and I've got to write it down now—in the car while Elizabeth's driving. When I said there'd be developments, I didn't expect this! My dad's law partner gave us six tickets to an L.A. Lakers' pro basketball game, which means there's one extra, and guess who Steven wants to take? Not Cara. Abbie! I just knew there was a reason that girl was trying to ingratiate (is that a word?) herself into this family! She's been putting the moves on Steven, right under our noses.

There's more, Diary, and this part is spooky. Elizabeth told me that Steven's been getting anonymous letters from someone on pink stationery. Remember how I saw him with a letter at Cara's birthday lunch? I guess there've been a whole bunch.

*And it turns out they're written on the same
stationery Tricia Martin used to use . . .
Steven's dead girlfriend! Elizabeth and I
just ran into Tricia's sister Betsy in town,
and Betsy said Steven called her recently,
wanting to know what became of Tricia's
personal belongings after her death. Isn't
this too weird? Naturally Elizabeth and I
decided to do some sleuthing—we went to
the Pen and Paper Shop at the mall. They
had the same pink-flowered stationery. We
asked the clerk if anyone had bought a box
recently, and she described a girl—dark
hair, pretty, petite—who sounds just like
Abbie! I bought a box, too. Maybe I'll use it
to entrap Abbie. . . .*

Elizabeth and I argued the whole way home
from town. "I think we should ask Abbie about the
letters right to her face," I told my sister. "Ask her
what she's up to."

"But we don't really have any proof that Abbie's
the one writing them," Elizabeth reminded me.

"You heard the clerk at the Pen and Paper," I
cried. "She described Abbie perfectly!"

"A lot of girls have brown hair," Elizabeth countered, turning the Fiat onto our street. "Cara has
brown hair."

"Yeah, but who's been hanging around Steven
constantly? Who has a killer crush on him?"

Elizabeth couldn't deny it. Anyone could see that Abbie worshiped the ground Steven walked on. "Maybe she has a crush on him," Elizabeth conceded. "That's not against the law. But she knows about Cara. Abbie's not the type to make a pass at somebody else's boyfriend."

"You've only been hanging out with Abbie for a week. How well do you really know her?" I challenged my sister.

Once again Elizabeth didn't have a good answer. But as she parked the car in the driveway she shook her index finger at me. "Just don't say anything to her or to Steven either," she said. "Until we have some firm evidence."

We walked into the house. I wasn't surprised to see Abbie sitting at the kitchen table, doodling on a pad of paper. "Oh, hi," she said with a big smile when she saw us. "I hope you don't mind that I came over, Liz. Steven let me in. I have a bunch of different story ideas for 'Jenny,' and I'd love to hear which one you think is the best. It's not a conflict of interest for you, is it? I mean, you're not judging the contest, but you are on the newspaper staff."

"I'm happy to give you my opinion," Elizabeth replied. "It's not a conflict of interest at all. I just have to make a quick phone call. You don't mind waiting a few minutes, do you?"

Obviously not, I thought. *Especially when she has Steven to keep her company!*

"Of course not," Abbie said. "Take your time."

Before Elizabeth left the room, she gave me a warning glance. "Don't worry," I whispered. "I won't say anything." It was the truth. I wasn't going to accuse Abbie. I didn't think I'd need to. I expected her to give herself away.

I stood at the counter with my back to Abbie. When she wasn't looking in my direction, I slipped the box of stationery out of the bag, leaving it on the counter. "So Steven's here, huh?" I asked Abbie.

"He went upstairs to get some old vintage comic books to show me," she replied.

"I see." I pretended to notice the stationery for the first time and lifted the box. "I wonder where this came from. Abbie, is it yours?"

I stepped closer to her and held the box so she could clearly see the pale pink-flowered paper. Abbie drew in her breath sharply. Her complexion turned pale and then beet red. *Aha!* I thought triumphantly. *She recognizes it. She's guilty, all right!*

"Uh, no," Abbie said, recovering her composure. "It's not mine."

I took another step and towered over her, my hands on my hips. "Are you *sure?*"

"Yes, of course," Abbie squeaked. At that moment my brother entered the room, followed by Elizabeth. I quickly slipped the box of stationery out of sight.

That's all the evidence I need to be convinced that Abbie's the culprit, but in typical

*fashion Elizabeth wants to give her the ben-
efit of the doubt . . . even if waiting means
letting Steven and Cara's relationship go
down the drain. We'll see who's right!*

Friday afternoon

*The sparks are really flying! Just as I ex-
pected, Diary, Abbie's sugar-sweet nice girl act
is just an act. I came home from cheerleading
practice this afternoon and when I walked
into the house, there was Abbie . . . with a letter in her hand. The pink stationery! When I
asked her about it, she mumbled something
and stuck the letter back in her purse. I told
Elizabeth as soon as she came home, and we
decided to confront Abbie right then and
there, in front of Steven. Talk about a scene!
Elizabeth doesn't usually get mad, but she
practically had smoke coming out of her ears.
She accused Abbie of writing the love letters
and using her friendship with Elizabeth as an
excuse to see Steven. Of course Abbie claimed
she didn't write the letters and only wanted to
be a friend to Steven and to all of us, but when
you're guilty, you're guilty. . . .*

Abbie had just marched out—the sound of the
front door slamming still echoed through the
house. Steven sat slumped on the couch, his whole

body limp and his eyes dull with shock. "I can't believe this," he said. "I really thought Abbie was my friend. I trusted her—I spilled my guts to her about what's been going wrong with Cara. And now it turns out—"

"It turns out she was behind it all," I cut in. "What a little schemer! First she writes anonymous love letters to you on Tricia's stationery just to throw you off balance. Then when things get tense with Cara, she plants herself conveniently nearby so you'll confide in her. And when your relationship with Cara totally falls apart, Abbie just happens to be right there to pick up the pieces!"

"I don't know," said Elizabeth, staring out the window after Abbie. "She really seemed upset. She was crying! Maybe we've got it wrong—maybe she didn't write the letters."

"She wrote the letters," I insisted. "The clerk at Pen and Paper described her to a *T*. And don't forget, I caught her red-handed!"

"I feel so stupid," groaned Steven. "Why didn't I see what was going on?"

"You didn't stand a chance," I told him. "Abbie was really sly. Just be thankful we exposed her before the two of you got involved."

"I never wanted to date Abbie, though," Steven said. "I liked her, but only as a friend. Cara's the one I'm crazy about. Do you think I'll ever be able to straighten things out with her?"

I thought about my recent conversations with

Cara. She'd been depressed at the prospect of breaking up with Steven, but Lila, Amy, and I had done a pretty good job convincing her that going solo would be a blast. "I don't know, Steven," I replied. "Maybe it's not too late, but I can't guarantee it."

Steven rose to his feet. "I've been acting like a jerk," he said with a troubled sigh. "There's no reason she should forgive me."

Elizabeth and I watched our brother shuffle sadly from the room. "Abbie," I muttered. "What a piece of work!"

Elizabeth bit her lip, still looking a little unsure, but I had absolutely no doubts. Abbie Richardson had made a royal mess of my brother's love life.

Friday evening

I'm back. To keep track of events in this household, I'd have to be a full-time scribe. Not my idea of a good time! It turns out we were a hundred percent wrong about Abbie. Of course, I was always pretty sure she was innocent. But when Elizabeth gets an idea in her head, there's no changing her mind. Don't you hate people like that?

Here's the dirt. Cara came over right after Abbie left and made this big confession. It turns out she was the one writing the anonymous love letters! Isn't that crazy? She says she was just trying to put some mystery into her relationship with Steven. Where did she ever get a wacky idea like that? Anyhow, she had no idea she'd bought the same kind of stationery Tricia always wrote on. That's what made the scheme backfire. When Steven got the letters, instead of guessing they were from Cara as he probably would have otherwise, he got totally freaked out. He acted secretive, which made Cara insecure because she decided that meant there must be another girl in his life, maybe someone at college. They had a total communication breakdown. What tangled webs we weave!

Once Cara broke the ice, it didn't take those two long to clear the air. They're moonier than ever, probably because they came so close to blowing it. But as soon as Steven and Cara were back together, Elizabeth and I remembered something. Abbie! We'd falsely accused her. What were we going to say to her now?

"I don't know why I should apologize," I said, crossing my arms with a scowl. "I didn't do anything wrong."

Elizabeth gaped at me. "Who was it who swore on the Bible she saw Abbie with one of the letters?"

"I *did* see her," I acknowledged, "and she *was* holding a letter. Of course it turns out she only had it because Steven showed it to her, trying to get her advice. Is it my fault, though, that you jumped to the wrong conclusion?"

Elizabeth started to splutter. "*I* jumped to the wrong conclusion? *I* jumped?"

"There you go," I said. "You admit it yourself!"

I could tell Elizabeth wanted to strangle me, and I was within easy reach—we were crammed in the backseat of Steven's yellow Volkswagen bug. Fortunately just then Steven pulled into Abbie's driveway.

"I'm not looking forward to this," he said under his breath. "We really hurt her feelings. It would serve us right if she refuses even to talk to us."

I personally didn't care if I never spoke to Abbie Richardson again, but Elizabeth, Steven, and Cara seemed determined to make it up to her. I followed them up the walk to Abbie's house.

Cara rang the doorbell, and we spent a tense minute waiting. Then the door swung open and Abbie looked out at us, her chin in the air and her eyes flashing with defiant fire. "Yes?" she said coolly.

Elizabeth had rehearsed an apology in the car, but as soon as she saw Abbie she broke down completely. "Abbie, we're so sorry!" she cried, throwing her arms around Abbie's neck.

"It was a huge misunderstanding," said Cara. "I was the one writing the letters to Steven."

"It was terrible of us to accuse you without any real evidence," Steven added, his expression contrite.

Everyone looked at me as if it was my turn to fall to my knees and kiss Abbie's feet. No way!

"They *are* really sorry," I assured Abbie.

Elizabeth explained the whole mix-up from start to finish. "We should have trusted you," she concluded. "We should have realized you're a true friend. Can you ever forgive us, Abbie?"

Slowly a smile spread over Abbie's face. "Of course," she said. "Isn't that what friendship is all about?"

She and Elizabeth hugged again. Then she hugged Cara, then Steven. Then Steven hugged Cara. It was a total hug fest. Before anyone could grab me, I made tracks for the VW, wedging myself into the bug's backseat. "Get me out of here!" I muttered.

My dad got an extra ticket to the Lakers' game, so we're all going together—Cara and Abbie. Everyone's buddy-buddy again—it's just so sweet. The frosting on the cake for Abbie is that her cartoon, "Jenny," won the Oracle *humor contest and is going to be a regular feature. Nothing like a happy ending, I suppose. Gag me!*

P.S. Speaking of basketball, Todd finally wrote back. It was a pretty good letter, I must say—he cracks me up. I think I'll wait awhile before I write back, though. If I write back, I mean. It's not a good move to let a guy (any guy, even your sister's exboyfriend!) think you have nothing better to do than sit around writing letters!

Part 3

Thursday evening

Dear Diary,

All week long I've felt like something really exciting was about to happen. As usual, I'm a hundred percent right. My cousin, Kelly Bates, is coming to Sweet Valley! The best part is, she's staying with us indefinitely—she'll go to school with us! Aunt Laura and Uncle Greg got divorced a long time ago and now Aunt Laura's getting married again, to some doctor with a couple of young kids. I guess Kelly's stressing out about it, and so she and her mom decided she needed a change of scenery to help her adjust. I don't really care about the reason. I'm just so psyched she's coming!

93

She lives in Tucson and we haven't seen her in eight years, since Aunt Laura left Sweet Valley for Arizona. But we've been pen pals, and I can tell from the pictures she sends that she's a knockout. She looks a lot like me, in fact! I can't wait to introduce her to Sweet Valley society—she's going to make a superbig splash. People will be talking about Kelly (and me!) for years and years to come. . . .

"These are so addictive," I said, reaching for one of my sister's french fries. Elizabeth and I were sitting at a big table in the Dairi Burger, our favorite after-school hangout, with Jeffrey, Amy, Cara, Enid, and Aaron. I dipped another fry into the pool of ketchup. "I was going to diet today, but I can't seem to stop myself!"

Elizabeth laughed. "I knew as soon as you saw our milk shakes you'd be pretty dissatisfied with your iced tea."

"I'm starving," I admitted with a resigned smile. "I'm going to the counter to order a burger. Anybody want anything?"

When I returned to the table, Nicholas Morrow had joined us. Nicholas is one of the best-looking guys in Sweet Valley—wavy black hair, emerald green eyes, and a cleft in his chin that makes him look like a movie star. He graduated from SVH last year, but he's still in town working at his dad's

94

computer company—he wants some business experience before he starts college. That's Nicholas—Mr. Mature. He's gorgeous, but way too serious for me. And he's been extra serious since his younger sister, Regina, died. It was good to see him looking relaxed and smiling.

"Hey, Nicholas," I greeted him as I slid back into my seat. "Did you cut out from work early?"

"Actually this is my lunch break," Nicholas said wryly. "It's one of those days."

"You know what they say," I warned him. "All work and no play . . ."

Elizabeth turned to me. "I was just telling these guys about Kelly," she said. "I'm enlisting their help. I really want Kelly to have a good time while she's here to take her mind off things back in Arizona."

"What's going on back in Arizona?" Aaron wanted to know.

"Her mom's remarrying," Elizabeth answered.

"And she doesn't like the new guy?" guessed Enid.

Elizabeth shrugged. "We don't really know the whole story."

I didn't want these guys to get the wrong impression. "Kelly's a lot of fun," I put in quickly. "She loves to dance and shop, and she's a great athlete." My gaze settled on Nicholas and a brilliant idea blossomed in my oh-so-clever brain. "She plays tennis *and* golf. Maybe you could take her to the country club sometime, Nicholas."

Nicholas looked a little surprised. "Oh, well, sure," he said politely. "I'd be happy to do that."

I took a big bite of my burger to hide my smile. Nicholas and Kelly—they'd be a perfect couple! Nicholas wasn't currently dating anyone, but just because I wasn't interested in him didn't mean he should go to waste. And I happened to know he liked blond hair and blue eyes. He used to have a crush on Elizabeth!

"Kelly's smart and spectacularly beautiful," I said to Nicholas, hoping to pique his interest. "But I don't need to tell you that. You'll find out for yourself soon enough!"

Tuesday night, late

Kelly's here! We've been so busy, I haven't had a chance to write for a couple of days. She's as gorgeous as ever. You should see the three of us: me, Elizabeth, and Kelly. We've been wearing matching outfits to school and really blowing people's minds!

Remember my plan to fix Kelly up with Nicholas? It's working out perfectly. Elizabeth and I introduced the two of them the other day and they really hit it off. Right on the spot Nicholas invited Kelly to a costume party at the country club! She's the first girl he's asked out since Regina died. Even though on the surface Kelly is always laughing and smiling, I sense there's something else going on deep inside her, and Nicholas is the exact same way. I think this could end up being true love, and they'll have me to thank. I'll be the maid of honor at their wedding, of course!

Wednesday afternoon

I thought I knew my cousin pretty well. Maybe we haven't spent much time together since we were little kids, but we always wrote letters and talked on the phone. And we're blood relatives, right? We look alike—I guess I expected us to think alike. But today Kelly surprised me and Elizabeth in more ways than one. . . .

We'd taken Kelly to Secca Lake after school to swim and windsurf. Now we were lying on a beach blanket on the grass, drying off. "It's so beautiful here," Kelly said lazily. "So green and lush compared to the desert in Arizona."

"It must get incredibly hot there," Elizabeth remarked.

"We roast in the summer," Kelly confirmed.

"I'd hate it," I declared, stretching my arms over my head. "I'd die if I lived that far from the ocean."

"I've missed Sweet Valley," Kelly confessed. Rolling onto her stomach, she pillowed her chin on her arms and gazed out at the sparkling blue water. "I'd like to move back here."

"It sounds like your mom's put down roots in Tucson, but maybe someday," Elizabeth said. "You could go to college here."

"I don't want to wait that long," Kelly responded.

"Do you have a choice, though?" I wondered.

"Yes," Kelly said firmly. "I could move in with my dad. He lives just a few towns away. Maybe I could even talk him into relocating to Sweet Valley!"

Elizabeth and I both sat up and stared at Kelly, stunned by this announcement. "Move in with your dad?" Elizabeth repeated.

Kelly nodded. "Why not?" she said, her tone defensive. "He's my parent too. And I'm tired of my mother trying to keep us apart. I get along so much better with him than I do with her. He's so much nicer and more understanding, and a million times more fun! Yes, I'm going to do it," she said, more to herself than to us. "Next time I talk to him, I'll tell him I want to live with him."

Elizabeth and I exchanged glances. I could tell exactly what Elizabeth was thinking. I didn't remember Uncle Greg that well, but from the way my mother talked about her sister's ex-husband, I got the distinct impression he was kind of callous and irresponsible. Apparently he'd remained single, and he traveled a lot and had no intentions of settling down again anytime soon. *I bet the last thing he wants is to be saddled with a teenage daughter,* I thought.

"You'll have to talk to Aunt Laura about this, huh?" Elizabeth said to Kelly.

Kelly shrugged. "Maybe."

An awkward silence fell over us. Not for long— I hate awkward silences. "Maybe you *will* have to move back to Sweet Valley," I said, a teasing note in my voice, "if you get involved with Nicholas. Long-distance relationships are such a pain!"

"I don't think I'll be getting serious with Nicholas," Kelly replied.

"Why not?" I asked. "The country club dance could be the start of something big!"

"To tell you the truth," Kelly said, "I only said I'd go with him out of politeness. He's not really my type."

"Not your *type?*" I couldn't hide my astonishment. Kelly was turning up her nose at Sweet Valley's best and brightest? "What's wrong with Nicholas?"

"Nothing's wrong with Nicholas," Kelly answered. "He's extremely nice. Maybe too nice. I like guys with more of a wild side, you know?"

We didn't know, actually. "What do you mean?" asked Elizabeth, curious.

"Well, there was this guy back in Tucson," Kelly

confided. "Dave." She got this starry look in her eyes just saying his name. "He was kind of a rebel, you know? Rode a motorcycle, drank beer, cut school a lot." A hard edge entered her voice. "Needless to say, Mom did *not* approve. That's part of the reason I'm here—she wanted to get me away from him."

Once again Elizabeth and I were speechless. This was the first we'd heard of a forbidden romance back in Tucson. "You're kidding!" I yelped at last.

"Nope, it's true," Kelly said casually. "Mom and I had a huge fight the night before I left. I threatened to run off with Dave instead of coming to Sweet Valley!" She smiled. "Of course I wasn't serious, but Mom had a fit. I have to say that was part of the attraction with Dave. Mom hated him, and I love making her mad."

Kelly's story was really an eye-opener—a new window on her personality. "Wow," I said simply.

She laughed. "Don't look so shocked, Jess. I happen to know that you have a naughty side too."

"Yeah," I admitted, "but . . ." *But it doesn't involve tormenting my parents by dating guys they don't like,* I thought. I didn't say it, though—I'm not Elizabeth, after all. I hate moralizing, and I try not to judge people. "Well, anyhow," I said. "Dave's history?"

"I'm open to meeting someone new," Kelly said. "And don't get me wrong about what I said before. I really like Nicholas. It was sweet of him to ask me to the dance—we'll have fun."

"I hope so," Elizabeth said sincerely.

I hope so, too, Diary. Maybe I should give Nicholas a few hints: if he wants to turn Kelly on, he'd better take her to the dance wearing black leather and riding a Harley!

Thursday night

I'm watching Rock TV, *but I can't give Jamie Peters's cool new concert video the attention it deserves because I'm too distracted thinking about Kelly. There's trouble in paradise, Diary. You will not believe who Kelly "Nicholas is too nice for me" Bates has decided to fall head over heels in love with. Kirk "the Jerk" Anderson! I really hoped I'd never have to write that name in here again. You don't have to remind me. I know I fell like a ton of bricks for him when he first moved to Sweet Valley—me and every other girl in town. But it didn't take me long to figure out what Kirk is really all about. He's the rudest, most arrogant and immature and insensitive male of the species.*

But he's also incredibly good looking

*and charming in this sleazy kind of way.
We ran into him at the tennis courts this
afternoon and he swept Kelly off her feet.
They went out to dinner together, and all
night she's been raving about what a great
guy he is. I tried to warn her about the
true Kirk the Jerk personality, but she just
wouldn't listen. . . .*

Kelly wandered into my bedroom, which she's
sharing for the first month of her visit, and flopped
onto her bed. Her arms folded behind her head,
she stared up at the ceiling with a dreamy look on
her face. Elizabeth and I were both sitting on my
bed, sorting through a batch of double prints we'd
just gotten back from the photo shop.

We exchanged glances. "Did you have a nice
time with Kirk?" Elizabeth asked, her self-control
admirable.

"Did I ever," gushed Kelly, sitting up and hugging her knees. "I think I'm in love, girls."

Fast work, Kirk, I thought grimly. "I hate to say
this, Kelly, because I'm the impetuous, fall-madly-
in-love type myself, but in the case of Kirk . . ."
Just in time I stopped myself from adding "the
Jerk." "In Kirk's case I'd go slow if I were you," I
counseled. "He might not turn out to be as nice as
you think he is."

To my surprise, Kelly's turquoise eyes crinkled
in a smile. "Kirk told me you'd say that. He said a

lot of people got the wrong impression of him when he first moved here. If you'd really taken the time to get to know him, Jessica, you'd have found out that he's an incredibly sweet, gentle person."

If I'd taken the time. Yeah, and you know him inside and out now that you've spent a whole hour with him at the Dairi Burger! "I got to know Kirk plenty well, thank you," I told Kelly dryly.

Kelly looked at Elizabeth. "What do you think, Liz?" she said, her tone playful. "Do you detect a note of jealousy?"

"Jealousy?" I barked. "Are you joking?"

Kelly shook a finger at me. "Now, Jess. Just because Kirk didn't like you as much as you liked him doesn't mean you should begrudge me my good fortune."

"Kirk didn't like me as much as I—" I spluttered. Elizabeth clapped a hand over her mouth, giggling. I glowered at her. "I think you got the wrong story, Kelly."

"It's OK, Jess," Kelly assured me. "Kirk didn't go into detail about what happened between the two of you. He's a real gentleman. And I don't blame you one bit for being jealous!" She sighed, her eyes misting over. "He has the best body you've ever seen, admit it. And those blue eyes . . ."

There was clearly nothing else Elizabeth and I could say. Kelly was a goner. It looked like one more girl was going to learn the hard way about Kirk the Jerk.

The worst part of it is, Diary, Kelly told us she wants to break her date with Nicholas. Kirk's family belongs to the country club too, and he asked her to the dance and she'd rather go with him!

I'm really worried about her, to tell you the truth. She acts so worldly and sophisticated, like when she told us about Dave, her bad biker boyfriend, but she must be pretty naive to fall so easily for Kirk's routine. I don't want her to get hurt. Kirk isn't the only problem either. Aunt Laura called tonight and Kelly wouldn't pick up the phone, even to say hi. I can't imagine not wanting to talk to my mom! Something must really be wrong between those two.

Then there are the bad dreams—Kelly wakes up crying practically every night. She tries to hide it, but it's starting to be obvious that deep down inside she's not happy. And I don't know what I can do to help.

Friday evening

Right now Kelly's in the bathroom putting on her makeup—she has a date with Kirk the Jerk. So I only have a minute, but I need to confess. I did something bad tonight. I can't tell Elizabeth because she'd chew me out, but I really wish I could get her opinion. I listened in on a phone conversation between Kelly and her mom. It was an accident. Really! Well, sort of. Anyway, talk about the Cold War. . . .

I was rummaging through Elizabeth's closet when the phone rang. Elizabeth was downstairs, so I picked up the extension on her night table. Kelly must have answered the phone in my room at the exact same moment. "Hello?" I heard her say.

"Kelly, it's your mom," Aunt Laura responded.

I knew I should hang up. The call wasn't for me, and Kelly deserved her privacy. It was probably hard for her, sharing a bedroom and bathroom with her cousins. But my curiosity got the better of me. I couldn't bring myself to put down the receiver—I stood paralyzed, the phone clamped to my ear.

"Hi," Kelly said, her tone curt.

"I know it's Friday night," Aunt Laura said in a rush, "so I won't keep you, but we haven't talked since you got to Sweet Valley. Are you settling in all right? Are you having a good time?"

"Yeah," said Kelly. "Look, I have to go. I'm trying to get ready for a date."

"A date? So soon?" Aunt Laura laughed nervously. "A friend of the twins', I assume."

"Actually, no." I could hear the malicious pleasure

105

in Kelly's voice. "They can't stand him. But you know how I feel about this kind of thing, Mom. It doesn't matter if other people don't like who I date as long as *I* like who I date."

"Kelly." Aunt Laura's voice shook as she fought to maintain her self-control. "I hope you're not giving your aunt and uncle any trouble. If I hear that you're not following the rules of their household, you'll be back home in Tucson in no time."

I held my breath, waiting for Kelly to drop the bombshell about not planning to go back to Tucson ever. But Kelly remained stubbornly silent. Finally Aunt Laura sighed. "Let's not do this, honey," she pleaded. "I really want this time apart to be constructive for us."

"You started it," Kelly snapped.

"OK, let me try again," Aunt Laura said with forced cheerfulness. "Tony and I want to fly to California to take you out for your birthday. Pick any restaurant you want and—"

"Sorry, Mom," Kelly cut in, "but Dad gets back from a business trip next week. I'm spending my birthday with him."

"Oh." Aunt Laura's disappointment was painfully audible. "Well, of course. That'll be fun."

"I've got to go. I think Kirk's here," Kelly said, although I hadn't heard the doorbell.

"Sure, honey. Bye."

"Bye."

Kelly hung up the phone and I did the same. I

let a few minutes pass and then I grabbed a couple of dresses at random from Elizabeth's closet and returned to my room via the bathroom.

Kelly was standing in front of my mirror, holding a pair of earrings up to her ears. "What do you think, Jess?" she asked. "Do you like these or . . ." She held up another pair. "These?"

"The first pair," I said, dumping Elizabeth's dresses on my bed. "So." I tried to sound casual. "Was that call for you?"

"Yep," said Kelly, slipping on the earrings and then examining an assortment of silver bracelets.

"Kirk, huh?"

"No, my mom," Kelly answered.

"She must miss you," I remarked.

"I suppose," said Kelly.

I didn't know what to say next. If Kelly was having problems with her mother, I wanted her to feel she could talk to me about it. But I didn't want her to pick up on the fact that I'd eavesdropped on the conversation. "I bet she was calling to ask you what you want for your birthday," I said.

"She doesn't have to get me anything. You know why?" Kelly answered her own question. "I'm already getting what I want most. I got a letter from my dad today, and he's coming home early from a business trip in Paris just to take me out to dinner at a fancy restaurant on my birthday!"

"Wow, what a nice thing to do," I said.

Kelly beamed. "That's the kind of guy he is.

He's so incredibly thoughtful and generous. He'll probably bring me a bunch of great presents too."

"Do you get to see him very often?"

"No, but that's just because he's so busy with his job," Kelly replied somewhat defensively. "He's a total workaholic. But when we *are* together, we have the best time. He doesn't try to restrict me with a million stupid rules. He lets me be me."

"He does sound terrific," I admitted. "It's funny, though. I hardly even remember him. I haven't seen him in eight years."

Kelly's expression darkened. "It's all my mom's fault," she burst out. "She tore our family apart."

I blinked at Kelly's vehemence. My mother doesn't refer to her sister's divorce very often, but when she does, it's pretty obvious that she thinks Uncle Greg was to blame. "I'm sure they both had something to do with the marriage ending," I volunteered. "I mean, it takes two to tango."

Kelly shook her head. "She walked out on him and she dragged me to Tucson, and then she never let me come back here to visit. It's my mom's fault," Kelly repeated. She took a deep breath and then smiled broadly. "But I don't want to talk about her. I'd rather talk about my father, and how much fun he and I will have on my birthday, and how great it will be when I'm living with him instead of Mom."

"Sure, Kelly," I said easily. But my own smile was forced. I wanted my cousin to be happy, but I couldn't help thinking she was looking for love in all the wrong places.

I just don't understand what's going on with Kelly. Aunt Laura is the nicest person in the world, but Kelly hates her and wants to move in with her dad, who from all reports hasn't paid that much attention to her since the divorce. Between that and her nightmares, a psychiatrist would probably have a field day with Kelly's brain. Judging from the fact that she ditched Nicholas Morrow for Kirk Anderson, I'd say she definitely needs her head examined!

Saturday afternoon

I've just got to tell you something, Diary, to get it out of my system. It's one of those terrible thoughts that I always hate myself for having, but I can't help it. I'm only human, right? So, Amy has this great new haircut and she really looks fabulous. Yesterday in school Paul Jeffries, this incredibly cute senior, asked her out. And I wasn't even psyched for her. In fact, I found myself wishing she'd break a fingernail or get food in her teeth at lunch and not realize it until dinner. Isn't that wicked? Am I just totally self-centered, so much so

*that I can't be happy if I'm not prettier and
more popular than all my friends?*

*I'll do something nice for Amy to make
it up to her, even though of course she has
no idea I'm feeling this way. But how come
Paul Jeffries never asked me out?*

Sunday afternoon

*What a weekend. Kelly is really hung
up on Kirk the Jerk. Yuck. Meanwhile Kirk
is up to his usual tricks. Like the other
night when they were going to the Beach
Disco, he was a solid hour late picking her
up. So Kelly's sitting around chewing her
fingernails, and then Kirk finally strolls
in, and instead of reading him the riot act,
she just melts all over him. It was truly
nauseating. But that's not the worst part.
Once again I've got some secret information that I actually have to keep secret even
though I'm dying to tell someone. I hate it
when that happens! Get this: I saw Kirk
kissing his old girlfriend Marci at the
beach today. . . .*

"Doesn't it bug you that Kirk's old girlfriend is
here?" I asked Kelly at the beach on Saturday.

Kirk had just joined the Frisbee football game,
but a few minutes earlier he'd been talking to

Marci Kaplan, his very attractive ex. Kelly un-capped a bottle of suntan lotion. "Kirk's here to be with me," she said with assurance. "And I really don't mind that he's still friends with Marci. He told me that her parents are splitting up and she's been kind of upset about it. I think it's incredibly sweet that he still cares about what's going on in her life."

I caught Elizabeth's eye. She looked as skepti-cal as I did. Kirk Anderson, "sweet"? I doubted it! "You're more understanding than I'd be," I told Kelly frankly. "When I date a guy, if he even speaks the name of one of his old girlfriends in my pres-ence, he's history."

"I trust Kirk," Kelly said. "If he tells me Marci's just a friend, she's just a friend." She hopped to her feet. "Anybody want to swim?"

Elizabeth got up and walked with Kelly toward the water. I rolled over on my towel to talk to Cara and Amy, who were sunning themselves a few yards away. "I really feel sorry for Kelly," Amy com-mented, adjusting her sunglasses. "She's setting herself up for a pretty big fall."

"Maybe Kirk *has* changed," Cara said.

"Yeah, and the sun's going to start rising in the west," I remarked dryly. "I'm going to the snack bar to buy a soda. You guys want anything?"

I headed down the beach to the snack bar at a leisurely pace. No point hurrying and denying the boys a good long opportunity to admire me in my black string bikini! I was carrying a couple of dollars—obviously I didn't have a pocket—and it was breezy. All of a sudden, a gust whipped the bills from my hand and I found myself chasing my money across the sand. I grabbed one dollar, but the other two danced up into the dunes. I waded into the grass after them.

Just as I was about to dive on the rest of my money, I saw something that froze me in my tracks. Hidden behind a dune, a guy and a girl were wrapped in a passionate embrace. The girl in the hot pink bikini was dark haired and willowy, and the broad-shouldered guy wore royal blue swim trunks. *I recognize these people*, I thought. Then they parted for an instant before resuming their clinch, and I got a good look at them both. Kirk and Marci!

Leaving my money in the sand, I scurried backward before they could see me. As I stomped back to my towel, watching Kelly and Elizabeth splashing in the waves in the distance, my eyes flashed with indignation. "That rat," I muttered to myself. "My poor stupid cousin. Kirk the Jerk strikes again."

I'm not really surprised that Kirk's cheating on Kelly. It's totally in character. He's an animal; it's that simple. I came really close to telling Kelly what I saw, but then I changed my mind. She's so infatuated with Kirk and she already thinks I'm jealous—it would only turn her against me. Shoot the messenger and all that. I can't tell Lila and Amy and Cara either, or the news will be all over Sweet Valley in thirty seconds. I can't even tell Elizabeth. She's even more naive than Kelly—she doesn't understand this kind of thing. No, the only thing to do is hope that Kelly realizes on her own what a loser Kirk is. And I hope it's sooner rather than later.

Saturday morning,
I mean afternoon

Yesterday was Kelly's birthday, and it was a certified disaster. Remember how I wrote that she was incredibly excited about her father flying home early from a business trip, supposedly to take her out for dinner at some fancy restaurant and shower her with fabulous gifts? If you think that's the way it happened, you'd be very wrong. You would not believe this man. He's just like Kirk the Jerk, only he should be old enough to know better. We had a little birthday party all set up, right? You know, appetizers and stuff so we could all toast Kelly before Uncle Greg whisked her off to La Maison Blanche.

113

*There's Kelly, all dressed up. And guess who
was an hour and a half late?*

*Uncle Greg breezed in full of excuses
that sounded totally bogus, if you want my
opinion. The man is handsome, I'll grant
you that, and he has this magnetism—
Kelly lit up like a Christmas tree when he
walked into the house. We were all ready
to give him a second chance, but then he
did something truly awful. He left. That's
right. He didn't take her out to dinner—he
didn't even stay for a drink! He gave Kelly
some lame story about a late business meeting in Los Angeles You should have seen
her face. "Give me a smile, princess," he
said, and she did her best, but it was obvious she was crushed. . . .*

Kelly went outside to wave goodbye to Uncle
Greg. Elizabeth and I just sat on the living room
couch, limp with surprise. My mother, meanwhile,
was fuming. "That man has no heart," she declared,
her voice shaking with anger. "Disappointing Kelly
like that when she needs him and looks up to him
so much . . . I don't know how Laura put up with
him as long as she did! And the way he thinks that a
charming smile can get him off the hook for the
most unforgivable behavior. It brings back so many
memories of times when Laura would call me up,
crying, and—"

My father put a hand on her arm. "Let's go in the kitchen, Alice," he suggested quietly, glancing in Elizabeth's and my direction.

Obviously my mother had forgotten that Elizabeth and I were there. As soon as my dad drew her attention back to us—unfortunately, since I wanted to know all the juicy details!—she pressed her lips together. Shaking her head, she let my dad lead her into the kitchen, but not before I saw her dash a tear from her eye.

At that moment Kelly reentered the house. She sat down on a chair on the other side of the coffee table and sighed dejectedly. "My poor dad," she said. "I can't believe those people in Los Angeles wouldn't let him reschedule this meeting. He works way too hard."

I cocked an eyebrow. "Your poor *dad?*" I exclaimed. "What about you? You're the one whose birthday just got wrecked!"

"My birthday isn't wrecked," Kelly said quickly. "My dad did his best. I'm happy I got to see him at all."

I wouldn't have been happy in Kelly's position, but I decided not to rub it in. "Well, at least you got lots of presents, right?" I said. "Let's see what he brought you from Paris!"

Spots of red started on Kelly's neck and crawled up to her cheeks. "Um, he didn't bring me anything," she mumbled, dropping her eyes. "He said he was too busy to shop, but he promised he'd pick me up something in Los Angeles."

Elizabeth and I both stared at Kelly with astonishment and pity. I knew I should keep my mouth shut, but the words burst out before I could stop them. "That's totally crummy!" I cried.

Kelly's blush deepened. "He did his best," she said again, but with less conviction. "He really does love me. He puts me first when he can."

"Look what came when you were out saying goodbye to him," Elizabeth interjected, trying to smooth the troubled waters. She pointed to an enormous bouquet of flowers standing on the hearth. "I think they're from your mom and Tony. And we have something for you too."

Elizabeth held out a package tied with a pink bow, but Kelly was walking toward the flowers, a dazed look on her face. She opened the card that came with the bouquet and read it silently. Then to my amazement, she burst into tears. "I don't want anything from her!" she shouted, ripping the card into shreds. Then she yanked the flowers from the vase and hurled them to the ground. "She can't make it up to me by sending me stupid flowers. I'll never forgive her. Never!"

Kelly ran from the room, sobbing, while Elizabeth and I stared helplessly at the trampled bouquet.

I wish I could help Kelly, but I don't know what to do or say. I also wish I knew more about what happened to her family

116

eight years ago, when Aunt Laura walked out on Uncle Greg. My mom was so upset by what he did yesterday, and I could tell it dredged up old—bad—memories. All I know is, I always took my parents for granted, but looking at Kelly's family makes me realize how lucky I am. From now on I'm going to do ALL my chores without complaining. At least as many as I can possibly fit into my demanding schedule!

Sunday night

I never thought there were any skeletons in my family's closet—we Wakefields are so clean-cut. Boy, was I wrong! Big time. Last night the whole truth about Kelly's father came out. And in a really weird way, we have Kirk the Jerk to thank.

It all started at the country club costume party. Elizabeth, Kelly, and I went as the see-no-evil, hear-no-evil, speak-no-evil monkeys—pretty clever, huh? Kelly was see-no-evil, which was pretty appropriate given her blindness regarding both Kirk and her father. First, Kirk. Apparently he sweet-talked Kelly into leaving the dance and driving up to Miller's Point with him. Then he really put the moves on her. He had a six-pack of beer, and he wanted to

117

get her drunk, probably so she'd have sex with him. What a total disgusting creep. But Kelly told him to bug off. That's when Kirk lost it. He started yelling at her and hurling beer bottles off Miller's Point.

Here's the really wild part: the sound of glass breaking on the rocks below triggered a repressed memory in Kelly, and all of a sudden she felt like she was eight years old again. And she remembered hiding under the kitchen table while her parents had a fight, and her dad just exploded and started throwing every single glass and plate in the cupboard against the wall. Aunt Laura begged him to stop, but he didn't—not until everything in the kitchen was trashed. Isn't that awful? That's the reason Aunt Laura left him, and who could blame her? I guess it was so terrible and scary that Kelly's brain tried to hide it in her subconscious. But it didn't disappear altogether—that must have been what gave her nightmares, the memory popping up while she was asleep. The poor, poor kid.

Anyway, Kelly ditched Kirk at Miller's Point, and luckily Tom McKay and Jean West saw her walking down the road and brought her home. The whole experience was pretty traumatic. But I suppose it's good that Kelly's finally coming to terms

with what happened to her family all those
years ago and who's really to blame. . . .

"Are you sure you're OK?" Elizabeth asked, her voice hoarse with worry. "Kirk didn't hurt you? Because if he did, I'll call the police this minute."

Kelly shook her tangled blond hair. "He didn't hurt me," she said softly. "He just made a lot of noise."

We were sitting on my bed, Elizabeth and I on each side of Kelly with our arms around her. For a while she'd been crying so hard she couldn't speak, and then the whole story of her repressed memories had spilled out. Now all three of us were feeling emotionally drained.

I patted Kelly's back and pulled away so I could look into her face. "Kelly, what are you going to do now?" I asked.

Kelly sniffled. Elizabeth handed her a box of tissues. "I—I'm not sure." Kelly blew her nose. "I feel like I've lost my father all over again." Her blue-green eyes brimmed with tears. "But I love him, you know? No matter what happened when I was a kid. He's still my dad. And Tony will never take his place."

"I'm sure Tony doesn't expect to take your dad's place," Elizabeth told Kelly. "He's going to be your mom's husband, though, and your stepfather. One of these days you have to start getting used to that idea."

"Tony's not a bad guy," Kelly conceded, reaching for another tissue. "I understand why Mom likes him. I mean, loves him. Mom . . ." Kelly's face crumpled again. "Oh, things are just so messed up!" she wailed, burying her face in my shoulder. "I can't live with Dad because . . . I just can't. And I can't go back to Tucson because I've been so bratty that Mom will probably never want to see me again."

I gave Kelly a hug. "Are you kidding? Aunt Laura loves you to pieces. She's dying to patch things up with you."

"I really miss her," Kelly admitted tearfully. "But I feel so bad. I've been holding it against her all these years—thinking the divorce was all her fault, blaming her for the fact that I hardly ever saw Daddy. She never told me what caused her to leave him. And do you know, she never once said a single bad thing about him to me?"

"She probably didn't want to prejudice you against him," guessed Elizabeth. "She wanted you two to be able to have a relationship separate from her own bad history with him."

"So what should I do?" Kelly wondered helplessly.

"Call her," Elizabeth urged. "Talk all this over with her."

"I can't," whispered Kelly.

"You can," I said, squeezing her hand tightly.

"Everything's going to be all right," Elizabeth promised.

For a long moment we all sat in suspenseful silence. Then Kelly drew a deep breath and reached for the telephone.

The minute Kelly called, Aunt Laura was on the next plane to California. You should have seen them hug—I thought they'd never let go. They had a long, really intense talk and then Kelly packed her bags and went back to Tucson with her mom. I miss Kelly already, Diary, but I know she made the right decision. Uncle Greg isn't necessarily a bad person, but he's not cut out to be a full-time parent. Meanwhile Aunt Laura is just so strong. Kelly is too. I really admire them. I don't know if I could handle a situation that tough. My life's been pretty easy so far, you know? I consider myself smart and strong, but what if I had a real problem? I guess a person doesn't know how much guts he or she has until a real challenge comes along.

Monday night

Two words, Diary: Alexander Kane. Isn't that name intensely sexy and masculine and romantic and glamorous? Tell me more, you say? OK, here's the breaking news! I discovered THE cutest guy on earth

*hidden in a cottage on the beach. I'm glad
Kelly's gone, because I just wouldn't have
any time for her now that I've met
Alexander!*

*It all started with a baby-sitting job, be-
lieve it or not—I was actually there to take
care of his younger sister. Yes, I despise
baby-sitting—you don't need to remind
me. But my parents just got their latest
credit card bill with a bunch of charges at
Lisette's (I lost control at the mall's
Midnight Madness sale), so I'm in desperate need of cash. Two afternoons a week
with a five-year-old—I was dreading it, let
me tell you. But talk about fate! When I
caught my first glimpse of Alexander, I forgot all about little . . . what's her name?
Oh, yeah, Allison. . . .*

"Maybe this won't be so bad after all," I mused,
pulling into the driveway at 1729 Coast Road.

The rose-covered cedar bungalow stood in a
grove of pines on a windy bluff. At the end of a
flagstone path I could see the top of a weathered
wooden staircase leading down to the beach. I
didn't mind baby-sitting if I could work on my tan
at the same time!

As I stepped out of the Fiat a child emerged
from the cottage. If the cottage looked like a doll's
house, then here was the doll. Bright golden curls

cascaded over the little girl's shoulders and dimples creased her round pink cheeks. "Are you Jessica?" she asked sweetly.

I bent down to shake her hand. "You must be Allison," I said with a warm smile. "Nice to meet you."

"I want to build sand castles today," Allison told me earnestly, "but first my brother said I had to bring you inside to meet him. Come on."

She gave my hand a tug. I followed her into the house. The living room of the cottage was sparsely decorated, but there was a fancy stereo system and shelves with about a thousand classical CDs. Sheet music and instruments—a flute, a saxophone, and something that looked like a giant violin—were lying all over the place. I stifled a yawn. *These people live right on the beach and they hang out indoors listening to music?* I thought.

"The piano is in the sunroom," Allison was saying, leading me through the cottage. "That's where Alex plays. He goes to college and he's writing a sym—sym . . ."

"Symphony?" I guessed.

"Symphony," Allison repeated with a pleased smile. "There he is. See?"

She pointed to a figure rising from the bench behind the grand piano. My heart fluttered erratically, threatening to stop altogether.

A Greek god was walking toward me: tall, broad shouldered, with fair skin, clear green eyes, and wavy, golden hair. "Jessica," he said, his voice deep and melodic. "You're wonderful to help me out like this."

For a second I couldn't remember what he was talking about. Help him out? I was only too glad to, but how? Then I felt Allison tugging on the hem of my shorts. "Can we go to the beach now, Jessica?" she asked.

That's right. Baby-sitting! I recalled. "It's no problem," I assured Alex Kane, flashing my most alluring smile. I patted Allison's head, praying for a sudden thunderstorm so we'd have to stay inside. Who needed a tan? "We'll go to the beach in a minute," I told her.

"Don't let me keep you from the sun and sand," Alex said, gesturing toward the sliding glass doors. "Allison will show you the way down. The cove is a safe place for her to swim as long as you keep a close eye on her."

"Of course." My head whirled as I tried to dream up an excuse to linger with Alex. "Um, what about . . . snacks?"

"She just had a carton of yogurt and a peach," Alex told me with just the faintest trace of impatience. "That should keep her for a while."

"OK. Well, uh . . ." I scanned the room desperately, my gaze falling on some sheet music. "Oh, Tchaikovsky's Piano Concerto number one in B-flat Minor!" I exclaimed, hoping I'd pronounced Tchaikovsky right.

Alex's beautiful green eyes lit up. "You like Tchaikovsky?" he asked, a new note of interest in his voice.

I spied some more sheet music resting on top of the grand piano. "Almost as much as I like Liszt," I replied with enthusiasm.

"You're a musician," Alex deduced, stepping closer to me.

I could smell his woodsy aftershave; I almost swooned. "Yes," I admitted shyly.

"What instrument do you play?"

I'd been bluffing pretty well up to that point, but now my mind went blank. For the life of me I couldn't remember the name of a single instrument. *Oh, help!* I thought desperately.

Just in time Allison piped up. "I play the recorder," she declared with pride.

"Why, so do I," I said.

"You'll have to bring your recorder next time, then, Jessica," said Alex with a warm smile. "You and Allison can play duets."

"That would be lovely," I lied, happily drowning in the emerald fire of his eyes.

"And now I have to get back to my . . . what is it I'm working on, Allison?"

"Symphony!" she chirped.

"Right." Alex tousled her curls, and I nearly fainted with jealousy. I wished he'd run his fingers through *my* hair that way! "Have fun at the beach, girls."

It was love at first sight for both of us, Diary. Alex is so wonderful! Unbelievably handsome, incredibly gifted, intelligent, mature, sensitive . . . SIGH. So from this day forward I'm Jessica Wakefield, musician extraordinaire. Notes for tomorrow: 1. Buy a recorder and 2. Learn to play as if I'd been born with one in my hand. Jeez, I hope I can do all that in less than a week!

Wednesday evening

Cheerleading has been a little dull lately, but today we had some real fireworks. I had something to do with the spat between Robin and Annie, but I didn't cause trouble on purpose. Is it my fault that Robin applied to and got accepted early decision at Sarah Lawrence College in New York, and she doesn't know whether or not to go, but her rich aunt Fiona is putting on heavy-duty pressure because she'll only pay for Robin's education if Robin goes to Sarah Lawrence? Is it my fault Robin was keeping all this a secret from her boyfriend, George Warren? Is it my fault George found out secondhand and got really upset with Robin, and Robin blamed Annie when really I think George found out from Elizabeth, who found out from me? Whatever. It was a real knock-down-drag-out, with Annie proclaiming her innocence and Robin accusing Annie of trying to sabotage Robin and George's relationship so Annie could steal George, which is ridiculous because George Warren simply isn't that special—Annie could do better!

Anyhow, it might have been indirectly my fault that George heard about Robin's secret college plans, but I don't know for sure, so I steered clear of the confrontation. To tell you the truth, Diary, I kind of hope Robin does go to Sarah Lawrence next year. I, for one, won't miss her. I still can't believe she was chosen Homecoming Queen over me. How could people forget so quickly that she used to be as fat as a hippo? If she graduates early, I'll be sole captain of the cheerleading squad. Sounds good to me!

I can't believe I wasted that much ink and paper writing about Robin. Who cares about her boring life? Back to me! I spent twelve bucks on a plastic recorder and already my investment's paying off. I'm really making progress with Alexander. . . .

The late afternoon sun cast a golden glow on Allison as she put the finishing touches on her sand castle. "See, Jessica?" she called excitedly, waving her plastic shovel. "It has turrets and a drawbridge and a moat!"

"It's splendid," I agreed, sitting up and sliding the straps of my bikini top down on my arms so my shoulders could tan. "Best sand castle I've ever laid eyes on."

I'm not that interested in castles, though—rose-covered cottages are more my taste these days. I cast a longing look up at the house on the bluff, where Alex was slaving away at his symphony. Then I blinked. Was it a mirage? No. Alex was walking down the wooden steps!

He was wearing nothing but faded blue swim trunks, and my heart started doing backflips. I always thought musicians were either bony and gaunt or round and doughy. Alex didn't have much of a tan, but his body was perfect: lean, muscular, rock solid. I couldn't wait to wrap my arms around his slim waist and walk my fingers up that strong, well-muscled back.

In the meantime I was speechless with admiration. "Hi, Jessica," Alex greeted me cheerfully.

"H-h-hi," I choked out.

Alex dropped down onto the beach blanket just inches away from me. "For some reason I'm really distracted today," he confided. "I couldn't concentrate on the symphony—I kept thinking about you two enjoying the sun and surf. Finally I just had to come down and join you."

You were distracted because you caught a glimpse of my red bikini from the sunroom window! I guessed. "I'm glad you did," I purred. "Some sun and a swim will renew your creative energy."

Allison marched up, shovel and bucket in hand. "I'm done with my castle," she reported, about to plop down on the blanket in between me and her brother.

"Maybe you could build some other things," I said quickly. "How about a sand town to go with the castle? I think you need a sand gas station and a sand library and a sand grocery store. Otherwise where will the king and queen do their shopping?"

"You're right," Allison said after a moment's serious consideration. As she skipped back to the water's edge Alex laughed. "You're really good with her," he observed.

"She's easy," I said honestly. "I've never baby-sat for a sweeter kid."

"May I?" He reached over casually and flicked some sand off my arm. I almost passed out. "This arrangement is going to work out well, then. I'm glad."

"Me too," I murmured, still tingling from his touch. "Like I said, it's no trouble at all. She's so adorable, I'd do it for free!" *Actually* you're *so adorable, I'd do it for free!*

Alex looked deep into my eyes. "You're really special, Jessica," he remarked. "Most girls your age don't have much patience for baby-sitting."

I decided not to tell him that ordinarily I considered baby-sitting worse torture than having dental work done without Novocain. "I love kids," I fibbed.

"I hope this job doesn't keep you too busy to practice your music, though," said Alex with genuine concern.

What *music?* I almost said. "Oh, I always find the time," I told him. "When something's that important to me." *Take right now, for example,* I added silently. *Getting to know cute guys is one thing for which I always have plenty of time!*

"Did you bring your recorder with you today?" Alex asked.

I snapped my fingers with fake regret. "I knew I forgot something."

"Next time," said Alex. "I'd really like to hear you play."

I thought about my most recent practice session. I'd studied the instruction manual and tried to get my fingers placed just right over the holes of the recorder, but even when I blew into it with all the air in my lungs, I couldn't quite get anything that sounded like music to come out of it. Elizabeth had finally run screeching downstairs with her hands clapped over her ears.

Time to change the subject, I decided. I wanted Alex to think I was musical, but I also wanted him to think I was attractive, desirable, sexy, and most of all available. *You have five minutes to get this guy to ask you out on a date, Wakefield,* I challenged myself.

"So, Alex." I fluttered my eyelashes. "What do you do for fun when you're not composing music?"

"That's right. I'm supposed to be working on my symphony!" Hopping to his feet, Alex flashed me a bright smile. "Thanks for reminding me, Jessica. See you in a bit—don't let Allison get too much sun, OK?"

So much for my five minutes! I thought with a sigh as Alex jogged back up the stairs.

> *He was really close to asking me out, Diary—I could tell. He's just so committed to his music! It's kind of annoying, but it's also one of the exciting things about him— he's so passionate and intense. One day soon he'll be that intense and passionate about me. I can't wait!*
>
> *Except I have to tell you, I absolutely HATE the recorder. I wish it had never been invented! Talk about boring. And it's really, really hard too. My mom said she heard me practicing and I sounded good, but I still have a long way to go before I'm ready to perform for Alex. I should have told him I played the tambourine!*

> *Monday afternoon*

> *I wouldn't dare say this out loud, Diary, but I'm beginning to wonder if I've lost my*

touch with the male species. I have to face the sad truth: Alex Kane doesn't even know I'm alive. Every time I'm over there, I come up with excuses to drop in on him at the piano, but he always shoos me away. Even when I try to discuss music with him (not that I know what I'm talking about!), he gets really impatient and I can tell he's dying to get back to his stupid symphony. He pays attention to me when we talk about Allison, but that's it. Lila tells me to forget it—she's convinced I'll never get his attention—but I'm not ready to give up yet. He is still so outrageously good looking! Desperate times call for desperate measures, though . . . and right now, I qualify as desperate!

Wednesday afternoon

Interesting. I just barged into Elizabeth's room to borrow a couple of CDs, and she was sitting on her bed looking at a photo album. She closed the album fast when I came in as if she didn't want me to see it, but I'd already caught a glimpse. They weren't recent pictures of her and Jeffrey . . . they were old pictures of Todd! I wonder what the story is. Does she still secretly have a thing for him? Maybe

he's on her mind because I keep getting let-
ters from him. I almost felt sorry for her. I
don't get the impression from his letters
that Todd spends much time looking at old
pictures of her!

Saturday night

Today was the day, Diary. I knew I could
do it if I really applied myself, and sure
enough, I had Alexander Kane kneeling at
my feet. While Allison played on the swing
set, I was in her brother's embrace. . . .

"I'm thirsty," Allison announced, hanging upside down on the monkey bars.

I'd already struck out once with Alex that afternoon. I'd hidden Allison's recorder in the bookcase
so Alex and I would have to hunt for it together, but
he found it after about ten seconds and kicked me
out of the sunroom again. I had one more trick up
my sleeve, though, and here was my opportunity.

"I'll go inside and get you some juice," I told
Allison. "Stay on the ground until I get back, OK?"

She hopped down obediently and busied herself
picking daisies at the edge of the lawn. I hurried
into the house, my pulse quickening. *This is it,
Alex!* I thought. *Ready or not!*

As usual Alex was seated at the grand piano, his
agile fingers racing over the keys. Lush, complex,

romantic music filled the room. The perfect sound track for our first kiss!

Alex didn't look as if he wanted to kiss me, though. When I entered the sunroom, he stopped playing abruptly, a frown creasing his forehead. "What do you need, Jessica?" he asked curtly.

You, you, you! I wanted to shout. "I was just getting Allison something to drink," I replied, "and I thought while I was at it, I could bring you some iced tea or maybe some—" My knees buckled slightly and I rested a hand on the piano for support. "But all of a sudden I feel . . ." I put a hand to my forehead. My eyelids fluttered. "Oh, Alex," I murmured as my body went limp as a piece of overcooked spaghetti and sank to the floor.

Alex leapt up from the piano bench. "Jessica! Are you all right?"

He ran to my side and slid his arm under my shoulders, cradling me gently. I smothered a satisfied smile. I deserved an Academy Award for this performance!

Alex brushed the hair off my forehead and gave my cheek a gentle pat. "Jessica, can you hear me?" he asked urgently.

I opened my eyes and gazed up at him. "What happened?"

"You fainted," he told me. "Jessica, are you sick? Should I call a doctor?"

"No, I'll be fine," I said, feigning embarrassment. "I'm really sorry to be such a bother, Alex. I'll just . . ." I tried to sit up, then sank back weakly in Alex's arms.

His embrace tightened. "Don't try to walk," he counseled. "I think you should lie down for a few minutes."

He gathered me up in his arms, only stumbling once as he carried me to the sofa. I clasped my arms around his neck, my face pressed against his silken gold hair. This was even better than my fantasies!

Alex helped me onto the couch, his touch strong and gentle. He continued to kneel beside me, still holding my hand. "I'll be OK," I assured him, allowing my voice to tremble just slightly. "You'd better get back to your symphony."

"Hang my symphony!" Alex declared, his eyes flashing. "Jessica, I've been wanting to ask you if—"

If you can kiss me? Yes, yes! "What, Alex?" I said, my lips puckering in anticipation.

He sat back on his heels, shaking his head. "You're such a beautiful girl, Jessica," he murmured sheepishly. "I came so close just now to getting carried away."

Get carried away, already! I wanted to shout. *What's stopping you?*

"But the time isn't right," he went on.

I blinked. I couldn't imagine a time that was *more* right, myself. "It's not?"

"No," Alex said firmly. "I'm devoted to my music, Jessica. Surely you've noticed that."

"Yes," I admitted, wondering where all this was leading. Was he going to kiss me or not?

"In a month I'm leaving for New York to study at Juilliard for a semester. But maybe a year or two from now, when I'm back in California . . ." He clasped my hand tightly. "You'll be older, and I'll have more free time. What do you say, Jessica? Can we stay in touch? Can I call you from New York?"

A year or two from now? Call me from New York? A long-distance romance? He had to be kidding! He really expected me to sit around getting "older" until he could make time for a relationship?

No guy, even one as cute as Alex, is worth waiting years for. I sat up, instantly recovered from my faint. "I just remembered—my boyfriend's taking me for a sail this afternoon," I lied, putting heavy emphasis on the word *boyfriend*.

I practically knocked Alex over as I sprang up from the couch. "But what about baby-sitting?" he asked, startled.

I was already halfway across the room. "I'm not going to be able to work for you anymore," I answered, waving goodbye. "It's been fun. Give Allison a hug for me!"

"But Jessica," Alex called after me. "The future—"

The future is for the birds, I thought as I sprinted out the door. *I live for today!*

So Alex is history—not to mention that heinous recorder (I'm never going to listen to classical music again for as long as I live!). One more guy bites the dust. C'est la vie, as Ms. Dalton would say in French class. Still, it's nice to know that Alex was lusting after me—not that I ever doubted it!

Sunday night

Robin really outdid herself at the regional diving championship today. Have I ever mentioned that she's not just the cheerleading cocaptain, but she's also SVH's star diver? Such an overachiever! Anyway, she got a bunch of perfect scores and totally creamed Tracy King, her biggest rival. I have to admit, it was a pretty exciting meet, and even though she's not my best friend, I admire Robin's skill and concentration. I actually felt kind of bad for letting her believe that Annie was the one who told George about Sarah Lawrence (Elizabeth straightened everyone out, by the way, and Robin and Annie are buddies again). Sometimes I do things that I know are selfish and mean, but I just can't seem to stop myself. It doesn't

137

*matter, though, because now Robin's life is
better than ever. . . .*

We were all squeezed into the bleachers at the
Sweet Valley Community Pool: the entire cheer-
leading squad, Elizabeth and Jeffrey and a bunch
of their friends, Robin's boyfriend, George, and
Robin's whole family. Even her witchy old aunt
Fiona!

"The meet's so close, I can't stand it," Elizabeth
exclaimed, gripping my arm so hard it hurt. "Tracy's
still ahead of Robin, though, and there's only one
dive left!"

We'd watched the springboard part of the com-
petition and the compulsory platform dives. Robin
and Tracy each had one more free dive from the
platform. "Robin needs a perfect score," George
confirmed. His hands were clenched on his knees—
his knuckles were white. "She can do it," he added
in a low, intense voice.

Tracy was diving first. We held our breath as
she slowly, steadily climbed the tall ladder and
walked to the edge of the platform. She turned
around and inched backward until she was hanging
on by her toes. "A back dive," Elizabeth whispered.

Each second seemed to last forever. Finally
Tracy coiled her body and then flung herself up
and out.

She tucked herself into a tight somersault. One
roll, two, three. . . . She unfolded her body and

knifed into the water, her feet kicking up a big splash.

"Did you see that? She was way over!" Annie cried, bouncing excitedly. "They'll deduct points for sure!"

Tracy climbed out of the pool, her expression grim. Clearly she knew the dive had been mediocre. The scores clinched it: two nines and some high eights.

"Robin has a chance," Elizabeth breathed. "She just has to nail this dive."

"And she will," said George, his eyes gleaming. "She will."

It was Robin's turn to climb up to the platform. At the top she paused to adjust the straps on her red tank suit. The pressure was palpable. But Robin moved with easy confidence.

"Robin Wilson's last free dive will be a flying forward, two-and-a-half-somersault pike, half twist," the announcer boomed over the loudspeaker.

Robin stood poised with her shoulders straight and her head held high. She looked like a statue, frozen and beautiful, but then all of a sudden she was in motion, dashing forward to the edge of the platform and soaring out into space.

Her body seemed suspended over the pool for an eternity, spinning and tumbling with speed, grace, and precision. When at last she sliced into the blue water, there was hardly a ripple. Her Sweet Valley friends jumped to their feet, screaming.

"A perfect dive!" I hollered as Elizabeth gave Jeffrey an excited hug.

Robin stood at poolside, dripping wet and smiling. It was obvious she knew she'd nailed the dive. When her scores were announced, the clapping and cheering got even louder and wilder. Robin had earned three perfect tens—and won the meet!

Elizabeth and I tossed our programs in the air. I stamped my feet, clapping until my hands tingled. Meanwhile George scrambled down the bleachers and fought his way through the crowd to reach Robin's side. He threw his arms around her even though she was soaking wet. Then in front of everyone he gave her a long, lingering kiss.

For some reason at that instant, even though I was happy for Robin, I felt a little sad for myself. There were hundreds of people around them, but George and Robin had eyes only for each other. Elizabeth and Jeffrey were also standing with their arms locked around each other, two people who'd become one. *It must be nice to care about someone that much,* I thought, a little bit wistfully. Would it ever happen to me, or was I doomed to a life of pointless crushes on wildly inappropriate people like Alexander Kane?

Not that I'm feeling sorry for myself, Diary. I like dating around. I'd be bored silly going out with just one guy. But some-

times I can't help wondering what it would be like. . . .

Robin told her aunt Fiona she's going to defer her acceptance at Sarah Lawrence College and stay at Sweet Valley High for senior year like the rest of us. And when the time comes, she'll go to whatever college she wants, whether Aunt Fiona pays or not. Apparently Fiona, who's a stubborn old biddy herself, was impressed by Robin being so strong-minded and sure of herself, so she caved in and now she says she'll pay for any college Robin wants. So Robin has her best friend and her boyfriend back, and she gets to decide her own future.

Speaking of the future, it's back to the romantic drawing board for me. I wonder who the next man in my life will be? Black hair? Blue eyes? Maybe I could get a sneak preview if I had a crystal ball. Do they sell those at the Valley Mall?

Tuesday night

I'm beat. Totally, utterly, completely beat. But I can't sleep because my lunatic twin is squawking away on the recorder she inherited from yours truly! I laughed until I cried when I found out Elizabeth had been playing my recorder in secret.

· 141

That's why my mom said I sounded pretty good that time—because she was listening to Elizabeth! Not that Elizabeth is ready to take her show on the road, but she's better than me, and now she's taking lessons from Julie Porter. Julie Porter, by the way, would probably be the perfect match for Alexander Kane—she's a very serious, quiet, musical type who plays the recorder and the piano. Those two could talk about études and concertos until they were blue in the face!

But I'm beyond Alex Kane, as you know—way beyond. If I can concentrate on anything besides Elizabeth's mournful tooting, I'll explain how I plan to take Sweet Valley High by storm—as a prima ballerina!

It was late afternoon and I'd really worked up a thirst playing beach volleyball, so I called a time-out and trotted over to the cooler Ken Matthews had brought. The rest of the gang cooled off by plunging into the surf; I twisted the top off a bottle of fruit-flavored seltzer and flopped down on the beach blanket.

DeeDee Gordon was the only person sitting out the game. She sat in a beach chair, a towel wrapped around her legs, studying a notebook. I took a swig of seltzer. "How can you do homework when the sun is shining?" I asked, mystified.

DeeDee pushed her sunglasses up on her glossy dark hair. "It's not homework," she replied. "It's the script for the drama club's next production, *You Can't Take It with You.*"

DeeDee had recently been voted president of the drama club. I guess that's an honor, but it's also a lot of work. Personally I'd rather be onstage, front and center—the star!—than backstage. "Is the play any good?" I asked.

DeeDee nodded enthusiastically. "But we have a casting problem," she told me. "We thought we could cast the play entirely with drama club members, but there's one part that requires dancing ability as well as acting. And no one in the club knows ballet! So Mr. Jaworski's holding a special audition just to cast that role."

"Ballet?" I sat up straighter, my eyes glinting. "You know, when I was a kid, I took ballet lessons for about a century at Madame Andre's dance academy."

"Did you really?" asked DeeDee with interest. "But it's been a long time, huh? You're probably pretty rusty."

"I'm sure I could pick it up again just like that." I snapped my fingers. "I'm in really good shape, and I'm limber from cheerleading."

"Maybe you should audition, then," said DeeDee.

I wanted to make sure I wasn't wasting my time on a bit part. "Is it the lead role?"

"Not the lead, but a really important secondary character," DeeDee assured me. "Let's put it this way. When Essie's onstage, she steals the show."

It sounded perfect. My eyes fogged up as I imagined myself bowing before a standing ovation in the SVH auditorium, long-stemmed red roses raining onto the stage at my feet. I returned for curtain call after curtain call, and still my fans wouldn't stop clapping! A Hollywood agent was in the audience—he begged me to let him make me a star. In no time I was the name on everyone's lips, arriving at movie premieres in my own stretch limo, blasé about the fact that Starring Jessica Wakefield flashed in bright neon lights on every movie marquee in the country.

I came back to earth when DeeDee spoke again. "Auditions are Thursday after school," she said.

"I'll be there," I declared.

I only have a few days to polish my technique, but luckily the barre is still set up in the basement from back when Elizabeth and I both took ballet lessons. I practiced my pliés and relevés all afternoon. My muscles are pretty sore and I'm hungry, but I can't eat because I need to lose a few pounds if I don't want to look like a hog in my new hot pink leotard. I just hope I don't try to do a jeté in my sleep!

144

Auditions were today. Guess who got a callback? I'm so talented, it's almost frightening. I have to admit, though, I had a moment of panic when I realized Danielle Alexander was trying out for the part, too. She's tall, blond, and thin as a rail, and she's been doing ballet since she was in the cradle—supposedly she's good enough to audition for the Los Angeles Ballet Company. But lucky for me, I guess, she really flubbed her tryout. She started out strong, and then all of a sudden she just crumbled and turned into a real spaz! Not that my audition didn't have its sticky moments. My pirouettes were a little shaky, and I fell right on my rear during an arabesque. I didn't lose my cool, though—I just asked Mr. Jaworski, the drama coach, if he liked my "Grand Floppe," and we both got a good laugh. So I got called back and snooty Danielle didn't! Isn't that fabulous? The role will be mine, all mine! Maybe one of these days I'll even get around to reading the play. Elizabeth keeps bugging me about it, but it never takes me long to memorize lines, so I'm not going to sweat it. My time's better spent working on my ballet.

Speaking of Elizabeth, I can hear her from her bedroom, and she's having one of

145

*her intense discussions with Enid. They're
probably talking about books, or maybe
world peace. No, wait a minute—I just heard
the name "Bruce Patman." Could it be gossip? I'd better investigate. . . .*

I've eavesdropped on Elizabeth about a million
times—I really don't have any qualms about it. If she
really, *really* didn't want me to listen, she'd go somewhere else to have her conversations, wouldn't she? I
mean, is it my fault that our rooms are connected, or
that the door on her side of the bathroom has this
tendency to pop open just a teeny bit so that if I'm in
there innocently brushing my hair or putting on
makeup, I can hear every single word Elizabeth says?

Not that it's terribly exciting most of the time.
Usually I tell Elizabeth what's happening around
town. But every now and then she comes up with a
choice tidbit.

I'd just gotten out of a hot bubble bath—I'd
been soaking my sore muscles. "Bruce and Julie
Porter?" I heard Enid squeak in surprise.

It surprised me, too. I wrapped a towel around
myself and put my ear to the door to hear more. "She
told me at my recorder lesson today that he asked her
to be his date for the Phi Epsilon pledge party at his
house tomorrow night," Elizabeth said to Enid.

"I thought Julie liked Josh Bowen," said Enid.

"According to Julie, they're just really good
friends," Elizabeth replied. "Although if you want my

146

opinion, Josh is crazy about Julie and would ask her out in a second if she gave him any encouragement."

"Poor Josh." Enid laughed. "He's having a tough week with all the stunts Bruce and the rest of the Phi Ep guys are making him do!"

"That's what he gets for wanting to pledge the frat," Elizabeth stated. "It's pretty stupid, if you ask me."

I rolled my eyes at my reflection in the mirror. Elizabeth was such a wet blanket sometimes. So what if the Phi Eps were making Josh and the other pledges walk around school with bowls of fruit on their heads and wash the frat members' cars and stuff like that? It was all in fun, and being in the frat would be really cool for a pseudo-geek like Josh. Elizabeth just doesn't get the importance of sororities and fraternities—she's always blowing off our Pi Beta Alpha meetings.

"Julie and Bruce," Enid mused. I couldn't see her, but I could picture her shaking her head. "Talk about the least likely couple. It doesn't make sense, you know? I mean, she's so . . ."

"Nice?" suggested Elizabeth.

They both giggled. "Exactly," said Enid. "So what about the rumor that Bruce is seeing Danielle Alexander?"

Bruce and Danielle? This was news to me, too! "I heard that rumor too, and they'd be a better couple," Elizabeth remarked. "They're the most stuck-up kids at school. But if Julie says Bruce asked her to the party, then Bruce asked her to the party."

"Julie just isn't his type," Enid said. "She's cute, but she's not gorgeous. She's not rich, she's not a snob. Why would he be interested in her?"

"He fell in love with Regina, remember?" Elizabeth pointed out. "So he has the basic capacity to like someone who's not shallow."

"Yeah, but since Regina died, Bruce has been up to all his old nasty tricks," Enid concluded. "Him asking out Julie Porter seems weird, that's all."

I had to agree. What was Bruce up to? *I'll find out at the frat party tomorrow night,* I thought as I finished toweling myself off and ran a comb through my wet hair. I just hoped the callback for *You Can't Take It with You* didn't run late and make me miss any of the action!

I don't know where Elizabeth digs up her dirt, but it's definitely not realistic. Bruce and Julie Porter? Not in a million zillion years!

Todd wrote back to me pretty fast—I got another letter from him today. I thought this was going to be a onetime thing, but we're becoming regular pen pals. It's très amusant, if I may borrow a phrase from Ms. Dalton. When Elizabeth saw the Vermont postmark, she automatically grabbed the envelope—I had to wrestle it away from her. You should have seen her face when she realized that once again the letter was for me! I re-

minded her that she'd discarded Todd for Jeffrey, but she still pouted. Ha!

Saturday

Goodbye, prima ballerina, hello, laughingstock of Sweet Valley. You will not believe what happened to me last night. Yes, I got the part in the school play, but get this: it turns out it's a comic role! That's why Mr. Jaworski liked my first audition so much—because I danced badly! Last night he had us read from the script and I found out that Essie just thinks she's a great ballerina, but really she's a total klutz. Gee, thanks for recommending me for the part, DeeDee! I was secretly praying they'd cast someone else, but Mr. Jaworski loved my "clowning around," as he called it. Naturally Elizabeth said, "That's what you get for not reading the play ahead of time." Sometimes I want to strangle her (especially when she's right!). But if Julie Porter can survive the embarrassment of last night, I suppose I can do a few Grand Floppes in front of hundreds of people. . . .

The Patman estate is built into a hillside—the basement, which is more enormous than most people's houses, has sliding glass doors opening out onto the lawn. It's a perfect place for a party, and

Bruce has thrown some wild ones. This party was hilarious, with the Phi Epsilon pledges dressed in wigs and evening gowns, wobbling around on high heels serving drinks and hors d'oeuvres.

After dancing for a while—Bruce has a great sound system—I found my way to the buffet. "Great party!" I shouted to Elizabeth, who was ladling punch into a cup.

She nodded, then gripped my arm and pulled me aside. "But have you noticed Bruce and Danielle?" she hissed into my ear.

It had been hard to miss Bruce and Danielle, who were cuddling by the stereo, their bodies pressed extremely close together. Bruce was saying something to Danielle that made her laugh, and he punctuated every word with a little kiss. "They look like they're very good friends," I observed dryly.

"But Julie's supposed to be his date!" Elizabeth reminded me. "Where is she, anyway?"

"I saw him take her to the alcove a few minutes ago, but then he came back alone. Maybe she's still back there."

"The alcove." Elizabeth frowned. The alcove is kind of famous. It's a private nook in the far corner of the basement, and there are a bunch of big, squishy couches, and the lights are very, very dim. Couples head to the alcove for one reason and one reason only—it's Make-Out Central!

"So Bruce has two dates tonight," Elizabeth said.

I shrugged. "It's probably not the first time."

"I still don't understand why he picked Julie. I don't have a good feeling about this."

All of a sudden the music changed. Bruce had put on a classical CD. "Ugh. What is this?" I asked Elizabeth.

"The Summer Wind Consort," she answered. "Julie's favorite—she's teaching me one of their recorder duets."

"Julie's favorite, huh?" I tilted my head thoughtfully. "It's pretty romantic sounding." Across the room I saw Josh Bowen whip off his blond Marilyn Monroe wig. A bunch of the Phi Eps were standing around him, laughing and prodding him. Finally Josh grinned and sauntered toward the alcove.

I had a hunch I knew what was about to happen. "Come on, Elizabeth. Let's watch," I said, dragging her through the crowd.

"Watch what?" she said, puzzled.

"I think Josh is about to do another pledge prank."

We stopped near the Phi Eps, with a good view of the alcove, which was still shadowy. I saw Bruce flick a switch on the wall and the overhead lights flashed on, illuminating the entire room in glaring brightness.

Only one couple was sitting in the alcove, and they had their arms around each other, locked in a passionate embrace. When the lights came on, the couple sprang apart, both gasping with surprise. It was Julie and Josh!

Julie sprang to her feet, her hand clapped over her mouth. "What are *you* doing here, Josh?" she cried. "I thought—Bruce went to change the CD and—"

Josh's face was scarlet. "It was just a joke. I had no idea it was going to be you," he swore. "The guys told me that—"

The rest of his explanation was drowned out by laughter. Bruce and the other fraternity members were doubled over, slapping their knees and guffawing.

I started to smile myself, but then I saw the tears glinting in Julie's eyes. She watched Bruce laughing, the pain of her betrayal evident. "Did she really think he liked her?" someone near me wondered loudly.

Julie's complexion went white as a sheet. "How could you," she choked out—to Bruce? Josh? both?—before escaping from the room, with Elizabeth running after her.

I saw a trick like that coming a mile away, as soon as I heard Bruce had asked Julie to the party. I probably should have warned her, but Patman is a lesson every girl needs to learn for herself. I'll never forget my first—and last—date with him. We went out to dinner and a concert, and we drove everywhere in a limousine, which at first I thought was pretty cool. But Bruce didn't stop talking about himself, and about his family and how rich and important they are, for a single minute. Usually I can hold my own in any conversation, but I couldn't get a word in edgewise. I was so bored, I just kept stuffing myself with crackers and peanuts and stuff and the other snacks that were stocked in the bar in the backseat of the limo. I really decided I'd had enough when Bruce had the nerve to call some other girl from the car phone!

Poor Julie. Kissing Josh when she thought it was Bruce . . . not that she missed out on anything great! As I recall, Bruce's lips are definitely mediocre. Some of the Phi Ep pranks have been pretty stupid, but this one was kind of funny, I've got to admit. Just don't tell Elizabeth I said that!

Sunday afternoon

I haven't written in here for ages—more than a week. Who has time? Rehearsals were a killer, but You Can't Take It with You *was a smash hit. I was bummed for a while about my comic role, but I wouldn't be surprised if I get some Hollywood agents calling me after all. . . .*

I stood perfectly still in the dressing room while one stagehand finished pinning my costume and another touched up my eye makeup. "You're ready," freshman Tina Ayala told me, brushing some lint off my costume and then giving me an encouraging pat on the arm.

At that moment DeeDee stuck her head into the dressing room. "You're on in two, Jess!" she hissed.

Two minutes. I felt my heart somersault in my chest. I'd been in school plays before, but there's something about opening night. I hadn't been able to eat all day—there was no room in my stomach for anything but butterflies.

I followed DeeDee down the hallway and joined the rest of the crew milling around backstage. Standing in the wings, I peeked through an opening in the curtain.

The auditorium was jam-packed. A sea of faces gazed at the stage, where Bill Chase and Maggie Simmons, who had the lead roles in the play, were engaged in rapid-fire dialogue. Flinging a scathing remark at Bill, Maggie turned on her heel and marched over to the record player.

"Here's your cue," DeeDee whispered in my ear, pressing my props—a paperback book and a lollypop—into my hands.

Maggie put a record on the turntable. Tinny music filled the air as she rejoined Bill. I counted to three and then launched myself onto the stage.

While Bill and Maggie had a very serious conversation front and center, my character, Essie, was supposed to dance across the room behind their backs. As I took my first step I remembered Mr.

Jaworski's final coaching. "This is broad physical comedy, Jessica. Let out all the stops!"

I held the book up to my nose, pretending to read and meanwhile pirouetting at a manic pace. I lost my balance, flapped my arms madly, then recovered and executed a serene if wobbly plié. The audience was already laughing at my wacky costume, and with every step I took, they laughed harder. As I continued to leap and prance, pausing occasionally to lick my lollypop and turn a page in my book, the other characters remained oblivious to my presence, which made the scene even funnier. By the time I stumbled offstage, the laughter was drowning out Bill's and Maggie's lines.

DeeDee ran up to help me with a quick costume change, but first she gave me a high five. "Great job, Jessica," she whispered triumphantly. "They love you!"

I was grinning from ear to ear. My character hadn't even spoken yet, and already she was stealing the show. I'd always wanted to be an actress, but I'd never considered comedy. I really have a flair for it, though. With a little work I could be the next Lucille Ball!

By the way, Julie Porter and Josh Bowen are SVH's newest item. Julie was furious at Josh for what happened at Bruce's party, but Elizabeth helped the two of them straighten things out. It turns out they both had secret crushes on each other, even though supposedly they were just friends. The best part was Josh telling off the Phi Epsilons. Right in the middle of the cafeteria he announced that he didn't want to be in their stupid fraternity after all, and then he dumped lime Jell-O all over Bruce! It was excellent. Bruce got dumped on twice in one day—Danielle blew him off because she thought he was being a jerk to the pledges.

The way everyone's pairing up, I'm wondering if there isn't something to this couple stuff after all.

P.S. I wrote to Todd again. I enclosed the rave review of my stellar performance in You Can't Take It with You. *I couldn't deprive the poor guy of that, could I?*

Part 4

Tuesday

Dear Diary,
I'm in love!

Wednesday afternoon

Being in love is the most miserable thing on the planet. Why didn't someone warn me? Not that I have a choice. What girl in her right mind wouldn't fall head over heels for A.J. Morgan? Diary, he is so cute, it's unbelievable. He's tall, with great muscles—he's a jock, the new center on the basketball team. And he has blazing red hair. I've never liked a guy with red hair before! And he has the most adorable

157

southern accent (he just moved to Sweet Valley from Atlanta). He's shy and really smart and he's just so sweet and polite, and I know you're thinking that this isn't usually my type of guy. I wouldn't have thought so either, but I have absolutely no control over my A.J.-crazy heart. I'm nuts about him! But it's horrible, Diary, because in order to get him to notice me, I have to pretend I'm someone else. Specifically my sister, Elizabeth!

I'd just left the locker room after school on my way to cheerleading practice when ahead of me on the path to the athletic fields I saw a flash of red hair. It had to be A.J. Morgan, the new boy at school. My heart started galloping like a runaway horse. Even though I hadn't met him yet, I had already decided he was the boy of my dreams.

I drew closer. Yep, it was A.J. He was talking to Aaron Dallas, the cocaptain of the soccer team, and two seniors on the basketball team, Jason Mann and Paul Isaacs. "Hey, Jess!" Aaron called when he spotted me. "Come on over here!"

For some reason my feet suddenly felt as heavy as lead. Hot color flooded my cheeks. This was it. I was about to shake A.J. Morgan's hand!

"Have you met A.J.?" Aaron asked as I joined them.

My tongue was tied in knots—not a usual occurrence for me. I looked down at the ground, studying the grass growing in the cracks of the sidewalk. "Um, no," I mumbled, sticking out my hand but still not meeting A.J.'s eyes.

"Nice to meet you, Jessica," A.J. said, giving my hand a warm squeeze.

His touch set my whole body on fire. I hoped the other guys couldn't feel the heat!

"You'll figure out soon, if you haven't already, that Jessica's got a double," Aaron told A.J. Aaron elbowed me gently in the ribs, grinning. "She and Elizabeth are the prettiest twins in Southern California."

Ordinarily I love that kind of compliment. After all, it's the truth! But just then I was mortified. From everything I'd heard, A.J. didn't go for flirty, glamorous girls. Lila and Amy had already struck out with him big time. Why did Aaron have to make such a fuss about my looks in front of A.J.? What if A.J. thought I was shallow and vain?

I risked a glance at A.J. He was smiling kindly. "You have a twin sister? How will I tell you two apart?" he asked me.

I wanted to tell him that he'd have to look *really* close—Elizabeth has a beauty mark on her left shoulder and I don't. Instead I shuffled my feet, overcome with shyness. "Uh—"

"It's easy," Aaron cut in. "Jess is the one in the short cheerleader skirt and Elizabeth works on the school newspaper."

159

Oh, great, I thought. *Make me sound like a brainless flake, why don't you!*

"I wrote for the paper at my old school," A.J. commented. I wanted to punch Aaron.

"Well, I like to write too," I blurted. Aaron raised his eyebrows. "I'm just more . . . private about it. I don't let other people read it."

A.J. looked interested. Aaron looked baffled. "I've got to get to practice," Aaron said to A.J., giving him a friendly clap on the shoulder. "Catch you later. *Ciao*, Jess."

Aaron, Paul, and Jason jogged off, leaving me alone with A.J. "I suppose I should go too," I mumbled.

"Are you going to practice?" asked A.J. "I'll walk you the rest of the way."

My jaw dropped. A.J. wanted to spend a few more minutes with me! He hadn't gotten a terrible first impression of me after all. The question was, what kind of impression *had* he gotten? I definitely wasn't acting like myself.

And I was still feeling totally foolish and awkward. As A.J. and I strolled side by side I struggled to think of something to say, but my brain was on the fritz. He was silent too. "So," I said at last. "You're from the South?"

Duh, I thought immediately. Was that a dumb comment or what?

A.J. smiled. "Atlanta. But I'm not a real southerner. My family's moved around a lot—Dad's in the army."

"The army—cool." Another dumb comment!

Lucky for me, A.J. was very tolerant. "How about you? Are you a native Californian?"

"You bet," I said, "and I wouldn't want to live anywhere else. I mean, I like to travel," I added quickly, so A.J. wouldn't think I was completely narrow-minded and provincial.

"Sure," he said. "Who doesn't?"

We'd stopped walking and he was looking at me expectantly. I didn't know what I was supposed to do next. Then I realized we were standing on the edge of the field and the entire cheerleading squad was gawking at us. My face turned cherry-tomato red. "Oh, um, I'd better . . ." I stuttered.

"Have a fun practice," A.J. said, touching my arm lightly. "See you around."

He walked off and I stared after him, my right hand cupping the place on my left arm where he'd touched me. I was still basically speechless, but that was OK, because it only took one word to describe how I felt about A.J. Morgan. "Wow!" I whispered.

A.J. is definitely the boy for me. The only problem is, I can't let him find out what I'm really like, and that's going to be hard with the slam books circulating all over school. Have I told you about the slam books? Amy started it—people had them at her old high school in Connecticut. Here's how it works: you buy a notebook and put a category at the top of each page. Things like "Best Dressed," "Best Athlete," "Biggest Brain," "Future Wall Street Whiz," "Mostly Likely to Have Ten Kids." Then you trade books and everybody writes in everybody else's. There are a couple dozen slam books being passed around school right now, and guess who's been written down about twenty times as "Biggest Flirt"? Me! Can you believe it? Is that fair?

I mean, OK, maybe I've flirted a bit. But those days are behind me. Now that I've met A.J., I'm ready to settle down and be a one-guy girl. But how can I do that if my past keeps coming back to haunt me? I'll die if A.J. sees the slam books. I can tell he likes quiet, studious girls—he'd probably hit it off great with Elizabeth. Which is why he has to think I'm the serious twin. It's really important, Diary, because I like him more than any guy I've ever met. This is different—I don't just want to date him, I want a RELATIONSHIP with him. So wish me luck. I'm sailing into completely uncharted territory, and I'm going to need all the luck I can get!

Thursday evening

I got a letter from Todd today. It must have been a gray, gloomy day in Burlington when he wrote it, because it's kind of melancholy and thoughtful. He confided a bunch of stuff about Elizabeth that really surprised me to hear. For example: "I don't think anybody knows how much it hurt me when Elizabeth started dating Jeffrey. We'd already broken up, so it wasn't like she was doing anything wrong—I mean, I expected to hear something like that sooner or later. I just thought it would be later rather than sooner! It made me wonder how much she could have cared about me if she got over me that fast. Maybe it would have been different if I'd been the first one to meet someone new. It's not that I didn't want her to be happy. I guess I just wanted her to miss me a little bit more, for a little bit longer."

I wrote back right away because he really seemed to need cheering up.

"Dear Todd,
I hope you're not wasting too much time bumming out about Elizabeth. That's ancient history now! Besides, she didn't deserve you. She's better off with Jeffrey, and take my word for it, you'll be better off with someone else someday. Hold out for somebody special!"

163

The funny part is, I really meant it when I said Elizabeth didn't deserve him. It kind of surprised me that I felt that way. I used to think, back when Elizabeth and Todd were dating, that he held her back. That she'd be more fun if she weren't dating somebody so boring and stodgy and predictable. Now that I know Todd so much better, I think maybe it was the other way around and she was holding him back.

In my letter I asked if Todd had any advice for me (from a guy's perspective) about snagging A.J. We still haven't gotten beyond saying "hi" in the hall at school!

Friday night, late

What's the penalty for murder in California? I'm not sure who I want to kill more—Elizabeth or Amy. We all went to the Dairi Burger after the basketball game tonight (A.J.'s first outing in a Gladiators' uniform—he was so cute, I kept messing up my cheers!), and stupid Amy brought out her idiotic slam book. Before I could stop her, she'd shown it to A.J., and somehow half a dozen more slam books materialized at our table. So there was A.J., reading all about me being the biggest flirt in Sweet

164

*Valley. But that wasn't the worst part,
Diary. Someone had invented a new category: "Future Couples." And guess who
some of the couples were? Jeffrey and
Olivia . . . and Elizabeth and A.J.! When we
got home, I really let my sister have it. . . .*

I undressed in my bedroom, my thoughts weary
and confused. Regarding my pursuit of A.J., I
wasn't sure if the night had been a success or a disaster. On the one hand, he'd sat next to me at the
Dairi Burger, when he could just have easily have
slid into the other side of the booth next to Amy.
And when he read the slam books, he really
seemed confused about the Jessica Wakefield as
Biggest Flirt stuff. "Somebody's pulling your leg,"
he'd said, giving me an incredibly sweet smile. But
he'd given Elizabeth a smile too, when people
started ribbing them about being one of the couples of the future!

I heard the sound of the faucet being turned on
in the bathroom. Somebody was splashing in the
sink—my twin sister. Stomping across the room, I
shoved open the door.

"If you don't mind, I'd like some privacy,"
Elizabeth said, patting her face dry with a hand
towel. "I'll be done in a minute."

"I *do* mind," I declared, my hands on my hips.
"I really, really mind that your name is linked with
A.J.'s in the slam books!"

Elizabeth pressed her lips tightly together. "I told you those slam books would cause trouble."

"They only cause trouble when people like *you* twist them to their own devious purposes," I countered hotly.

"Me?" Elizabeth said. "What are you talking about?"

"You wrote it, didn't you?" I accused. "I thought it looked like your handwriting. Are you tired of Jeffrey all of a sudden? Is that why you put your name down with A.J.'s?"

Elizabeth stared at me. "Tired of—but I didn't—" Suddenly she burst into tears. Without even trying to defend herself, she bolted into her room, slamming the bathroom door behind her.

I turned on the faucet and stuck my toothbrush under the stream of water, my heart pounding. Her tears proved it—Elizabeth was guilty. She had a crush on A.J. too! A serious crush. *What should I do next?* I wondered. I was going slowly with A.J. because he was the old-fashioned, romantic type—aggressive girls turned him off. But what if my twin sister stole him away before I could make him mine?

I can't believe I'm getting so worked up about a guy I've only known for a few days. But there's a lot at stake, Diary. My feelings are new, but they're also intense. I've never really worried about my grades

166

before. Academics aren't that important to me—I'd rather focus on other stuff. Now I wish I was as smart as Elizabeth. I'm popular for all the wrong reasons. I like A.J. so much. But what if he doesn't like me back?

Saturday night

This is the worst night of my entire sixteen years. I'm so depressed, I can hardly write. After a disgustingly brazen display at the beach, Elizabeth is now out on a date with A.J.! Yes, a date, as in two people who like each other doing something alone so as to get to know each other better and probably end up in each other's arms, kissing madly . . . oh, I could SCREAM! She was out of control today, Diary—it was shocking. . . .

"I'm really sorry, Liz," I said sincerely, putting a consoling hand on my sister's arm.

We'd been at the beach for a couple of hours, but it hadn't exactly been a typical relaxing and fun Saturday afternoon. Elizabeth had been waiting for Jeffrey, who was off taking pictures of Olivia Davidson for a photo essay he was submitting to SVH's new arts journal, *Visions*. She wasn't too worried about Jeffrey being late, though, until Cara arrived. It was clear right away Cara was bursting with gossip, and she blurted it out almost instantly. Driving on the coast highway, she'd spotted Jeffrey's car pulled over at a rest area. And in the car she'd seen Jeffrey with his arms around Olivia!

"I can't believe he'd do something like this," she said angrily, dashing a tear from her cheek. "And Olivia! I thought she was my friend!"

Elizabeth and Olivia both work on the newspaper—Olivia's the arts editor. They've been close pals for years. I guess I could see why Jeffrey might go for Olivia. She has wild, curly brown hair and huge hazel eyes, and she wears long, gauzy dresses and dangly earrings. She's very feminine and romantic looking. "You know how some girls are," I said. "When they're interested in a guy, friendship goes out the window."

"But Olivia was never that type." Elizabeth rummaged around in her beach bag until she found a packet of tissues. She blew her nose loudly.

"Maybe she's changed since she broke up with Roger," I suggested.

"Maybe." Elizabeth wrapped her arms around her knees, looking out at the ocean. Fresh tears spilled down her face. "I know those two have been spending a lot of time together lately trying to get *Visions* started. But it never occurred to me not to trust them. How could Jeffrey do this to me?"

At that moment I saw someone approaching us across the sand. Jeffrey . . . and Olivia!

"The nerve!" I exclaimed.

Elizabeth followed my gaze. She flushed with distress. "I can't face them," she choked out.

"Tell Jeffrey that you know what's going on," I urged her. "Get it over with."

But Elizabeth was already hurrying off in the opposite direction.

I didn't want to deal with Jeffrey either, so I trotted after Elizabeth. To my surprise, she made a beeline for a bunch of guys hanging out by a windsurfer at the water's edge. Bruce, Ken, Winston, Aaron . . . and A.J.!

My mouth got dry, the way it always does around A.J. I licked my lips, wondering if I'd be able to utter a single word.

It didn't matter. Elizabeth suddenly decided to be chatty enough for both of us. "Whose board?" she asked, walking over to A.J. and standing right next to him.

"It's mine," Bruce said, adjusting the sail. "Want to try it out?"

Elizabeth didn't even glance at Bruce. Her eyes were fixed on A.J.'s face. He smiled down at her, his expression shy and somewhat uncertain.

"I'd love to try it, but I'm not very good," she confessed. "Do you know how to windsurf, A.J.?"

"I know the basics."

"Good," Elizabeth declared. "Would you give me some pointers?"

"Well, sure," A.J. agreed, sounding a bit surprised. "But I bet Bruce knows more than I do."

169

"I want you to help me, though." Elizabeth put a hand on his arm, fluttering her eyelashes. "Pretty please?"

I stared in astonishment as Elizabeth hauled A.J. and the windsurfer into the water. The boys were staring too. "What's gotten into Elizabeth?" wondered Aaron.

"Where's Jeffrey?" asked Ken.

I knew the answers to both questions, but I was too distraught to speak. My sister was making a play for the boy with whom I'd fallen in love! And it looked like he was going to let her!

Talk about on the rebound. That's no excuse, though, in my opinion! Jeffrey and Olivia tried to explain about what Cara supposedly saw them doing, but Elizabeth wouldn't listen. After practically tackling A.J., she proceeded to monopolize him for the rest of the day, flirting like crazy and not letting anybody else (me!) even talk to him. And now they're probably sitting in a dark movie theater, holding hands! When she was getting ready for her date, I really wanted to strangle her. . . .

"How do I look?" Elizabeth asked me, twirling.

I eyed her short, clingy blue dress with hostility. "OK for someone who's about to cheat on her boyfriend," I grumbled.

"What are you talking about?" Elizabeth peered into my mirror and fluffed her hair with her fingers. Instead of pulled back in a headband or barrettes, her hair was loose . . . the way I usually wear mine.

"Don't you think Jeffrey's going to be a little hurt when he finds out about this?" I asked.

"He cheated on me first," Elizabeth answered in a grim voice. "I don't see why I should sit around at home and mope when he's probably out with Olivia."

"You don't know for sure that something's going on between those two," I pointed out. "You didn't give Jeffrey a chance to explain."

"What's to explain?" countered Elizabeth. "Cara saw them with their arms around each other. She's not the kind to make up a story like that." She grabbed my new denim jacket off the back of my desk chair. "Mind if I borrow this?"

I shrugged. What did I care? She'd taken A.J. . . . . she might as well take my jacket, too!

The doorbell rang, and Elizabeth hurried to the door. Before stepping into the hall, she turned back, giving me a probing look. "Is something else bothering you?" she asked. "I just don't know why you'd care about me going out with A.J. unless . . ." Her eyes widened. "*You* don't like him, do you?"

"Of course not," I sniffed. I wasn't going to give her the satisfaction of knowing she'd snagged the one guy in the world I'd set my heart on.

171

"I didn't think so," Elizabeth said as she breezed off. "I mean, he's not your type at all!"

I listened to her feet pounding down the stairs, and then I walked over to my bedroom window. Pushing aside the curtain, I looked down just in time to see Elizabeth step out onto the front walk and smile up at A.J., who looked absolutely adorable in baggy khaki trousers and a faded green polo shirt. They chatted animatedly for a minute, and then A.J. took Elizabeth's arm and helped her into his car.

As I watched the car back out of the driveway, I realized that the scene was growing blurry. I put a hand to my face—my cheeks were wet with tears.

"It's just not fair," I whispered, sniffling. Elizabeth didn't care about A.J.—she was just trying to get back at Jeffrey. But I *did* care, more than I'd ever cared about a boy before. And now I'd never have a chance with him.

A.J.'s car drove off down Calico Drive, picking up speed. As it disappeared from sight I thought my heart would break.

I have to get busy doing something or I'll go crazy thinking about Elizabeth and A.J. Maybe I'll write to Todd again. He's always glad to hear from me. Who'd have thought it, you know? I mean, we used to barely tolerate each other. I thought he was so boring, but maybe that was just

172

Elizabeth's influence! It turns out we have a lot in common. I'll just write to him in here and tear the pages out later.

"Dear Todd,

Believe it or not, I'm sitting home on a Saturday night. No, the world hasn't ended—last time I checked, the earth was still orbiting the sun! I know this is totally out of character, moping around my room because this new guy I like is out with someone else tonight. But I can't help it. I'm really hurt.

Promise you won't tell anyone I said that! I can't talk to my friends because they'd just laugh at me. "Oh, please," Lila and Amy would say. "Stop sulking! You could have any other guy in town. Let's go to the Beach Disco and find you someone cute to dance with." And I know it's true, I COULD have any other guy, but I don't WANT any other guy. I want A.J. So how come he doesn't want me?

Don't answer that, Todd! Seriously, though, if you talk to Ken or Winston or anyone, don't you dare breathe a word of this. I'm only spilling my guts to you because I know I can trust you to keep my secret. I kind of wish you still lived in Sweet Valley—I could use a shoulder to cry on."

I just finished my letter to Todd, Diary. I was surprised when I reread it before sticking it in the envelope. It was pretty personal. Since when did Todd Wilkins become my closest confidante? Maybe because he's far away, it feels safe. Whatever. I feel better now—think I'll go downstairs and raid the fridge and find a good movie on TV.

Tuesday afternoon

I'm hanging out with Lila by the pool at her house. When I was getting ready to come over here, I grabbed some magazines and accidentally stuck my journal into my shoulder bag, too. Lila thinks I'm writing an English paper—I don't want her snooping!

Li thought it would cheer me up to be pampered a little. I certainly don't mind being waited on. Theresa, the Fowler Crest maid, just brought out a pitcher of iced tea and a tray with all these delicious miniature sandwiches. Later a masseuse is coming to the house to give us massages and aromatherapy! Lila really knows how to live.

Still, I can't think about anything except

the fact that Elizabeth is out with A.J. right now.

I think I'll move in here. Lila could use the company—her dad travels a lot for business, so she's usually alone with the servants. And Fowler Crest is huge. I could have my own private wing!

One thing's for sure. I won't be able to bear living in the same house as Elizabeth if she's going to be A.J.'s girlfriend.

Friday afternoon

Well, Elizabeth is back on my good side. It's been a wild week! Strangely enough, I have Olivia Davidson of all people to thank for how things worked out. She was pretty upset about the fact that people were gossiping about her and Jeffrey—like being paired up in the slam books, and the time Cara thought she saw them kissing. It turned out Jeffrey and Olivia had pulled over because Olivia had a giant speck of dust in her eye and Jeffrey was helping her get it out. They were just friends and had never been anything else.

Olivia came to me, desperate to find a way to patch things up between Elizabeth and Jeffrey and also repair her own friendship with Elizabeth. I thought things looked *pretty hopeless—why would Elizabeth want Jeffrey back when she had A.J.? But Olivia came up with a great idea: figure out who started writing that "Future Couple" stuff in the slam books. It occurred to us it might have been a scheme to make Elizabeth and Jeffrey insecure with each other and wreck their relationship.*

So I pretended to be Elizabeth doing research for the "Eyes and Ears" column and collected all the slam books. Sure enough, someone had written Olivia and Jeffrey in every single slam book but one. Lila's! Therefore, Olivia and I deduced that Lila was behind the whole mix-up. Just call us Holmes and Watson—Lila should have written in her own slam book to cover her tracks. As for a motive, Li's always wanted to get her claws into Jeffrey. She had the hots for him when he first moved to Sweet Valley and was totally burned when he fell for Elizabeth instead.

It was a happy ending for everyone (except Lila!). Elizabeth and Jeffrey made up, and Elizabeth and Olivia are friends again. And best of all, guess who asked me out on a date?

"There you are. I've been looking for you all over the place!" a deep male voice drawled behind me.

I'd just slammed my locker shut. Now I turned, hugging my books to my chest, my cheeks bright pink. A.J. Morgan was smiling down at me.

I wanted so much for that smile to be meant for me. But I knew he was making a mistake. *He probably hasn't heard that Elizabeth got back together with Jeffrey,* I thought. "Oh, A.J. Hi," I squeaked. "I—I think you have the wrong twin."

He cocked one auburn eyebrow. "I do? But I just saw Elizabeth going into the cafeteria. So you must be Jessica."

I blinked in confusion, my blush deepening. "Yeah, but . . ."

"You're the twin I'm looking for," A.J. declared. "Take my word for it."

I was more than happy to, but I was still baffled. "What's up?"

"I need to ask you something," A.J. said mysteriously. "Come on. Let's go someplace where we can talk privately."

I followed A.J. down the hall toward the library. There was a reading area just inside the library door—he sat me down on one of the plush couches. I looked at him expectantly and noticed that now he was the one blushing. "Jessica, you'll probably think I'm way out of line," he began. "But I was wondering . . . are you free tonight? Would you like to go to a movie with me?"

I stared at him with wide eyes. "Would I— would I like . . ."

"I'm putting you on the spot." A.J. made a wry face. "This is awkward, isn't it? Because I went out a couple of times with your sister. Elizabeth and I had fun, but it's not going to lead to anything. To tell you the truth, she's not my type at all."

"She's not?"

"Don't get me wrong. She's smart and beautiful and a lot of fun. But she came on kind of strong, you know? Maybe I'm old-fashioned, but I like to be the one to make the first move. I go more for girls who are shy and a little reserved. Poetic, romantic." He took my hand and gave it a squeeze. "Like you."

A.J. continued to hold my hand, gazing into my eyes with hopeful admiration. I felt as if I were floating away on a cloud of happiness. *He likes me!* I thought, delirious. *He likes me, not Elizabeth!*

Of course, there was the slight complication that he'd been turned off by Elizabeth when she was acting like me, and he liked me when I acted like Elizabeth. But if pretending to be shy and poetic was what it took to win A.J. Morgan's heart, then I could be shy and poetic. I was an actress, after all!

"So will you go out with me?" A.J. pressed. "I really want to get to know you better, Jessica."

"Yes," I said, my eyes shining. "I want that too."

Diary, it was like a scene in a romance novel. It was worth going through so much

178

torture to have A.J. look at me like that!
SIGH. So how many people should A.J.
and I invite to our wedding? Three hun-
dred? Four hundred? Jessica Wakefield
Morgan. Sounds good, huh? And guess
what I just did? I tossed my slam book in
the trash!

Monday night

Dear Diary,
If A.J. doesn't kiss me in the next
twenty-four hours, I may self-destruct. I've
done absolutely everything I can think of
to please him. I wore a boring one-piece
bathing suit to the beach instead of my
usual skimpy bikini, and then—the ultimate
sacrifice!—I left the beach early, right dur-
ing prime tanning hours, to go to the li-
brary with him. I thought he was about to
kiss me right there in the stacks, but I got
so nervous, I dropped the poetry anthology
I was holding. . . .

"Did you find the book you need for your
English report?" A.J. asked.
We were standing in the stacks at the Sweet
Valley Public Library. "Yep," I said, holding out
what was probably the most boring book ever writ-
ten, about boring dead American poets. But I had

179

to pretend to be intensely interested in it. A.J. liked poetry, and he liked girls who took their classwork seriously. "I'm so excited to learn more about Emily Dickinson," I told him, my eyes radiant.

A.J. shook his head and smiled. "I really admire you, Jessica. It's hard to concentrate on academic stuff on Saturday when everybody else is playing beach volleyball."

"Work always comes before play with me," I lied. "If I want to keep my grades up, I have to hit the books on weekends too." I just hoped A.J. never got a look at one of my report cards!

"Well, maybe when you're done, we can go sit in the park and read," he suggested. "Combine work and pleasure."

"OK," I agreed. "But first, listen to this." I didn't jump at his suggestion because I didn't want him to pick up on the fact that I was desperate to get back outside. He had to think I was more at home in the dim, chilly library than on a warm, sunny beach. "This is one of my favorite Emily Dickinson poems," I informed him, opening the poetry anthology I'd borrowed from Elizabeth. I didn't mention that before last night, I didn't have a favorite poem. I'd never even heard of Emily Dickinson!

"'If I can stop one heart from breaking, I shall not live in vain,'" I read, my voice vibrating with emotion.

I read the whole poem, A.J. listening with a

somber expression on his face. "Wow," he said when I was done. "That's pretty intense stuff."

"She wrote these poems sitting in a garret," I told A.J. Not that I knew exactly what a garret was! "And she never showed them to anybody. Isn't that wild? Imagine pouring your heart onto the page, without any expectation that another human soul would ever read your words." I dropped my eyes modestly. "That's how I feel about my own writing," I confided. "Poetry is an outlet for my deepest, most private feelings."

A.J. looked suitably awestruck. "You're really something else, Jessica," he said at last.

You'd better believe it! I thought.

We were standing next to each other, surrounded by books. In my opinion, the library stacks were a depressing backdrop for a first kiss, but hopefully A.J. thought it was romantic. I leaned closer. "Let me read you one more poem," I whispered provocatively. *To get you in the mood!* I almost added.

A.J. gazed down into my eyes. I fluttered my lashes; my lips parted invitingly. He put a hand on my arm and a thrill ran up my spine. This was it. He was going to kiss me!

I was so excited, I forgot I was still holding Elizabeth's poetry anthology, which weighs a ton. It slipped from my hand, crashing to the floor with a thunk that sounded particularly loud because in general the stacks are as silent as a tomb. A.J. and I jumped apart, startled. He backed into the stacks, sending more volumes cascading to the floor.

The noise brought the librarian running. "What on earth . . . !" she exclaimed, bending to help us pick up the books. I clapped a hand to my mouth to keep from exploding into giggles. The librarian scowled at me. "This isn't the place for *rambunctious* behavior," she lectured sternly. "Perhaps you should *remove* yourselves to the park next door."

A.J. and I grabbed our things and sprinted for the exit. As soon as we were outside, I doubled over, hiccupping with suppressed laughter. "Oh, gosh, did you see her face?" I snorted. "We'll probably be blacklisted—they'll never let us back in there again." I remembered that I was supposed to love the library and quickly rearranged my face into more sober lines. "I mean, that would be awful," I added. "I think I'll come by tomorrow and volunteer to help shelve books for a few hours. Maybe they'll forgive me for disturbing the peace today."

A.J.'s smile was a bit uncertain. "You probably don't need to do that, but gee, Jessica. That's generous of you."

"Yeah, well . . ." I tossed my hair to signify that it was business as usual for Jessica "The Serious Twin" Wakefield. I looked at the watch I'd had to borrow from Elizabeth—I'd never in my entire life owned a wristwatch. "Oh, look," I declared. "If we

182

hurry, we still have time to get to the Save the Whales rally!"

I almost blew it in the library this afternoon. I just couldn't help laughing when A.J. landed in that pile of books! Don't you hate that feeling? It's always when I'm in a situation where I know I'm not supposed to laugh, like during an exam or something, that I want to burst out laughing the most. But I can't let myself forget that A.J. doesn't like giggly, frivolous girls. I'm going to have to beef up the studious spinster routine. It's exhausting, not to mention BORING (a Save the Whales rally when I could have been at the Dairi Burger!), but what choice do I have? I'm mad about A.J. He's worth it.

Tuesday

Just scribbled a funny postcard to Todd. Have to keep him up to date on my exciting life! He knows about A.J., but I feel kind of weird going into detail now that A.J. and I are actually an item. I wonder why.

Todd and I are writing a couple of times a week. I write to him almost as often as I write in here!

The A.J. situation has reached a crisis point, Diary. We've gone out a bunch of times now, and he still hasn't kissed me! I don't know what I'm doing wrong. I'm trying so hard to be his dream girl. We went hiking at Secca Lake, and I brought binoculars and a field guide even though birdwatching is so boring it makes me want to cry. We went to a poetry reading, and we spent an afternoon serving meals at a soup kitchen. I can tell A.J. thinks I'm wonderful for caring so much about serious things, but the problem with being so serious all the time is that it doesn't exactly put you in the mood for romance. I mean, we can't exactly go from a homeless shelter to Miller's Point for a make-out session. It would be too weird!

I guess I could be more patient if it weren't for what happened at the beach today. We were jogging along the shore and I was telling A.J. about my plan to raise money for the new wing at the children's hospital. Just then we saw this girl out in deep water, flailing her arms and shouting for help. I guess she swam out and got a cramp. So A.J. dashed into the surf and rescued her.

184

The whole thing was fine with me until they waded into the shallows and I got a good look at her. Her name is Pamela Janson, and she's our age but she goes to Whitehead Academy, this exclusive private girls' school up the coast in Bridgewater. So she's rich and spoiled . . . oh, and did I mention she's a knockout? You should have seen her playing the "I almost drowned, you saved my life" routine for all it was worth, clinging to A.J.'s arm like a barnacle. And poor stupid A.J. just stared at her like he'd never seen a gorgeous, dripping wet girl in a practically nonexistent bikini before, which maybe he hasn't, because I always wear my dowdiest one-piece when I'm with him! Argh.

You know what's the worst thing, Diary? Pamela was flirting with A.J. the way the old Jessica would have flirted with him. But the new Jessica can't act that way because A.J. thinks she's earnest, down-to-earth, conscientious, and all that baloney. And that's the kind of girl he prefers . . . isn't it?

A.J. and I stood in the beach parking lot, watching Pamela Janson drive off in her white Mercedes convertible. I was still seething at the look Pamela had given me when A.J. was opening the car door for her, his back turned—a sly, challenging smile that could mean only one thing. Pamela had made up her mind to go after A.J. in a big way, even though she knew he was someone else's boyfriend! As for A.J., he stood stock still, staring after the Mercedes with a glazed look in his eyes.

I snapped my fingers in front of his nose. "Earth to A.J.," I said, masking my impatience as best I could. "Are we going to leave or what?"

"Right, sure," said A.J., blushing hotly. He jingled his car keys. "Yeah. Hop in."

I settled myself in the passenger seat of A.J.'s car and put on my belt. I was seething about what had just happened with Pamela, but also confused. Was it my imagination or was A.J. panting after Pamela like a dog after a rib roast? *He's not supposed to like that kind of girl!* I thought.

"It's pretty lucky we came along when we did," I remarked, trying to sound sweet and concerned even though in retrospect I would have voted to let Pamela drown.

"It sure was," agreed A.J. "That beach was deserted except for us. It's really fate that we were there when Pamela needed us."

I wanted to gag, but I forced myself to smile. "Pamela thinks you're a hero."

He blushed again. Redheads just can't hide their feelings—their fair skin always gives them away! "Do you think so?" he asked. Then he cleared his throat. "Uh, but of course it's more important that *you* think I'm a hero."

"You were very brave," I told him.

A.J. smiled at me. "Thanks, Jessica."

We drove for a few minutes in silence. I couldn't tell what kind of silence it was, though. Comfortable . . . or awkward? Was A.J. quiet because he was daydreaming about Pamela?

"Pamela was kind of . . ." *All over you like a cheap suit.* "Friendly," I said, testing the waters. "Maybe overfriendly. If you know what I mean?"

A.J. nodded, his face still pink. "She came on pretty strong."

"I guess she was just so grateful," I said.

A.J. also seemed eager to excuse Pamela's behavior. "And she was still a little scared. She really had a close call out there."

A close call that she turned into a close encounter! I bit my lip hard. I couldn't say it out loud. I didn't want A.J. to think I was catty.

A.J. pulled up at the curb in front of my house. "Thanks for going jogging with me, Jessica," he said.

"Anytime," I responded cheerfully, even though my muscles were aching. Didn't A.J. know that beaches were for lazing around, preferably in a horizontal position? "Bye."

I waited a few seconds, giving him a chance to lean over and kiss me. He did put a hand on my arm, but he kept the other hand on the steering wheel. "See you, Jessica," he said.

I climbed out of the car, trembling with disappointment. A.J. still hadn't kissed me, and I wasn't sure anymore why he was holding back. Was it because he didn't want to move too fast with the prim and proper (or so he thought) Jessica Wakefield? Or was he just not that interested in me? Pamela Janson wanted to sink her claws into A.J.—was he going to let her?

I really don't know what to do, Diary. Keep up this too-good-to-be-true charade, or change course and be myself? I could out-Pamela Pamela in a minute! No, that would never work. Remember what A.J. said when he first asked me out? He didn't like Elizabeth because she was too flirtatious and forward. But what if Pamela . . . no, I refuse to even think about it.

All I can say is, my life has somehow become much too complicated when I really only want two simple things: 1. to kiss A.J. and 2. to win the modeling contest at Lisette's. As you know, that's my absolute favorite store at the mall, but I haven't shopped there lately because the clothes are really stylish and sexy, and A.J. thinks I'm conservative and demure. Hold on—I haven't shopped anywhere lately. Cara, Lila, and Amy go to the mall without me because I'm always busy doing serious things with A.J.!

*That's why I can't even enter the con-
test, and it's killing me. Nadine, who de-
signs all the fabulous clothes at Lisette's, is
having a fashion show to promote her line.
The girl who wins will get a free, custom-
designed wardrobe of Nadine originals!
Isn't that incredible? I know I'd be a shoo-
in if I entered—even Lila agrees. But a
modeling contest just doesn't agree with
my new image. What if A.J. found out
about it and realized I'm not the girl he
thinks I am?*

Saturday morning

OK, Diary. Here's my latest poem:

> *My heart is heavy
> Heavy as cement
> Heavy as a tire iron. I would tear it out
> Of my body
> But I'll need it if
> You ever smile at me again.*

*Writing poetry is a lot easier since
Elizabeth told me about blank verse. A
poem doesn't have to rhyme to be good! In
fact, in modern poetry rhyming is totally
uncool. What a relief—that was definitely
the hardest part. All I can say is, A.J. better*

flip over this—I spent a whole half hour on it! I really, really hope he likes it. What if he doesn't, though? What if after all this hard work, I blow it with A.J. and he dumps me for Pamela? She's really putting the moves on him, Diary. Yesterday he was late picking me up at the library because she lured him over to her house on the pretense of returning his beach towel. Can you believe her nerve? Elizabeth says Pamela would be no threat to the real Jessica— Elizabeth thinks I should come clean with A.J. and just be myself. But then A.J. would think I was a total fake.

No, I'm committed to this strategy—I have to stick with it. I did let Elizabeth talk me into entering the modeling contest at Lisette's, though. A.J. can't disapprove too much, can he? Maybe he'll even be psyched to have a smart, serious girlfriend who's also well dressed. I'm crossing my fingers!

Saturday evening

I'm back, and I'm mad. Guess who I bumped into at Lisette's today when I was signing up for the Modern Girl Fashion Show? Pamela Janson! She's entering the contest, too. Isn't that awful? And she was

*so snotty and disdainful to me. She doesn't
make a secret of the fact that she's hot for
A.J.'s body, and it's pretty plain she thinks
she'll have no problem stealing him away
from a mousy thing like me. I warned her to
keep her hands to herself—not in so many
words, but she got the message. And she just
laughed! I can only imagine what lengths
she'd go to for a little of A.J.'s attention.
Some girls just don't know when to quit!*

Sunday afternoon

*I just got around to reading the letter I
got from Todd yesterday. It really cheered
me up, and heaven only knows I needed
cheering up. A.J. and I double-dated last
night with Elizabeth and Jeffrey, and it
was a disaster. I was trying so hard to be
the kind of girl I think A.J. wants me to
be—talking about things he's interested in,
picking songs he likes on the jukebox—but
he still didn't seem to have fun. I'm really
starting to worry that I'm blowing this
relationship. . . .*

We were squeezed into a cozy booth near the
artificial waterfall in the back of Guido's Pizza Palace.
Guido's is a great place for a date because it's cheap
and casual, but it's also kind of romantic—dark

paneling, cushiony red leather booths, low lighting. And the pizza's not bad, either!

Elizabeth studied her menu. "I don't know why I'm bothering, though," she remarked. "We always order the same thing, don't we, Jeffrey? It's Jessica's favorite too," she told A.J. "The Guido's Special."

A.J. read the description in the menu. "Sausage, pepperoni, green peppers, garlic, mushrooms, olives . . . I've got to tell you. I'm not wild about garlic and olives," he confessed.

"I'm not, either," I said quickly. I wanted A.J. to think I was easy to get along with, easy to please. I didn't want him to think I was the kind of girl who had to have her own way. "We can order something else, A.J. Whatever you like."

Elizabeth frowned. "But Jess, you always—"

I kicked her under the table. She winced. "What kind of pizza do you like, A.J.?" I asked.

"You'll probably think I'm boring," he said with a laugh, "but I like plain cheese with maybe one thing on top. Pepperoni or Canadian bacon."

"That's the way I like my pizza too," I told him. "If there are too many different flavors, they cancel each other out."

Elizabeth and Jeffrey both stared at me as if I'd spoken in Russian. A.J. gave me a quizzical smile. "But if you want the Guido's Special, Jessica, I'm sure we can order more than—"

"I want cheese and pepperoni," I insisted. "Let's just get that, OK, guys?"

Elizabeth and Jeffrey just nodded dumbly.

The waitress brought the pitcher of root beer we'd ordered. As A.J. filled everyone's glass there was a minute of awkward silence. I couldn't decide which topic to bring up—poetry? nuclear disarmament?—so I looked to my sister and Jeffrey for help. *Start talking,* I pleaded with my eyes. *Say anything!*

"So, A.J.," Elizabeth began. "I know Jessica told you about the fashion contest at Lisette's. How do you like the idea of your girlfriend being a model?"

I wanted to slug her. Sure, I'd told A.J. about the contest. But I was trying to downplay it. I didn't want him to think I placed a lot of importance on clothes and beauty and stuff. "It's not that big a deal," I blurted before A.J. could answer. "I kind of wish I hadn't let Amy and Lila talk me into signing up. I really don't have the time, you know? With the history test to study for, and the poem I'm submitting to *Visions,* and my volunteer work at the library . . ."

"But it sounds like fun, Jessica," A.J. said. "I think you should do it."

I pretended to still be up in the air about it. "We'll see. You're right—it could be fun. It's just not my top priority, that's all I'm saying."

A.J. smiled halfheartedly. "Hey, I think I'll go put some quarters in the jukebox. Any requests, Jessica?"

"I want to hear whatever you want to hear," I replied.

As A.J. got to his feet I saw him steal a quick glance at his watch. I know how to read body language, and that gesture only has one interpretation. My stomach tied itself into an anxious, unhappy knot. A.J. and I were supposed to be in love, but he was counting the minutes until this date was over. Why? What was I doing wrong?

Elizabeth and Jeffrey were no help— they just think I'm off my rocker. I ended up in the ladies' room at Guido's, crying my eyes out. Pathetic. I don't even try to be seductive anymore when A.J. and I say good night. We just shake hands. We might as well be sister and brother!

I reread the funny part of Todd's letter to make myself laugh. Then I reread the serious part. It's pretty wild, Diary. When Todd and I first started writing, our letters were breezy and superficial. Now we really open up to each other. I think I started it by telling him the whole A.J. saga. As it turns out, Todd's been having some romantic troubles himself. Listen to this:

"Kathy was the most serious relationship I've had since I left California. Actually what drew me to Kathy in the first place was that she reminded me a little of Elizabeth. She writes for the school paper,

she's an honor student, all that jazz. But after a while I realized something pretty intense. I don't want to go out with another Elizabeth. I want something different this time around. Do you know what I'm saying?"

A lot of the letter was really personal like that. Really intimate. Elizabeth would faint if she knew some of the stuff Todd tells me! One goofy coincidence: it turns out Todd and A.J. went to the same basketball camp when they were little! Isn't that a riot? Todd asked me for A.J.'s address. I just hope he doesn't regale A.J. with stories about the "real" Jessica Wakefield.

Friday night

Tomorrow's the big day. The modeling contest. And A.J. will be watching! I have a sinking feeling it's going to turn into a showdown between me and The Horrid Girl Whose Name I Won't Even Deign to Mention. And what if she beats me? What if she wins the contest and wins A.J.'s affection too? Tonight at Lisette's we tried on the Nadine outfits we'll wear in the show tomorrow and had a little rehearsal. My outfits were just OK, but Pamela looked incredibly good in all of hers. . . .

195

"Try this one on first," Amy said, holding out a short blue dress made out of clingy, nubby fabric.

Lila, Amy, and Elizabeth had come with me, and we were all crammed into a dressing room at Lisette's. Like the other contestants, I was supposed to try on the outfits Nadine had assigned me. Then we'd get a chance to practice walking down the runway, with Nadine critiquing our style.

For some reason I was incredibly jittery. I stripped off my skirt and tank top, hoping my sister and my friends didn't notice my shaking hands. Lila slipped the dress off the hanger, and Elizabeth helped me shimmy into it. Then Amy zipped it up the back.

We all looked at my reflection in the mirror. The dress hugged my curves, and the wide neckline showed off my shoulders. The material was the exact same color as my eyes.

"You look fabulous," Amy breathed admiringly.

"That dress was made for you," Lila agreed.

"The other girls don't stand a chance!" Elizabeth concluded.

I was the only one who wasn't convinced. I frowned at myself, tugging on the hem of the dress. "I don't know," I mumbled. "I think it makes me look fat."

"No way," Amy said.

I pivoted to get a rear view. "It doesn't do anything for me," I argued.

196

Amy tipped her head to one side. "Well, now that I take a closer look . . . yeah." She nodded. "It does sort of make your butt look big."

I hadn't expected her to agree with me—in fact, I'd assumed she'd keep trying to convince me I looked great. "It does?" I asked indignantly.

"Just a little," Lila assured me. "Come on. Let's take a look in the mirror outside—the light's better there."

We all trooped out of the dressing room. Someone was already positioned in front of the nearest full-length mirror, admiring herself shamelessly. Pamela!

"What a great dress," Amy gushed to Pamela.

"Now *that's* a perfect fit," agreed Lila.

I stood stock still, my arms hanging limply at my sides. Pamela did look fantastic, in a strapless cranberry red satin cocktail dress. Her skin was smooth and golden; her hair tumbled in raven waves over her bare shoulders; her blue eyes sparkled like jewels. She twirled in front of the mirror, every move radiating grace and confidence. "It *is* a great dress, isn't it?" she purred, flashing a brilliant smile. "I can't wait to have a closetful of these. I'll wear a Nadine original every time I have a special date with A.J."

I wanted to scratch her eyes out, but I couldn't even think of a good comeback. *Because she's right,* I thought, my self-esteem plummeting to new lows. *She looks ten times better than I do. I don't stand a chance.*

197

Elizabeth, Lila, and Amy looked at me expectantly, waiting for me to put Pamela in her place. Instead I turned on my heel and fled back into the dressing room.

The whole night all Elizabeth and Lila and Amy could talk about was Pamela, Pamela, Pamela. I was ready to strangle them. I guess I just have to do my best tomorrow, but what if my best isn't good enough? Do I still have what it takes?

Saturday evening

Mirror, mirror, on the wall, who's the fairest of them all?? Yep. ME!! Not only did I win the Modern Girl Fashion Show, but I made Pamela Janson's name MUD. I haven't felt this good in ages!

You wouldn't believe how low that girl was willing to stoop to wreck my chances of winning the contest and make me look bad in front of A.J. She actually sabotaged my outfits. First she "accidentally" snagged her ring on the nubby fabric of that blue dress. Then she broke the zipper on another. I didn't fall to pieces like she expected me to, though. Lila and Cara helped me hide the flaws, and I really strutted my stuff on the runway so the audience would be too busy noticing me to notice a tiny flaw in my outfit. And it worked—I got more applause than any of the other girls, even Pamela!

Then Pamela made her fatal mistake. She should have just been a good sport about losing the contest, but instead she tried one last time to put me out of the running. I was about to go onstage for the last time wearing Nadine resort wear, a strapless bikini and cover-up, and Pamela dumped a huge glass of water all over me. That did it. I started yelling at her, accusing her of damaging my clothes so she'd have a better chance of winning. The plot backfired, I told her, because I still looked ten times better than she did. Pamela said, "I bet A.J. doesn't think so," and right then Lila yanked open the curtain. The audience—including A.J.—had heard every single word!

Pamela realized that she'd blown it big time, and she ran off in total disgrace and humiliation. I was a little worried that Nadine would be mad about all the fuss, but she had just the opposite reaction. She ran right up to me and gave me a big hug. "Here's my modern girl," she declared. "Jessica Wakefield knows what she wants and goes after it with all she's got!"

The audience went wild, needless to say. I was psyched, and not only because I'd just won a new designer wardrobe. Pamela's underhanded tricks had brought out all my old fighting spirit. Standing up to her, I felt like myself for the first time in weeks. The real Jessica Wakefield was back. And did she ever make an impression on you-know-who!

As I stepped off the runway at Lisette's people crowded around me, trying to congratulate me on my victory. But I only had eyes for one person. A.J.

He made his way toward me, his expression sober and hard to read. My palms started to sweat. Suddenly I didn't care about the prize I'd just won. If I lost A.J., nothing else would matter.

He reached my side, and for a moment we just stared searchingly into each other's eyes. Then slowly a broad grin spread across his face. He wrapped his arms around me and lifted me into the air, twirling me in a circle. "Good for you, Jessica!" he exclaimed.

I hugged him tight, relief and happiness fizzing like seltzer water in my veins. "You mean you're not furious with me?" I asked.

"Are you kidding? I'm proud!" he swore. "But confused too, I'll admit. Come on, let's go someplace we can talk."

He led me to a quiet corner of the store and sat

down. There was only one chair, so he pulled me onto his knee. "Jessica Wakefield," he began. "You *are* Jessica Wakefield?"

I giggled. "Guilty as charged."

"I hardly recognized you up on that runway. You're a different person today than the one I've been seeing. What's going on?"

I took a deep breath. Now that I had to explain myself, I realized how idiotic the whole thing was. "Up until today I've been putting on an act," I confessed.

"But why?" asked A.J., his brow furrowed.

"Because I wanted you to like me!" I looked at him earnestly. "And I knew the real Jessica Wakefield wouldn't stand a chance with you. You said yourself that you don't like girls who come on too strong." I made a wry face. "And that's me in a nutshell. Remember the slam books? 'Biggest Flirt'?"

A.J. laughed. "I can't tell you what a relief this is," he said, holding me close. "Our relationship was going nowhere fast. I was starting to think you were way too serious for me!"

"*Too* serious?" I blinked. "You mean you *don't* care about poetry readings and no-nukes rallies and volunteering and fund-raising and all that stuff?"

"Sure, I care," said A.J. "But I don't feel like I have to be saving the world every minute of the day. I also like to have fun."

"You do?"

"Yes." His gold-flecked eyes twinkled. "To be

201

absolutely honest, you were starting to get a little boring."

I folded my arms, my eyes flashing. "I am *not* boring!"

"Not now," A.J. agreed. "Not since you stopped campaigning for the Nobel Peace Prize."

It was a few minutes before we stopped laughing. I wrapped my arms around A.J.'s neck, sighing happily. "So you don't mind that I'm selfish sometimes?" I said. "And a little bit vain and a little bit catty? You don't mind that I'd rather party than do my homework?"

A.J. smiled. "How could I mind?" He lowered his voice, declaring solemnly, "I'm crazy about you, Jessica Wakefield. About you and only you. Don't ever change."

Pretty hot stuff, huh, Diary? I should have known that being myself was key. After all, I'm irresistible!

Saturday night, LATE

We kissed!!!!! I'd go into detail, but the pages might burst into flame. On second thought, that's a chance I'll have to take. This kiss was too good to keep to myself. . . .

After the fashion show A.J. took me out for a celebration dinner at the Box Tree Café. Then we drove to the beach to watch the sunset.

We'd been talking nonstop—there was so much to tell each other. A.J. couldn't get over my transformation. "So this is the real Jessica Wakefield," he said, swinging my hand as we strolled by the water's edge. "She's amazing." He lifted my hand, kissing it lightly. "I think I'm falling for her pretty hard."

"You mean you don't want to ask out Pamela Janson?"

A.J. wrinkled his nose. "Pamela who?"

I laughed happily. "Come on, though. Admit it. You were attracted to her."

"Just a tiny bit," A.J. said, "and only because I was frustrated with how things were going with you."

"But now things are OK?"

He wrapped his arms around me. "More than OK."

The mood was getting pretty romantic. We were on the verge of our first real kiss . . . finally! I pushed A.J. away from me slightly. I knew exactly how—and where—I wanted this to happen. "There's someplace I've wanted to take you for the longest time," I told A.J., leading him back to the parking lot. "Do you mind going for a little drive?"

"I'm yours," A.J. replied. "Do with me what you will."

On the road I pointed him in the direction of Miller's Point. A.J. raised his eyebrows. "Miller's

Point, eh?" he said. "I think I've heard about it."

"It's got a great view," I promised.

"But it's dark," he pointed out.

I smiled. "Exactly!"

We weren't the first car to arrive at the popular parking spot in the hills above Sweet Valley—it was Saturday night, after all. A.J. pulled up to the guard-rail and turned off the engine.

For a minute we sat quietly, looking down at the twinkling lights of town. Then we turned to each other.

We'd talked enough for the time being. Now all we wanted to do was stare into each other's eyes. For a long time we didn't even touch. It was so thrilling, and such a tease, that I thought I was going to spontaneously combust. Then at last A.J. reached over and traced his finger along my cheekbone and down to my chin, tipping my face up to his. I closed my eyes, my whole body trembling with anticipation. When his lips met mine, the heat between us was so powerful, I was pretty sure I was going to melt.

I pressed my body against his as he locked his arms around me. I planned to stay there forever.

It was incredible, Diary. We'd waited so long, when the moment finally came, we couldn't hold each other close enough. We probably would have kissed for a year or two, but eventually we had to take a break and catch our breath. Which was fine, because it was so much fun to start all over again!

Monday afternoon

I got another letter from Todd today. I've quit mentioning the letters to Elizabeth because I really don't think she'd be interested. I mean, at this point Todd and I don't even talk about her. It's funny how much more I like him on paper than I used to in person. Why is that? Maybe because he's finally learned to appreciate me! Listen to this:

"So, Jess, has A.J. finally come to his senses and figured out that you're the hottest babe in Sweet Valley? Just kidding, of course. I mean, you are hot, but looks aren't everything. You've got more than a little extra in the personality department—if A.J. doesn't realize that, then hold out for someone who does!"

Isn't that nice, Diary?

P.S. A.J. Morgan is the best kisser in the entire world, and he's mine, all mine!

Part 5

Wednesday night

Parents always complain about teenagers being hard to live with, but they should look at themselves sometimes. I think my dad may be certifiable. His twenty-fifth high-school reunion is coming up, and it's catapulted him into an early midlife crisis. All of a sudden he's obsessed with how many gray hairs he has, and he's furious at himself for gaining a whopping eight pounds since college. I tried to make him feel better by telling him he was definitely the best looking of all my friends' fathers, but for some reason that didn't cheer him up. It's getting a little out of hand, Diary. Not only did he join a health club and buy

*an exercise bike, but he's wearing all these
groovy clothes on the weekends (not to the
office, thank goodness!). He probably thinks
they make him look younger, but actually
they make him look like an idiot.*

*So, with a little help from Elizabeth
(she's really busy producing the student variety show at SVH), I've come up with another one of my typically brilliant plans.
By the time we're through with him, Dad
will wish he was already old and gray!*

Thursday evening

*I can't believe I wrote in here yesterday
and forgot to mention that I'm in love with
A.J. Completely, sickeningly in love. We
could be one of those ultra-nauseating couples on a long-distance phone commercial.
We're inseparable. We can't keep our hands
off each other (and why would we want
to?). So here's the question, Diary. Why did
I rush home to the mailbox today?*

Cheerleading practice is usually my favorite part
of the school day. Robin and I take the squad out to
the athletic fields (where we have a prime view of
the football team doing wind sprints and push-
ups!), and basically we just goof off for an hour.
Actually that's not completely true. We're serious

athletes. We work hard on our cheers, and I bet we're in as good as or better shape than the girls who play basketball and field hockey and whatnot. But hanging out gossiping at the end of practice is what we all look forward to the most.

Today the gossip was particularly interesting . . . because it was about me. "I never thought this day would come," said Amy, flopping on the grass and twisting the cap off a bottle of water. "Jessica Wakefield is whipped."

"I'm not whipped!" I protested as the rest of the girls burst out laughing. I smiled sheepishly. "OK, maybe a little. You know me—I like to try everything at least once. This devoted girlfriend thing is a new experience."

"I give you and A.J. one more week as a couple," Amy groused. "Then I bet you're itching to play the field again."

"You're just jealous," I said sweetly, "because A.J. never gave you a second glance. We happen to be madly in love—this is going to last. Ta-ta, girls—I have to run."

"But we haven't even talked about Caroline Pearce's horrible new haircut!" said Jean.

"You'll have to rake her over the coals without me," I replied, swinging my backpack over my shoulder. "Later."

I set off for the student parking lot at a slow trot. I hadn't told everybody why I was in such a hurry to get home, because I wasn't really admitting it to myself. Elizabeth was in the newspaper office, helping lay out the next issue of the *Oracle,* but what if she finished early and beat me home? I had to get to the mailbox first. *In case the new* Ingenue *magazine came,* I told myself. *I'm dying to read about the supermodel diet and exercise plan.*

I buzzed home in the Fiat—top down, radio blasting, pushing the speed limit more than a little. When I turned onto Calico Drive, I realized my pulse was racing faster than the engine. "Whoa, girl," I muttered. "Take it easy. The U.S. Postal Service is nothing to get excited about!"

But as I pulled into the driveway and dashed to the front door, I couldn't keep the expectant smile from my face. Who was I kidding? There might be a letter from Todd!

I opened the box and pulled out a stack of mail. "Phone bill, letter from Grandma, bank statement, catalog, catalog, catalog," I noted. Where was it? Where was my letter? I hadn't heard from Todd in a week—I was *sure* there'd be something today!

I sifted through the pile again, even shook the catalogs to see if anything had gotten tucked into their pages. Still no letter.

I'd been holding my breath. Now the air escaped from me in a loud sigh. Feeling like a popped balloon, I sank onto the front step, dropping the mail to the sidewalk in disappointment.

"Jeez, get over it already!" I mumbled to myself. "Todd didn't write to you this week—big deal.

What, are those letters the high point of your life or something?"

I didn't answer the question. The way I'd started to feel about my correspondence with Todd couldn't bear close examination.

I picked up the mail and unlocked the front door. Walking into the house, I tossed the mail onto the hall table. I didn't get a letter from Todd, but I didn't care, I tried to convince myself. I really didn't care.

Thursday, later

Never mind what I said before about the mailbox. I don't know what I was thinking—I must have bumped my head in cheerleading practice! When I see A.J. tomorrow, I'm going to give him a kiss he'll think about all day . . . and all night!

Friday evening

I have a date with A.J. tonight and I just put this gloppy conditioner on my hair, so I have to sit for half an hour with my head wrapped in a warm towel. Yawn. Just wait till he runs his fingers through my hair, though—he'll go WILD.

I gave him an earthshaking kiss as promised, and the poor boy practically passed out. . . .

We were standing outside the boys' locker room, leaning against the wall, with our arms wrapped around each other. "I really should get going," A.J. murmured into my hair. "I'm late for practice."

"OK, get going," I teased, tightening my arms around his waist. "So long. See you later. Bye."

A.J. groaned. "You could make this easier, you know."

"Why would I want to?" I asked.

He laughed. "You're right. You're absolutely right. I know how to play basketball. Who needs to practice?"

"You're already perfect," I agreed.

I slid my hands up his chest and around to the back of his neck, pulling his face down to mine for a kiss. Our lips met, softly at first, and then the kiss got hotter and deeper. I was on fire from head to toe. I could feel A.J.'s body tremble.

"Wow," he gasped when we parted at last. "I think you just liquefied every bone in my body, Jess. I'm not going to be much use on the court today, that's for sure!"

I smiled. "It's a small price to pay, don't you think?"

We kissed one last time, and then A.J. reluctantly stepped free from our embrace. "I'll see you tonight," he said, his voice husky. He touched my cheek with the back of his hand. "Seven-thirty?"

"Make it eight," I said, turning his hand and pressing a light kiss on the palm.

A.J. opened the locker room door, lifting his arm in a goodbye wave. As I waved back I had a strange sensation. It was like I was floating above the scene, looking down on myself as I sent my boyfriend off to basketball practice . . . only the boy who gave me one last lingering look wasn't A.J. It was Todd!

The locker room door swung shut behind A.J. I stared at it, my cheeks flaming. *Todd Wilkins used to date your twin sister,* I reminded myself, rapping my head lightly against the wall to emphasize the point. *He was never your boyfriend. A.J.'s your boyfriend. A.J., A.J., A.J.!*

I turned my back on the locker room and headed back down the hall, silently chanting A.J.'s name like a mantra. I was still blushing with dismayed confusion. Todd and I were pen pals—that was one thing. What on earth was he doing elbowing his way into my fantasies?

Maybe lunacy runs in the family, Diary. My dad's a nut and so am I!

Saturday afternoon

Elizabeth and I are quite a team. I'm pretty sure Dad wishes he'd never heard of the Beach Disco! Last night we told him

212

that if he wants to be young again, he has to act young. And he could start by going dancing with us. He was into the idea at first—got all duded up in his baggy khakis and skinny purple tie—but then we got there and this new heavy-metal band The Razors was playing, and the music was deafening and all our friends took turns dragging Dad onto the dance floor, and by eleven o'clock—things were just starting to hop!—he was ready to collapse. We took him home to Mom and she delivered the final blow. "Hope you saved some energy for tomorrow, dear," she said. "I signed you up for a ten-mile run with the Marathoners Club!"

Dad hasn't admitted it yet, but he's more or less cured of whatever disease he had. Actually Elizabeth didn't help as much with our plan as I expected. She's directing the student variety show at school—it's a fund-raiser for the new dance department at SVH. The show's next week, and she's working long hours trying to get all the performers ready.

The mailman's here. Gotta go.

Wednesday afternoon

I have a new hobby, Diary. Not that I

have a lot of free time, between dating A.J., cheerleading, parties, keeping this journal, and writing to Todd! But the other day I was flipping through a fashion magazine and I saw these earrings that I just loved. I'm short on cash, though (as usual!), so I decided to try to make a pair of earrings just like the ones in the picture. I bought a bunch of stuff at a crafts store, and it actually turned out to be a lot of fun. It's not that hard, and the earrings are totally hot! I've gotten a million compliments on them.

So I'm making a bunch more to give to Mom and Elizabeth and to mail to Kelly and Aunt Laura. I really should explore this artistic streak—I didn't even know I had it!

Friday night, late

The whole family went to see the show Elizabeth has been slaving away on. The highlight was Jade Wu's modern dance solo. She was amazing! I guess the variety show was a pretty big deal for her. Elizabeth says Jade has these really strict, traditional Chinese parents and at first they didn't want Jade to dance in public. Can you imagine that? They also didn't let her date! Luckily Mr. and Mrs. Wu have seen the light and now Jade gets to have a normal life. She's seeing this other sophomore, David Prentiss. He's tall, sandy haired, freckled—they make a cute couple.

We finally got Dad to admit that he was better off being a forty-something father than a teenager. Thank goodness! I would've died if he'd started coloring his hair or wearing gold chains. Yeow!

Saturday afternoon

Dear Diary,

I'm waiting for A.J. to pick me up to go to the beach. But that's not why I'm writing. The truth is, I got another letter from Todd today. Why do I care? Maybe because—

Oops! The doorbell. He's here. A.J. The love of my life.

Sunday

I think I need to set the record straight. It probably seems like lately I've been making a big deal about Todd's letters. They're really not that newsworthy, so don't get the wrong idea. I was about to start analyzing Todd's latest letter yesterday when A.J. came over. There was this one part that seemed really significant and meaningful, like Todd was hinting at something kind of surprising. Something about his feelings for me.

But I just looked at the letter again, and I think I was reading stuff into it that wasn't there. I should spend my time doing something more constructive, like making jewelry. I gave some of my earrings to Cara, and now everybody's clamoring for a pair. I'm just so talented!

Wednesday evening

I'm RICH! At least, I will be soon. Treasure Island Boutique in downtown Sweet Valley is going to showcase my jewelry! Elizabeth encouraged me to try to sell my stuff, and when I showed Ms. Lussier, the manager at Treasure Island, some of my pieces—earrings, bracelets, and necklaces—she went wild for them. It didn't hurt that Lila and Amy happened to casually stroll into the store (pretending not to know me, of course!) and raved over my jewelry. Ms. Lussier and I made a deal on the spot for Treasure Island to have an exclusive on the Jessica Wakefield line!

Now I need to stock up on materials—feathers, beads, semiprecious stones—and get to work making more jewelry. Mom said

I could borrow two hundred dollars from her to get my business launched, but when I called Classic Land Imports, it turns out it makes a lot more sense to buy in bulk. I'm going to need more like nine hundred dollars. Gulp! Mom will never go for it, but as luck would have it, I know someone else I can hit up for a loan. Remember my classmate Ronnie Edwards? He's never been my favorite person, as you know. He's a jerk, basically. But lately he's been coming to school in these really hot designer clothes, driving a new Mustang, treating everybody at the Dairi Burger, just throwing cash around like you wouldn't believe.

No one knows where he's getting it. His family isn't rich or anything—his dad owns an all-night convenience store. Maybe some rich old relative of Ronnie's died, or maybe he won the lottery. Whatever. The other day at school, before I even went to Treasure Island, Ronnie offered to invest five hundred dollars in my venture. If I flirt with him enough, maybe he'll make it a thousand. So I'm sitting pretty!

Friday afternoon

Well, Ronnie really let me down. After all his talk about how much money he has,

217

he won't give me a cent for my jewelry endeavor. . . .

When the final bell rang, I sprinted down the hall to waylay Ronnie outside his math classroom. "Ronnie, wait up!" I called as he started down the hall.

He stopped to wait for me, his expression guarded. "Jessica," he said in greeting. "What's up?"

"I wanted you to be the first to know," I told him, flashing my most appealing smile. "Treasure Island is going to market my jewelry!"

"That's great," Ronnie said dully.

He wasn't acting very enthusiastic—not like the other day in the cafeteria when I first told him I wanted to start my own business. "I'll back you up with some cash—whatever you need," he'd boasted. "I bet you'll turn out to be a good risk."

"Ronnie," I said now, placing a hand on his arm. "I thought maybe we could go someplace quiet and talk about our arrangement. I mean, I don't know if you want me to sign a contract or something or if we can just have a verbal agreement."

Ronnie narrowed his eyes. "What are you talking about, Jessica?"

"Don't tell me you forgot already," I said, shaking his arm playfully. "The money you're going to loan me!"

"Don't have it," he said curtly.

"You don't *have* it?" I stared at him. "But you promised! I was counting on you!"

"Sorry." Ronnie shrugged. "I'd give it to you if I could, but my situation's changed. My situation's . . ." His voice trailed off and he looked over his shoulder, a haunted expression in his eyes.

Now that I took a good look at Ronnie, I noticed that his nice new clothes were rumpled, almost as if he'd slept in them. He looked worried and weary, with dark circles under his eyes. Something was wrong with Ronnie, but I didn't have a whole lot of sympathy—I was too mad about not getting my loan. "Well, thanks anyway," I said in a huff. "I really thought we were in this together."

"You'll figure something out," said Ronnie.

I'd better—I owe Classic Land Imports nine hundred dollars! I thought, chewing my nails anxiously as I watched Ronnie slouch off down the hall.

I was superannoyed at Ronnie. What a rat for backing out of his promise! But when I whined to Elizabeth about it, she said she thinks Ronnie's in major trouble. Supposedly he's been hanging out with this bookie, Big Al Remsen—Elizabeth says that's where Ronnie got the money he's been throwing around, by gambling. But I guess Big Al let Ronnie gamble on credit, and now Big Al's calling in the debt but

219

Ronnie doesn't have the cash. Ronnie's actually tried to borrow money from his friends, including Jeffrey!

I don't know what else is going on. I got the feeling there was more to the story, but Elizabeth clammed up when I asked her. Her eyes were blazing when she mentioned Ronnie's name, though. It's not easy to get my twin angry, but when she is, watch out!

Saturday night

I should be out dancing with A.J., but I'm grounded. And it's not my fault! I mean, sure, I charged nine hundred dollars on Mom's credit card when she thought I was only charging two hundred. But it wouldn't have mattered—I would've been able to pay her back no problem as soon as I sold my jewelry. I worked like a dog, with Cara and Amy helping, to make dozens of pieces for Treasure Island. But then Ms. Lussier decided she didn't want to feature the Jessica Wakefield line after all!

"Nine hundred dollars," my mother said, her tone disbelieving. *"Nine hundred dollars."*

"I know, I know," I said. "Do you have to keep repeating it?"

We were sitting at the kitchen table—the spot

where all serious discussions in my family take place. I knew I was in for it. It just remained to be seen how bad my punishment would be.

My dad shook his head. "What on earth were you thinking, Jessica?"

"Capitalism. The great American dream!" I told them, trying to put a good spin on my mistake. "I have a talent, and I wanted to see if I could make some money off it. What's wrong with that?"

"What's wrong is that you didn't have permission to charge that much on my card," my mother said.

"I've had a little setback, that's all," I assured her. "I'll pound the pavement—I'll take my samples around to other stores. Someone else will be interested, I'm sure of it."

"In the meantime you need to start paying off this bill," my father pointed out.

"You can keep my allowance for a while," I suggested generously.

My father had the nerve to laugh. "It would take about a century of your allowance. No, you'll need a steady job if you expect to meet the minimum credit card payment every month."

"I saw a Help Wanted sign in the window of a store downtown," my mother commented.

I raised an inquiring eyebrow.

"Treasure Island is looking for a salesclerk," she told me.

"No way," I burst out. "I won't work for them. Not after the way they treated me!"

"You'll apply for the job or you'll find something comparable by the end of next week," my father declared sternly. "And in the meantime you're grounded. Just for the weekend, but you can spend it looking through the classifieds."

I gaped at him. "Grounded? But I have a date with A.J.!"

"You should have thought of that before you abused your credit card privileges," my mom said.

I could tell from the looks on their faces that pleading wasn't going to get me anywhere. They were cold as ice—they had zero sympathy. I stomped out of the room, muttering under my breath. "This is outrageous. It's so unfair! My parents are inhumane dictators. I'm calling Amnesty International!"

In my room I hurled myself on my bed, still fuming. I knew I should call A.J. and tell him our date was off, but I was too steamed even to pick up the phone. Instead I grabbed a pad of paper and a pen and started to scribble furiously.

"Dear Todd,
You would not believe what my parents have done to me. I'm grounded! Isn't that the worst? And just because I charged a few hundred bucks on my mom's credit card. It's not like she didn't give me permission to use it . . . she just didn't expect me to spend that much. But I swore I'd pay

it back, and you'd think they'd trust me—
you'd think they'd give me the benefit of
the doubt for once. BUT NO! They sat me
down at the kitchen table and gave me the
standard lecture. YAWN. I could tell what
was running through their heads, though.
'What a Jessica thing to do.' And I guess it
was a Jessica thing. I mean, that's me. But I
can be responsible too. Maybe I'm not a
paragon of virtue like Elizabeth, but I'm
not all bad. Why can't they see that?"

I ended up writing a five-page letter. By the time I was finished, I was feeling a lot better. Maybe my parents didn't understand me, but I knew Todd would.

Saturday night, later

At least Elizabeth is enjoying her free-
dom. She's out with Jeffrey, celebrating
Sweet Valley's soccer win over Big Mesa.
The game almost didn't have such a happy
outcome, though. You'll never believe what
Ronnie Edwards was up to! He actually
asked Jeffrey to fix the point spread on the
game—hold back so Sweet Valley would
win by only two goals instead of four like
we were favored to. It was a betting
thing—Big Al put Ronnie up to it and said

if Ronnie didn't fix the game, some of Big Al's thugs would beat him to a pulp. Jeffrey would never have gone along with it in a million years, but he was pretty upset—he knew Ronnie might get pulverized. Luckily the police busted Big Al right there at the game, so Jeffrey was able to play his best and not worry about Ronnie.

So Elizabeth and Jeffrey are dancing cheek to cheek under the stars at the Beach Disco right now while I'm stuck here! I'll bet you anything Lila's dancing with A.J. I'll kill her.

Monday night

I'm not grounded anymore, but life still stinks. I think A.J. and I had our first fight today.

Well, not a fight, really. He just did something that really bugged me. We were at the Dairi Burger with the gang, and Dana Larson was talking about the party she's having on Friday. You know Dana— tall and slim, short funky blond hair, lead singer for the Droids, the band that plays at the Beach Disco a lot and at parties. Very cool girl in my class.

Anyway, Dana's parties are always great. I wouldn't miss one. So I told Dana

I'd be there with bells on. Then A.J. jabbed me with his elbow. "Jessica, don't you re-member we have other plans?" he said. He claimed we had a firm date to have dinner at his uncle's on Friday, which is like a two-hour drive round trip and would hog up our whole evening. I don't think so!

"Why did you pick a fight with me in front of all my friends?" I asked irritably as I climbed behind the wheel of the Fiat.

A.J. folded his long body into the passenger seat. "I didn't pick a fight," he said. "We made this plan to go to my uncle's a week ago. There's really nothing to argue about."

"The way I remember it, we talked about the *possibility* of going to your uncle's," I corrected him, starting the engine and flipping down my sun visor. "If nothing better came along. Now there *is* something better—Dana's party!"

"Uncle Brad's expecting us," A.J. insisted.

"Can't you tell him we'll come up next week in-stead?" I asked as I drove out of the Dairi Burger parking lot.

"Why is missing one party such a big deal?" A.J. wondered. "We go to parties all the time. I thought maybe you'd want to meet some of my relatives."

He sounded a little hurt, so I patted his arm. "I do, A.J. I just don't see why it has to cut into our

225

social life. Visiting relatives should be like a Sunday brunch type of thing."

I thought I was being completely fair and reasonable, but A.J. got all in a huff. "I don't see it that way," he said stiffly. "My uncle's a lot of fun—I know you'll like him."

"I'm sure I will." I reached over and rubbed his shoulder, then tickled the side of his neck. "But I can meet him anytime. It doesn't *have* to be this Friday, does it?" I cajoled.

"Well." A.J. sighed heavily. "If you *really* want to go to this party . . ."

"I really do," I said, pulling up at the curb in front of A.J.'s house. I shifted into neutral and leaned over to plant a kiss on his cheek. "Thanks, A.J.!"

A.J. gave me a brief hug and then got out of the car. He waved goodbye and I waved back. Then I shifted back into first gear and hit the gas.

When I got home, Elizabeth asked if everything was OK with A.J. (she was at the Dairi Burger and witnessed our little tiff). I didn't feel like going over it all again, so I told her we were fine. And we are fine. Like I said, it wasn't really a fight. But just between you and me, Diary, being part of a heavy-duty couple is getting old fast. . . .

"We don't have to talk about it." Elizabeth finished unloading the clean dishes from the dishwasher and shut the cupboard. "I didn't mean to be nosy. Things seemed kind of tense between you and A.J., that's all."

I hitched myself onto the counter and reached for the fruit bowl. "It was just one of those couple things," I said breezily, twisting the stem off an apple. "*You* know."

Elizabeth smiled. "Yeah, I do. It's not all romance and roses."

Well, it should be! I thought. "But it's worth it," I said, a question in my voice. I wanted to be convinced, and I supposed if anyone could do it, it was my sister, the Commitment Queen.

"I think so," said Elizabeth, leaning back against the counter and gazing at me with thoughtful eyes. "But everybody's different when it comes to this sort of thing. Everybody has different needs."

And I need to be free. I squelched the disloyal thought. "You and Jeffrey set the standard, though," I told her. "If A.J. and I end up half as devoted as you two, we'll be doing OK."

"Don't worry too much about it," Elizabeth advised. "Just have fun."

Elizabeth rummaged in the cupboard, pulling out a bag of tortilla chips. She ripped open the bag and we munched for a while in silence. Then I cleared my throat. "Um, Elizabeth," I said hesitantly. "I was just wondering, while we're on the subject of relationships . . ."

"Yeah?"

227

"I know you're happy with Jeffrey. But do you—do you ever think about Todd? I mean, think about him in that way?"

Elizabeth blushed slightly, and for a millisecond I regretted asking such a personal question. But I couldn't help myself—I was dying to know.

"Yes," she said softly after a long moment. "I do."

"Oh," I said, wishing now that I hadn't raised the subject.

I didn't press Elizabeth to elaborate, but she did anyway. Maybe she was glad for an excuse to talk about her old boyfriend. "I think about him, and I think about how different things would have been if he hadn't moved away. And I think about the future. What if we end up at the same college or something? Would we get back together?"

"Hmm," I mumbled, snapping a chip in two.

"I love Jeffrey," Elizabeth said earnestly. "Don't get me wrong. But I'd be lying if I didn't admit that deep inside, part of me still loves Todd—and will *always* love Todd."

I gulped. "Yeah, well . . ." I tried to lighten up the conversation a bit. "Things change. You're leading separate lives now. You've got a new boyfriend, and Todd probably has a new girlfriend." I didn't mention that I knew for a fact from his last letter that he was currently single.

"Maybe," Elizabeth conceded. "I'd rather not think about it, to tell you the truth. I mean, I know in theory that he got over me. He dates other girls. I can live with it because it's not happening right in front of me. But if I had to *see* him with someone else . . ." Elizabeth's voice dropped to a whisper. "It would break my heart."

I stared at my sister, not speaking. Somehow when I'd asked about her feelings for Todd, this wasn't the answer I'd been hoping to hear.

Wednesday afternoon

I was like five minutes late to meet A.J. today and he practically had a cow right in my backyard. I wanted to strangle him!

I parked the Fiat and strolled into the house, swinging my backpack in one hand and humming the song that had just been playing on the car radio. In the kitchen I grabbed a glass of juice before sauntering out to the patio.

A.J. was sitting at the edge of the pool with his pants rolled up and his feet dangling in the water. "Hi!" I called cheerfully.

He looked up at me, his eyebrows wrinkled in a frown. "It's about time!" he replied.

I gazed at him blankly. "What?"

"Don't you know what time it is?" he asked. Then he smacked the heel of his hand to his forehead. "Duh. I forgot. Jessica Wakefield doesn't wear a watch. The party never starts until she gets there."

I laughed. "You got that right." I knelt next to him and ruffled his hair. "Sorry I kept you waiting," I said, even though I wasn't. It's good for guys to stew a little, in my opinion. Keeps them on their toes.

A.J. wasn't amused. "I have better things to do, that's all," he told me. "And we were going to catch the early movie before dinner. Now we've missed it."

I shrugged. "So we'll go to a later show. It's not like the night is ruined."

"This happens all the time, though, Jess," said A.J. "We make plans and you mess them up."

"What, by being five minutes late?" I exclaimed, my irritation growing. I couldn't believe A.J. was worked up about something so trivial. "Big deal!"

"It's more like twenty minutes," A.J. said. "If you know you can't be punctual, you shouldn't tell me to meet you at a certain time."

"I can too be punctual," I responded indignantly. "When I want to," I added.

"So you're saying you just don't want to?" A.J. sounded hurt. "Seeing me isn't that important to you?"

"Don't be silly," I exclaimed. "Really. Talk about a waste of time—I can't believe we're having this conversation! And I was *not* twenty minutes late. Five."

"Twenty," said A.J., tapping the face of his watch with one finger.

"Fifteen, maybe," I conceded grudgingly.

A.J.'s lips twitched as if he were trying not to smile. "Seventeen and a half."

I wriggled onto his lap, twining my arms around his neck. "OK, so here's the question," I purred. "Will you let me make it up to you?"

"You're not going to kiss me, are you?" A.J. said in mock horror.

"Maybe I will . . . ," I murmured, bringing my lips closer to his, "and maybe I won't."

I brushed his lips softly with mine. He wrapped his arms around my waist, pulling me closer. We kissed more deeply, passion flaming between us. In fact, we got so into it, we almost toppled into the swimming pool.

A.J. pulled me back from the edge just in time, laughing. "You win again, Wakefield," he said. "You can be late all you want if you'll keep giving me those kisses."

I grinned. "You've got a deal."

> *I hate to admit it, Diary, but I know I can say it here—it won't go any further. I'm starting to wonder if A.J. and I are really made for each other. I really thought so at first. I mean, I'm still crazy about him. But he's also starting to drive me crazy in the other sense—he can be a total pain in the you-know-what! Like that stupid fight about being late, and also the*

other day when he walked by the athletic fields to pick me up after cheerleading practice. I was hanging out with some guys from the soccer team—Aaron, Mike Schmidt, Brad Tomasi—and we were just chatting. OK, maybe I was flirting. Just a teeny bit. And A.J. got all upset about it! He didn't say anything, but he gave me the silent treatment for a while, and there's nothing I hate more. I mean, I've known those guys longer than I've known him— lots longer. And we always flirt—it's just a game. Does A.J. expect me to ignore them?

Oh, and then I could tell he disapproved when he heard me and Amy and Maria talking about the "Best Kisser" category in the slam books. He's such a puritan. Lucky for him he's the best kisser! Every girl thinks her boyfriend is, though, right? Elizabeth is too much of a goody-goody—she wouldn't write under the Best Kisser category. I wonder who she thinks is a better kisser, though, Jeffrey or Todd?

Thursday night

Guess what, Diary? I got a package in the mail today. From Todd! He put a bunch of goofy stuff in the box: a little jug of Vermont maple syrup, a T-shirt with the logo of his new high school, a black-and-white stuffed cow (I guess there are a lot of cows in Vermont!). But there was also this cassette tape. He made it himself—picked out all the songs, even drew a fancy cover. Can you believe he went to all the trouble? Isn't it sweet? Elizabeth is at the hospital with John Pfeifer and Jennifer Mitchell, so she doesn't know about the package yet. Should I tell her when she gets home?

I guess I should explain the John and Jennifer stuff. It's quite the saga. You know John—he's the sports editor for the Oracle *and he's on the tennis team. Well, he's good friends with Jennifer, this really pretty sophomore. Maybe he likes her better than a friend, but she's been hanging out lately with Rick Andover. Remember Rick? He's a high school dropout with tattoos all over his arms, and he drives a souped-up Chevy, plays the guitar, and thinks he's going to be a rock star someday—but I doubt it. He's cute, though, I'll admit . . . I went out with him once! I can see why Jennifer fell for him. But he's still a lowlife.*

ANYWAY. I got the story from Elizabeth—I think this is accurate. Rick was trying to talk Jennifer into running away with him. I guess she's been kind of unhappy at home—her parents are really strict or something. And she has a major crush on Rick. So to get cash for the trip, Rick pulled an absurd stunt—he ripped off a music store right in the middle of town. In broad daylight!

He got caught because Elizabeth and John happened to be there and saw him running away from the store, so they tipped off the police. You'd think Jennifer would have been furious at Rick. Instead she got mad at her father—she thought he was the one who got Rick busted. When Mr. Mitchell went into the hospital a couple of days ago for emergency heart bypass surgery, Jennifer refused to visit him! Meanwhile, John was afraid to tell Jennifer the truth, that he called the police, because he didn't want her to hate him (since as I said before, I think he's secretly in love with her).

Enter my sister, Ms. Diplomacy. She should really work for the United Nations when she grows up. Elizabeth persuaded John to come clean with Jennifer, which he did. Jennifer did get mad, but only for a minute. I guess she's finally gotten a clue about how rotten Rick really is, and she appreciates that John did what he did because he cares about her.

So right now Elizabeth is driving John and Jennifer to Fowler Memorial to visit

*Mr. Mitchell . . . and I'm listening to the
tape Todd sent me. Some of the songs are
actually kind of romantic. What does this
mean?*

When someone knocked on my bedroom door,
I assumed it was Elizabeth, home from the hospital and ready to give me a John-Jennifer update.
"Come in," I hollered over the sound of the stereo,
flipping a page in my *Ingenue* magazine.

The door swung open, and A.J. stepped into the
room. "Hey," he drawled with one of his slow,
sweet southern grins.

I gaped at him. "A.J.!" I squeaked. "What are
you doing here? I'm half naked!"

This wasn't true, but I *felt* half naked, wearing
an old T-shirt with the sleeves ripped off and with
my hair an uncombed mess.

"That's the way I like you," A.J. teased, coming
over to sit next to me on the bed.

"You caught me by surprise, that's all," I said,
giving him a quick kiss.

"That's OK, isn't it? I was just out doing some
errands and I started thinking about you, and I decided not to waste any time—I wanted to see you
right away."

"Sure, it's OK. I like a guy who acts on his im-
pulses," I responded, reaching up to run my fingers through his hair.

We kissed again, then flopped back on my bed

235

in a cozy tangle of limbs. "I suppose we should go downstairs," A.J. murmured lazily as he dropped feathery little kisses on my jawline. "In case your parents suspect there's some hanky-panky going on up here. But I'm so comfortable . . . and I really like this song. What group is this?"

I sat up abruptly, remembering. It was the tape Todd made for me, but I couldn't exactly tell A.J. that! "Um, it's an East Coast band," I answered. "The Rain Buckets."

"Never heard of them," remarked A.J. He reached over toward the stereo and grabbed the plastic tape cover, which was lying right on top. "Hey, look at this!" he exclaimed. "Cool art." He scanned the list of song titles. "Wow. Did you make this?"

"No. It was a present from . . . Enid," I said after a desperate pause. "She made it for Elizabeth and I borrowed it. Neat, huh?"

A.J. looked a little surprised. "I didn't know Enid was such a rock fan."

"You didn't?" I said. "Yeah, well, she follows all the hot new alternative bands. She even subscribes to a bunch of those cutting-edge rock music magazines, you know? You should see her collection of live bootleg tapes." Sometimes when I start telling fibs, I get carried away and go into too much elaborate fictional detail. I said a silent prayer that A.J. and Enid would never find themselves engaged in a conversation about modern rock.

Idly A.J. started to pull the paper insert out of the plastic cassette cover. My heart stopped. If he unfolded it, he'd see the inscription from Todd, which happened to be very personal. He'd realize I was lying about the tape, and he'd definitely want to know why.

"Come on." I snatched the tape cover from A.J. and tossed it aside. It bounced into my open closet where, thankfully, it was immediately devoured by the mess within. "Let's dance!"

I grabbed his hand and thrust out my arm, then put my cheek next to his, tango style. A.J. laughed. "You're a nut, you know that?" he said fondly.

As we danced around my bedroom I tried to feel as if I deserved A.J.'s affection. *I should have told the truth about the tape,* I thought. *I don't have anything to hide. Todd used to go out with my sister—he's a friend, nothing more.* But even as I considered this, I knew I was lying to myself as well as to A.J.

Todd had become something more than a friend to me, and the tape proved it.

Part 6

Monday afternoon

A.J. and I are getting along great—sort of. But I keep listening to the tape Todd sent me. There's this one song in particular, "Harvest Moon," by a pretty cool band called the Starving Artists, and it's definitely on the steamy side. Make-out music. It puts me in the mood to go to Miller's Point . . . but not with A.J. I don't know what's happening to me, Diary. I feel so strange.

Tuesday evening

I'm trying to distract myself from thinking so much about The Boy I Won't Name

238

Who Lives in a Scenic New England State Famous for Its Fall Foliage, but who is right with me in spirit whenever I read one of his letters or listen to the music he sent me. So I spent hours and hours and tons of physical energy making up all these cool new cheers for the squad. Sandy, Cara, and the rest of the girls loved the new routines, and they especially loved the music we're going to dance to at the next game . . . songs from Todd's tape! So much for getting him out of my brain. It's impossible!

Saturday night, late

Dear Diary,
    Bruce's family threw a big gala at the country club tonight, and A.J. and I had a great time. But I had this really weird hallucination. I was dancing with A.J., and I thought I saw Todd!

Every year Mr. and Mrs. Patman host a huge party at the Sweet Valley Country Club. It's the only reason I stay friendly with Bruce—it's the social event of the season, and I wouldn't want to miss it!

"This is really something," A.J. said in a low voice. "I don't think I've ever seen so much diamond jewelry in one place!"

As A.J. popped a salmon puff in his mouth, I surveyed the scene with approval. The country club was packed with elegantly dressed people— men in tuxes and women in satin, sequins, chiffon, and velvet. A.J. was right—the glitter from the diamonds was almost blinding. "The band is better than last year," I told A.J., delicately lifting an hors d'oeuvre from a silver tray passed by a waiter. "Jazzier."

"Then let's go show 'em what we're made of," suggested A.J., taking my arm.

We strolled under a high archway into the ballroom, and A.J. took me in his arms. We swayed gently to the music. "Did I tell you that you look incredible tonight?" A.J. murmured, his lips close to my ear.

I knew I looked dynamite in the long, close-fitting peacock green dress I'd borrowed from Lila. "Yes, but tell me again," I said, my voice sultry.

A.J. pulled me closer. I rested my head on his shoulder, letting my mind drift. Then it happened, the way it always did. I started thinking about Todd.

It was horribly disloyal, but I couldn't help myself. I looked up at A.J., suddenly feeling critical and dissatisfied. When we first met, I thought his red hair was adorable, but now I decided that it made him look goofy. And his rented tuxedo didn't fit right—the pants were too long and the jacket was tight across the shoulders. I couldn't resist mentally comparing him to Todd. I remembered the time Todd picked up Elizabeth to take her to a holiday dance at school. Todd had looked great in his tux, accented by a red bow tie and cummerbund. Elizabeth teased him about needing a haircut, but I'd liked the way his wavy brown hair brushed the top of his collar in back. . . .

I shook my head, forcing myself back to the present moment. *You're dancing with A.J.,* I reminded myself. *Pay attention!*

"Let's take a break," A.J. said when the band paused between numbers. "My appetite's back—I could go for some more of the excellent grub they're serving."

I wrinkled my nose. *Grub? It must be one of his dad's army expressions,* I thought distastefully. *Does he think he's in boot camp or something?* It didn't show a lot of class. Todd would never refer to caviar on toast points and prosciutto and melon kabobs as *grub!*

We filled small plates at the buffet and then went outside to sit on wrought-iron chairs under a grape arbor. As A.J. chowed down, my gaze roamed the lawn, which was illuminated by a whimsical path of paper lanterns. A lone figure stood at the edge of the grass, his back to the festivities. He lifted his drink to his mouth, then lowered it again. I stared, fascinated. There was something romantically melancholy about him . . . and something vaguely familiar. His height, the curly dark hair, the broad shoulders . . .

My heart leapt into my throat. Todd!

I jumped in my chair, nearly spilling my plate onto the grass. A.J. looked at me, his expression quizzical. "What's the matter, Jess?"

"It's—it's . . ." I stammered.

On the other side of the lawn the figure turned and began to walk toward us. I held my breath, the tension unbearable. Then I let it out with a disappointed sigh. The young man had light eyes, not brown ones, and although his tuxedo was elegant, he wasn't all that handsome. It wasn't Todd after all. Of course it wasn't. What would he be doing here?

"Jess?" A.J. said again.

"Just a mosquito," I said quickly, slapping my arm. "I got bit."

"Maybe we should go back inside, then."

"Sure," I agreed. I'd be better off inside, definitely. My thoughts might still wander, but in the clear glow of the crystal chandeliers my eyes wouldn't play such cruel tricks on me.

Bruce was at the party with Kristin Thompson, which struck me as a little strange. She's in my class at SVH, but nobody knows her that well because she spends all her time playing tennis. She's always in the paper for winning junior tournaments and will probably turn pro soon.

Maybe it's not so strange—Bruce is a good tennis player, too. Anyway, she's a pretty girl, but she had this totally tacky flowered sundress on, like she was going to a backyard barbecue instead of a black-tie ball. I guess she doesn't get out much! I can't see Bruce getting seriously interested in her—he's pretty picky when it comes to appearances.

But back to me. You know I don't usually waste my time pining over guys who aren't around, unless you count my crush on Jamie Peters. If J.P. ever knocks on my door in between recording albums and touring, I'll definitely let him in! But in general I'm the "love the one you're with" type. So I don't know what's come over me lately. I THINK ABOUT TODD ALL THE TIME. (I hope Elizabeth never reads this!) Like tonight at the ball. I have these daydreams, and I also keep remembering times when he still lived in Sweet Valley, when he'd be over to see Elizabeth but he and I would shoot the breeze, joke around a little. Did it mean more than it seemed to at the time? Was there a spark between us way back when? Not that it matters. Todd lives three thousand miles away. That's why he and Elizabeth broke up—long-distance relationships stink. What

*am I talking about, anyway? This is what
I mean. I'm losing my mind! I don't have
a "relationship" with Todd Wilkins. And I
never will!*

Sunday . . . midnight or later

*I don't know what to do, Diary. Some-
thing big happened and I can't tell a soul.
Todd called today while Elizabeth was at
Kristin's tennis match!*

My sister had tried to talk me into going with
her to the finals of the Avery Cup Tournament.
Supposedly it was Kristin's big chance—if she won
her match against Rachel Rose, she'd earn a spot
on Nick Wylie's pro team. It was Sunday, though,
and I just didn't feel like getting up early to clap
for Kristin, who wasn't exactly my best friend. So I
slept in, had a leisurely brunch with Steven, who
was home for the weekend, and then took the
Sunday paper—OK, just the comics and the fashion section—out to the pool.

I'd spent half an hour tanning my back and had
just rolled over to get some sun on my front when
the phone rang. I'd brought the portable out with
me just in case—I was expecting to hear from A.J.
I answered the phone. "Hello?"

"Is this Jessica?"

The words sent a warm shiver up my spine. My

heart started to gallop like a Kentucky Derby winner. I knew that voice. And it wasn't A.J.'s.

"Yes, it's Jessica. Todd?" I said weakly.

"Hi! How's it going?"

I'd imagined this moment a thousand times—hearing his voice and actually talking to him instead of just writing letters back and forth. But now that the moment had come, my mouth was dry as dust. I was speechless.

"Jess?" Todd said.

I coughed. "Sorry," I choked out. "I was just—want me to get Elizabeth? Oh, I forgot. She's at a tennis match. She'll have to call you back. Is that OK?"

Todd laughed—a husky, sexy laugh that made my whole body tingle. "No, it's not OK," he declared.

"It's not?"

"No, silly. I called to talk to *you*."

"Oh." I swallowed a nervous giggle. It was so easy to be myself on paper with Todd—why couldn't I relax? "Well, um, great. What's new in Vermont?"

"Not a lot," said Todd. "Just got back from windsurfing on Lake Champlain."

"Sounds like fun," I remarked.

"The wind was really kicking," he agreed. "I had a couple of major wipeouts. How about you? How come you're not at the beach?"

"The sun's just as bright in my own backyard," I

told him. "Besides, this way the other girls can get some attention for once. It's only fair."

Todd chuckled. "That's generous of you, Wakefield."

I smiled, stretching my body out on the chaise lounge. "You know me, Wilkins. Always putting other people first!"

Todd laughed again. When he responded, his tone had grown thoughtful. "Yeah, you know, I *did* used to think I knew you, Jess. But these last few weeks . . . your letters. It's been like getting to know you again for the first time."

"What's the verdict? Can you stand me, or do you still think I'm a brat?"

His voice was warm and vibrant. "I never thought you were a brat. And yeah, I can stand you. Easy."

I blushed hotly, glad that Todd couldn't see my face. There was another brief silence, and I wondered what would happen next. Would we keep making idle chitchat and then say "so long"? Would either of us have the nerve to say what we were *really* thinking?

I realized that I didn't want to hang up without telling Todd something important. "Um, Todd," I said softly. "I've been thinking about you. A lot."

"I've been thinking about you too," he confessed. "You should see me race home after basketball practice. The mailman's my new best friend."

I laughed. "I'm the same way. I *really* race

because I want to get the mail before . . . in case there's a letter from you, I wouldn't want—" I didn't finish the sentence, but it was pretty obvious what—or rather, whom—I was talking about. *Before Elizabeth sees that you're still writing to me—that you write all the time.*

"Does she know?" Todd asked after a moment.

"I showed her the first letter, but after that . . . I decided I wanted to keep them to myself."

"That was probably a good idea," he said.

It was time to change the subject—I didn't feel like talking about Elizabeth, even if we never actually mentioned her name. "So should I keep writing, or are you getting bored of Sweet Valley High gossip?"

"I'm not bored," Todd said, "but to be honest, I'm tired of writing letters."

"Really," I said, just a teeny bit hurt. I thought my letters were great!

"I want to talk to you face-to-face, Jessica," Todd went on. "I want to come to Sweet Valley and see you."

I nearly dropped the telephone. For a moment I was too stunned to speak. Up until now corresponding with my sister's ex-boyfriend had kind of been like a game. Flirting and sharing secrets, falling a little bit in love—it was safe when you did it long distance. No one could get into trouble that way. But now . . .

"You want to *see* me?" I croaked.

"Maybe I shouldn't have put it so bluntly," Todd apologized. "You probably think I'm way out of line. Why don't we forget I even said that and—"

"No," I broke in quickly. "No, I . . ." My voice dropped to a breathless whisper. "I want to see you too. But how can we—how can you—there's no way. It's crazy!"

"I know," he conceded. "It'd probably be impossible. First I have to scrape up the money for a plane ticket, and then we'd have to work it out so that . . ."

He stopped speaking, but I knew what he was getting at. *So no one else finds out,* I thought. *So A.J. doesn't find out. So Elizabeth doesn't find out!*

"I don't know, Todd," I said quietly. "Maybe we should think about this a little longer."

He laughed. "I thought Jessica Wakefield was the type to take chances and do things on the spur of the moment and—"

"OK, OK." I had to laugh too. "Caution is a little out of character, but this is pretty out of the ordinary."

"You're right." He sighed. "Let's sleep on it. I'll call you again soon, though, all right?"

We said goodbye and I hung up the phone. For a minute I just sat on the chaise lounge. My whole body trembled as the significance of my conversation with Todd sank in. We'd crossed a line into new, uncharted territory. What was going to happen next?

I wasn't sure, but I knew one thing. I couldn't wait to find out. My secret relationship with Todd terrified me, but it was also the most exciting thing that had ever happened to me in my entire life.

When the phone rang, I was so sure it was Todd again that when I picked it up, I didn't even bother saying hello. "Did you forget to tell me something?" I teased. He'd gone on and on about how much he wished I lived in Burlington, but I was happy to hear it again.

"Jess, is that you? Forget to tell you what?" A.J. said.

Oops! I winced at how close I'd just come to making a major blunder. Thank heavens I hadn't used Todd's name! "Uh, last night when you dropped me off after our date," I said, recovering quickly. "You didn't tell me you loved me."

"Yes, I did," A.J. protested. "I know I did. Right before we kissed good night. Or was it after? Or during?"

I forced myself to laugh lightheartedly. "Well, anyway. How was the tennis match?"

A.J. launched into a point-by-point rehash of Kristin's surprising loss to Rachel Rose, and I lapsed into a daydream. Todd was in Sweet Valley, and we were walking hand in hand on the beach at sunset. As the fiery sphere sank beneath the waves he pulled me into his arms and then . . .

I gave myself a mental slap. How could I have such disloyal thoughts about another guy when I was on the phone with my devoted boyfriend? And when that "other" guy happened to be my twin sister's old flame, a flame that still flickered warmly in the deepest corners of her heart?

But I couldn't help myself. I couldn't stop thinking about what it would be like to see Todd again, to be alone with him. Would it ever happen, though? *Maybe we should stick to writing letters,* I thought. But could we? We'd taken the next step. Was there any going back?

Tuesday,
no idea what time it is

I just got off the phone with Todd. At one point Elizabeth actually picked up! When she heard my voice on the line—thank goodness Todd wasn't talking!—she apologized and hung up, but I still almost had a stroke. I feel so guilty I want to die. But I'm aching to see Todd, and he really wants to visit—in SECRET! He'd stay in a motel and we'd have to meet on the sly, and it would be horrible and wonderful and I just don't know what to do. I still love A.J. . . . don't I?

Wednesday morning

Dear Diary,
I dreamt about Todd last night, and my

dream was so wild, I have to write it down before I go to school. I really, really, REALLY hope nobody EVER reads this . . . especially Elizabeth! OK, are you ready? 'Cause this is intense.

In my dream Todd came to Sweet Valley and we couldn't tell anyone for the obvious reasons—it might get back to Elizabeth, and Todd knew she still had a thing for him, and I would never want to hurt her, etc. etc. But for some reason while he was here, Todd ended up staying at my house! He was sleeping in Steven's room, and we had to do incredible gymnastics to keep my parents and Elizabeth from finding out. Of course, in real life it would never happen like that in a million years, but you know how in dreams the weirdest things seem totally plausible? So there was Todd, right down the hall from me. And in my dream, at night when the rest of the family was asleep, he'd sneak into my room and . . . I don't think I can write it—I'm blushing just thinking about it. Let's just say it was intensely romantic. I haven't done anything like that even with A.J.! So, Diary, if you think I'm the naughtiest girl on the planet, you're probably right!

Back in the real world, it turns out

Kristin made the pro team after all. Rachel Rose sprained her ankle, so Kristin's taking her spot. Kristin also had the good sense to dump Bruce, so I'd say in general things are going her way.

Gotta run. I need to grab some breakfast before school. Must've burned a lot of calories dreaming about Todd—I'm ravenous!

Thursday afternoon

Dear Diary,

A.J. gave me flowers for no particular reason today. "Because they're beautiful and so are you," he said. I'm usually not the sentimental type myself, but I almost started to cry. He's so sweet—I don't deserve him. Why did I ever think I could be happy with just one guy? I have this horrible feeling I'm going to end up breaking A.J.'s heart in a million pieces . . . and maybe breaking my own while I'm at it.

Friday evening

I should be getting dressed—A.J. and I have a double date with Cara and Steven tonight. Instead I just phoned Todd's favorite radio station in Burlington. I requested "Harvest Moon" and dedicated it to Todd from Jessica. I wonder if Todd will be listening when the DJ plays the song?

I haven't spoken to Todd for almost a week, but I got a letter from him today. It turned my insides to oatmeal! He heard my dedication on the radio, and while describing how it made him feel, he got very passionate. We're not even bothering to pretend anymore that we're "just friends." I can only hope and pray Elizabeth never opens one of his letters by mistake. We haven't made a decision yet about a visit, but I can tell Todd's just waiting for me to give him the green light.

Something else: I found out today that A.J.'s going away this weekend. There's a big Morgan family reunion in Dallas for his grandparents' fiftieth wedding anniversary. The timing's perfect from my point of view. Maybe with him gone, I'll be able to get some perspective on the crazy situation I've gotten myself into. I need space. I need help!

Thursday night

I said goodbye to A.J. this afternoon. I want to miss him while he's in Texas,

253

Diary, I really do. I want to be a good girl-friend. But it's hard when actually I'm just relieved to have him out of the way. I've been looking forward to him not being around! Isn't that terrible? I'm out of control. One of these days I'll have to deal with this situation head-on, but in the meantime. . . .

"I don't know how I'm going to stand it," A.J. grumbled, his face buried in my hair. "I won't see you for three whole days!"

He'd driven me home after cheerleading practice, and now we were parked in front of my house. I gave him a brotherly pat on the shoulder. "You'll survive," I replied, trying not to sound impatient. "You know what they say, anyhow. Absence makes the heart grow fonder."

"I thought it was 'out of sight, out of mind,'" said A.J. "You won't forget me, will you, Jess?"

"In only three days?" I made myself smile playfully. Poor A.J. If he only knew! "Not a chance."

I pecked him on the cheek, hoping that would satisfy him. I was dying to make my escape. But A.J. pulled me close again, finding my mouth with his. We kissed for what seemed like an eternity, but instead of making me all warm and tingly as his kisses used to, this one left me feeling cold as a stone.

"A.J.," I said, wriggling away at last. "I should

254

go. It's my night to cook dinner, and if I don't get started pretty soon, we won't eat until midnight."

This was a pretty thin excuse—A.J. knew as well as anybody that I didn't take my household chores very seriously. More often than not, when it was my turn to cook, the family ended up ordering take-out. But A.J. had no reason to suspect insincerity. He released me with a reluctant sigh. "I'll miss you like crazy," he told me, his eyes a little misty.

I'm a pretty good actress. I sniffled, dabbing at an imaginary tear. "I'll miss you too."

"I'll call the minute I get back."

"I'll be waiting by the phone."

I climbed out of the car, breathing a sigh of relief. A.J. shifted into first gear and drove slowly forward, waving as he went. I stood at the curb, waving back, until he rounded the corner. As soon as the car was out of sight I felt an enormous weight lift from my shoulders. I sauntered toward the house, smiling. *I'm free,* I thought.

Why does A.J. have to like me so much? It would be easier if he were more like Bruce "Casual Relationships Only, Please" Patman. But then, if he were like Bruce, I would never have fallen for him. Oh, it's just so complicated. I know what I should do, Diary. I should tell Todd that it's not a good idea for him to visit. DEFINITELY not a good idea. We should stop writing to each other too—we should just stop, period. And I should try really hard to fall back in love with A.J., because he's the sweetest, cutest guy in the world and he worships the ground I walk on. I'm incredibly lucky to be going out with him. But. BUT.

Friday night

How's this for wild and unexpected—I met a guy at the beach today! His name is Christopher, and he's gorgeous: green eyes, curly brown hair, dark tan, great body. I was moping around all by myself, trying to solve the problems of the world, starting with my own tangled love life. Out of nowhere he just walked up to me with his surfboard. We started talking, and I flirted a little because that comes naturally when a cute guy's around, and then he asked me out and I said yes, and maybe I shouldn't have, but I'm hoping dinner with him will take my mind off T.W.!

Saturday night

Christopher is something else. Dinner last night was really romantic, and we saw

each other again today. In fact, we were to-
gether for like ten hours! He's very inter-
ested in me and I know I shouldn't
encourage him, but for some reason I can't
hold him at arm's length. At any other time
in my life I'd have been unbelievably
psyched to meet a guy like Christopher,
but why did this have to happen now,
Diary? I'm more confused than ever. . . .

It was my idea to meet at the Main Street Café
in Pacific Shores on Saturday morning. It's a
quaint, touristy little town—art galleries and gift
shops. Not a place kids hang out, which was just
the point. I didn't want to bump into anyone I
knew.

Christopher had greeted me with an armful of
red roses. After brunch we went to the aquarium
and planetarium. Then we bought some bread,
cheese, and fruit and found a deserted stretch of
beach.

It all seemed like a dream to me. I didn't want
to think about what I was doing or about what the
consequences might be. This was uncharted territory for me. I'd never cheated on my steady boyfriend before because I'd never *had* a steady
boyfriend before. *I haven't done anything bad yet,*
I reminded myself. *We haven't even kissed.*

Christopher lay on one side, propped up on his
elbow. He watched me eat grapes, a seductive half

smile on his face. "What?" I said, self-conscious. The intensity of his gaze made me feel naked.

"I can't get over how beautiful you are," he said, taking my free hand and rubbing his thumb across my knuckles. "You must be used to people staring at you, though."

I *was* used to it, but that didn't mean I didn't enjoy it when the person staring was a gorgeous guy like Christopher. "Brie or Gouda?" I asked, tearing off a hunk of bread and offering it to him.

"I can't eat food," he said. "I only have an appetite for you."

If A.J. had said something that corny to me, I would have burst out laughing. But Christopher, with his smoldering eyes and sexy voice, pulled it off. I sensed something was about to happen between us. It was wrong, but it was also inevitable.

"Well, nibble on my earlobe, then," I invited, smiling.

Christopher sat up and reached out for me. I dropped the bunch of grapes and melted into his arms. As I gazed into his eyes it occurred to me that Christopher was still really a stranger. I didn't know where he lived, how old he was—I didn't even know his last name. *Maybe that's what makes being with him so exciting. He can fulfill all my fantasies*, I thought, closing my eyes as his lips met mine. *He can be anyone I want him to be.*

Then we were kissing, and no question about it, it was even better than kissing A.J. *Why?* I wondered, running my hands up Christopher's broad back and massaging his shoulders. Then the answer came to me, hitting me like a bucket full of icy ocean water. I pulled away abruptly, flushing with confusion.

"What's the matter?" Christopher asked.

I turned my head, hiding my eyes. "Nothing, but something just bit me." I slapped my ankle. "A fly." I hopped to my feet. "Ready for a swim?"

We jogged down to the waterline. Christopher looked relaxed—he was oblivious to my inner turmoil. It was a safe bet he would've been bummed to know the truth, though.

If I'd told him that his kiss only turned me on because I'd imagined I was kissing Todd.

Am I messed up or what? You know me pretty well, Diary. I've done some crazy things in the past when it comes to guys, no question. But this takes the cake, wouldn't you say? I'm dating one guy, having a fling with another, and secretly pining over a third. Yikes! But as of tomorrow, things will get a little bit more manageable again. I'm meeting Christopher at the beach in the morning, and he doesn't know it yet, but I'm going to tell him I can't see him again . . . because A.J. gets back in the afternoon!

I'm exhausted, Diary. Leading a double (make that triple!) life really tires a girl out. How am I supposed to explain my fatigue to Elizabeth, though? She thinks the new pal I'm hanging out with ("Chris") is a girl!

Sunday evening

I broke the news to Christopher today, and he took it pretty well. Of course he was crushed—who wouldn't be? But he didn't make a scene or anything when I told him I already had a boyfriend. So that's that. Fun while it lasted.

A.J.'s back. We went for a drive tonight and I tried really hard to fall in love with him again. We made out at Miller's Point for at least an hour. But I don't think it worked. Being attracted to a total stranger—Christopher—made me realize that I feel zero passion for A.J. these days. I'm not sure if it's because of Todd or if it would've happened anyway. What am I going to do? I'm not ready to break up—I still want to go to the Citizens' Day Ball with him next weekend. Did I tell you about that yet? A.J. entered an essay contest sponsored by the Sweet Valley Samaritans' Club, this bunch of old geezers who do charitable things for the town. The topic was "Sweet Valley in the Year 2000" and my oh-so-creative boyfriend won first prize, which means he'll be king of the Citizens' Day Ball . . . and yours truly will be queen! If we broke up, A.J. would ask someone else to the dance. We have to stay a couple for at least another week, and that's all there is to it!

Sunday, later

Brace yourself. Todd just called and he did it—he bought a plane ticket. HE'S COMING TO SWEET VALLEY! In just ten days!

Wednesday evening

This has been a terrible week. I'll never have a thoughtless fling again. Remember how I told Christopher I couldn't see him again and he seemed cool about it? Well, it turns out he's some kind of psycho. He keeps calling me—he must've gotten my number from directory information. He's following me too. He actually showed up at the Dairi Burger the other night! Luckily A.J. and I were on our way out, so I escaped before Christopher could talk to me.

It's too, too weird. When he called the house last night, I didn't mince words. I *told him to leave me alone or else. He got really mad. He started to say these sick things, so I hung up. I was praying that he finally got the message, but then today he sent a big bouquet of flowers to me at school! I gave the flowers to Cara, pretending they were from Steven. A.J. still doesn't suspect anything. It's only a matter of time before he finds out about Christopher, though, especially if Christopher keeps pulling stunts like the one at A.J.'s house this afternoon. Diary, I'm scared. REALLY scared. . . .*

A.J. turned on the hose and directed the spray of water at the old Toyota parked in his family's driveway. "I spent all afternoon cleaning and vacuuming the inside," he told me, rinsing off the soap bubbles. "Looks like new, huh?"

I squinted at A.J.'s car. "New" wasn't the word I'd have chosen, but it definitely looked better. "I can't believe you're going to sell this baby," I replied. "You two seemed like you were meant for each other."

"Well, my dad's been after me to start putting aside some money for college," said A.J. He dropped the hose and started wiping the car dry with a soft cloth. "If I get fifteen hundred for the car, which is what I'm asking, that'll be a good start for my savings account."

I grabbed a rag and bent to polish the front fender. Behind me I heard a car brake to a stop. "Must be the guy who called about the Toyota," said A.J., putting a hand to his forehead to shade his eyes as he gazed out at the street. "He sounded pretty interested on the phone—he wants to take it for a test drive."

I straightened up and turned just as a boy stepped out of the VW bug parked by the curb. He was tall and dark haired, wearing faded orange shorts and a baggy white T-shirt. As my eyes fixed on his face my stomach contracted into a small, icy ball of dread.

It was Christopher.

Oh, no, I thought, biting my lip until I tasted blood. My brain spun in panicked circles. *He's going to tell A.J. about us, about last weekend. What am I going to do? What am I going to say?*

Christopher strode up the driveway, a friendly smile on his face. A.J., who hadn't noticed my traumatized expression, stuck out his hand in genial fashion. "You must be Christopher," A.J. said.

Christopher shook A.J.'s hand. He still hadn't met my eyes, and in an instant of mingled relief and terror I realized he was pretending he didn't know me. *Why?* I wondered, my knees quaking. *What is he up to?*

"A.J., right?" Christopher asked.

"Right." A.J. turned to me. "And this is my girlfriend, Jessica."

Christopher extended his hand. I wanted to run in the opposite direction, but I had to act normal if I didn't want A.J. to figure out there had been something going on between Christopher and me. Slowly I held out my hand to Christopher.

He grasped my fingers so tightly I almost gasped. "Nice to meet you, Jessica," he stated, his voice and eyes deadly calm.

It was so strange. Just a few days earlier I'd relaxed happily in his arms. Now my skin crawled at his touch. "N-nice t-to . . ." I mumbled, unable to spit the words out.

Mercifully A.J. still hadn't picked up on my tension. He was pacing around the car, pointing out its virtues to Christopher. "Eight years old, but the mileage is pretty low," he declared in classic used-car-salesman fashion. "No rust, new tires, really good stereo system."

"Brakes?" asked Christopher.

"Had them done last year," A.J. replied. "All the service receipts are in the glove compartment if you want to look them over. The previous owner took good care of the car too—regular oil changes, scheduled tune-ups, the whole nine yards."

Christopher stuck his hands in his pockets and rocked back on his heels, studying the car in a thoughtful and deliberate manner. I clenched my hands into fists, stifling a scream. "It looks good, but I'd like to take it for a spin before I make up my mind," he told A.J.

"Of course," said A.J., tossing Christopher the keys.

All of a sudden I thought I knew what was about to happen. The two guys would drive off, and when he had A.J. alone, Christopher would tell him about last weekend. And I was helpless to stop him.

A.J. put his hand on the passenger-side door handle. At that moment his mother appeared on the front porch. "Phone, A.J.!" she called.

"Can you take a message, Mom?" A.J. shouted back.

"It's someone else about the car," Mrs. Morgan replied. "He has a lot of questions and I'm in the middle of cooking dinner, so you'll have to answer them."

A.J. turned to Christopher with a shrug. "Can you hang out for a few minutes?" he asked. "This shouldn't take long."

Christopher glanced at his watch. "Actually I have to be somewhere and I'm late already. Maybe I can come back another time."

"Hey," said A.J., brightening. "Why don't you go with him, Jess?"

"Me?" The color drained from my face. "But I—"

A.J. was already trotting toward the house. "Go on out to the highway if you want," he yelled back to Christopher. "Just don't run off together, OK, you two?"

Christopher laughed at A.J.'s joke. To A.J., it probably sounded lighthearted, but to me the sound was menacing. Christopher opened the car door for me. "Come on," he said pleasantly.

I stood rooted to the spot like a statue. "Come on," he repeated, anger seeping into his voice.

I climbed into the passenger seat, my movements jerky and robotlike. As Christopher started the engine he tossed me an eerie smile. Reaching across my body, he pushed down the lock on my door. I was trapped.

As he gunned the engine, driving much too fast for local streets, my eyes stung with tears. "Why are you doing this?" I whispered, digging my fingernails into the vinyl armrest.

"I thought we needed a chance to talk in person," he said. He smiled again, and a shiver of fear ran up my spine. He looked and sounded perfectly normal—just as he had when I met him the past weekend. But I knew his mood could change in an instant. Christopher was unpredictable and unbalanced. Christopher was dangerous.

"We weren't communicating very well on the phone," he went on, his tone still reasonable. "You kept saying you didn't want to see me again, and I knew that just couldn't be true."

"I told you," I said through clenched teeth. "I already have a boyfriend. I made a mistake going out with you and—"

"A *mistake?*" Christopher slammed on the

brakes. My body was flung violently forward against the shoulder belt. "You're calling the most wonderful weekend of my life—of both our lives— a *mistake*?"

The most wonderful weekend—was he joking? For me it had been the beginning of a nightmare. "I'm sorry if I hurt your feelings," I said, trying to keep my voice steady. "I really didn't mean to. But I'm dating A.J., and I'm not going to cheat on him again, and that's all there is to it. Will you please take me back now?"

"Not until you promise to tell him about us," said Christopher. To my horror, he was pulling onto the coast highway. "You know you'd rather go out with me than with him, Jessica."

Christopher hit the gas. I watched the speedometer climb. Sixty miles an hour, seventy, eighty. *Where's the California Highway Patrol when you need them?* I wondered, praying we'd get pulled over. "I'm not telling him, and you'd better not either!" I shouted over the roar of the Toyota's engine.

Christopher slammed on the brakes. As the car spun around in a full 360-degree circle, I hid my face in my arms, screaming. We skidded to a stop on the sandy shoulder. The engine shuddered and died. My sobs sounded loud in the sudden silence.

"You shouldn't have made me do that," Christopher said, patting my shoulder gently. "We're lucky there's no one else on the road. Now what were you saying? You don't want to tell A.J.? That's fine. This can stay our little secret. As long as you go out with me again. How about this Saturday night?"

"Fine. Sure. Whatever you want," I cried, hunching my shoulders and leaning as far away from him as possible. "Just take me home. Please. Now!"

Christopher beamed. "We'll have fun, Jessica," he promised as he drove slowly and safely back to A.J.'s neighborhood. "We could go to a movie, or maybe hear some live music. There's a concert on the town common in Pacific Shores and . . ."

As Christopher babbled cheerfully about his expectations for our date, I wiped the tears from my face with a tissue and tried to compose my features. The way I was looking now, A.J. would know in an instant that something was terribly wrong.

Saturday night. The Citizens' Day Ball was Saturday night, and I planned to be there with A.J. On no account would I go out with Christopher, under any circumstances, ever again.

I glanced at Christopher out of the corner of my eye. He was humming along to the radio, a contented smile on his lips. He looked adorable—charming, sweet, handsome.

I shuddered. By giving in to Christopher's demand, I'd bought myself some time. But what was I going to do on Saturday? How could I get rid of Christopher before he did something *really* crazy?

I admit I've always liked male attention, but this is ridiculous. Christopher is totally over the edge. I really don't know what to do. Should I get Elizabeth's advice? Should I call the police and put a restraining order on Christopher? Then A.J. would find out. Maybe it would be just as well if he did. Our relationship is over—he just doesn't know it yet. Todd's coming next week, and I can't keep pretending I'm hot for A.J. when I'm really burning up for someone else. I wish Todd were here now. He'd straighten out Christopher! Oh, help. I'm in trouble. BIG trouble.

Saturday morning

I still don't know what to do about Christopher. I've been on the verge of a nervous breakdown all week, and yesterday I finally told Elizabeth the whole sordid story. I thought she'd be scandalized, but she took it in stride. . . . I have a feeling that says something not very flattering about me, that she's not surprised I'd get myself into such a mess!

Anyhow, predictably, she urged me to come clean with A.J. She says if I tell A.J. the truth, then Christopher won't have any power over me—he won't be able to black-mail me into dating him. But A.J. would never understand how I could have gone out with another guy behind his back, because he'd never in a million years two-time me. He'd be so hurt—he'd break up with me on the spot. So what's the problem, you say? I know, I know. I've been griping nonstop about how I'm ready to be single again. But I guess I don't want our relationship to end that way. I do care about A.J. It's not just because I want to be queen of the Citizens' Day Ball. At least, I don't think it is. I'm not that shallow . . . am I?

In the meantime Christopher's going to call any minute now to make plans for to-night. What am I going to say?

Sunday night

I'm still shaking, Diary. Last night was one of the strangest of my entire life. I keep dashing into Elizabeth's room to check on her and make sure she's all right. She could have been kidnapped or killed or some-thing, and it would have all been my fault!

Here's what happened. When Christopher called yesterday afternoon, I faked this really hoarse voice and told him I had strep throat so we'd have to put off our date, but of course I'd want to see him the minute I was feeling better. He was really understanding, so I thought I was off the hook. I even thought—stupidly—that maybe he'd decide he was tired of harassing me and he'd leave me alone from now on. I went to the dance with A.J., and we were having a pretty good time. But then, just as A.J. was about to read his prizewinning essay and receive the king's crown, Jeffrey came up to me. He was worried about Elizabeth, who'd gone off with some guy Jeffrey had never seen before. When Jeffrey described the guy to me, I almost fainted. It had to be Christopher!

At the exact same moment I had one of those twin things. It's like ESP—Elizabeth and I have this connection, and when one of us is in trouble or in pain, the other feels it. This time the intuition hit me like a tidal wave. I was suffocating—I couldn't breathe! I knew Elizabeth was in serious danger.

Jeffrey and I ran outside, and thank heavens we did. Christopher was about to drive off with Elizabeth locked in the trunk of his car! It turned out she'd been trying to do me a favor. When Christopher approached her, thinking she was me, she *guessed right away who he was. She thought if she talked to him for a while, he wouldn't interrupt the coronation. But Christopher had totally cracked—the minute they were out of sight, he pulled a knife. He said he wanted her—or rather me—to be with him forever, and there was only one way to make sure of that.*

I start shaking all over again when I think about what a close call Elizabeth had. Jeffrey and I got there just in time. Jeffrey tackled Christopher, and then a couple of security guards ran up, and after that Christopher sort of crumbled. One minute he was a brutal maniac and the next he was like a frightened little boy. It was very, very weird. He was really docile with the police and told them he wanted to talk to his psychiatrist—it turns out he's been getting some heavy-duty therapy. He has a lot of problems, and he'd latched on to me as a focus for his obsessions. Anyhow, they hauled him off, and I guess they'll keep him locked up until he stabilizes again.

When the whole drama with Christopher was over, I knew I was free to walk back inside and rejoin A.J. Elizabeth and Jeffrey agreed not to tell him what had happened—I could pretend everything was

fine. But it wasn't fine, even with
Christopher out of the way. If anything, it
was more clear to me than ever that I
wasn't cut out to be anyone's girlfriend. It
was going to hurt us both, but it was time
for me and A.J. to have a talk. . . .

When I walked back into the club, leaving
Jeffrey and Elizabeth sitting outside on the terrace,
A.J. had just finished reading his essay aloud.
Everyone was clapping. A.J. smiled shyly, looking a
little uncomfortable at all the attention. I could tell
he was glad to turn the microphone back over to
Mr. McKormick, the president of the Samaritans,
who launched into yet another speech.

When A.J. saw me, he hurried to my side.
"There you are!" he said. "We're on next. First
they'll crown me, and then I get to choose my
queen and—"

As he spoke, his voice full of love and enthusiasm, my eyes filled with tears. A.J. stopped,
frowning. "Jess, what's wrong?" he asked.

I didn't want to cry, but I couldn't help it. The
tears spilled down my cheeks. "I don't deserve to be
your queen," I sobbed, turning to run from the room.

A.J. dashed after me. We huddled behind some
potted palms, A.J. patting my shoulder as I continued to cry. The tension of the past week had finally
exploded inside me, and I wasn't sure I'd ever be
able to stop the flood of tears.

A.J. just stood quietly by my side, handing me tissues. At last I blew my nose and looked at him with relatively dry eyes. "A.J., I'm sorry," I said. "I don't want to ruin this evening for you. Go back in there and get your crown. You earned it."

"I'm not going anywhere until you tell me what's wrong," he insisted kindly. "I can't stand seeing you unhappy."

I felt more tears tickle my throat. I had to get this over with before I collapsed entirely. "A.J., it's . . . it's us," I said, my voice a ragged whisper. "I—I care about you so much. But . . ."

My last word seemed to hang in the air, dark and heavy and sad. A.J.'s jaw tightened. His own eyes grew damp. "But," he repeated.

"I'm sorry. We've had a lot of fun together. But I guess I've realized that I'm not cut out for a steady relationship."

A.J. mustered a smile. "I knew it was too good to last. I'm probably too boring and old-fashioned for you."

"It's not that at all. You're wonderful." I squeezed his hand, smiling through my tears. "My friends can tell you, I've never been as serious about a guy as I've been about you. For a while you had me convinced I was ready to settle down! But I'm not ready, and I guess it's better to deal with that now, instead of down the road when we're more involved."

A.J. nodded. "I won't pretend it doesn't hurt,

though," he said quietly. "Because it does. A lot."

"It hurts me too." My lips quivered. "Oh, A.J."

He wrapped his arms around me and we stood that way, embracing, for an endless moment. Neither of us wanted to let go, probably because we knew it was the last time we'd hold each other.

Finally we stepped apart. "You'd better go back in," I told him. "Mr. McKormick must be wondering what happened to you."

"You're coming with me," A.J. said.

"But A.J.—"

"Please, Jessica." He gazed into my eyes with a wistful smile. "You're the most special and beautiful girl here. No one else even comes close. Maybe we're breaking up, but tonight I still want you to be my queen. Can we have this one last dance?"

I nodded, my eyes brimming. A.J. took my hand. We walked back into the party together.

Breaking up is definitely a drag. By the end of the ball word had gotten around, and people kept coming up to me and asking really seriously, "Are you OK? Are you sure you're OK?" like maybe they thought I was about to throw myself off a balcony or something. I didn't mind pretending that it was as much A.J.'s decision as mine. Nobody was really surprised—I mean, we were kind of an odd couple. Me being part of a steady couple with any guy would seem odd! Of course, I'd never admit to ANYONE that my feelings for Todd had a teeny, weeny bit to do with me and A.J. calling it quits. Everyone—including A.J.!— bought my "no commitment" line, which is basically true anyway.

So I'm single again, Diary. It feels right, I've got to admit. A.J. and I had fun, but the fact that I had feelings for other guys when we were together obviously means I'm not cut out for fidelity. Although maybe I'd feel differently on that subject if Todd moved back to Sweet Valley . . . !

He'll be here in just three days, Diary. I can't wait. He's staying in a motel, can you believe it? It's so racy and forbidden. I really can't believe we're doing this! No one else knows he's coming, not even Ken or Winston or Aaron. He's coming to see ME. All the way from Vermont! Whenever I think about it, my heart starts pounding double time and I get out of breath like I've just finished a really vigorous cheerleading routine. Right now Elizabeth is sleeping peacefully in the next room, and she doesn't have a clue what I'm up to. She'd be really upset if she knew, though. Am I just a terrible, selfish person? I don't care! I want this more than I've ever wanted anything. I want Todd.

I'm so on edge about Todd's visit, I can't sit still. I need to study for my French test tomorrow, though. I thought if I scribbled in here for a few minutes, it might calm me down. I wish I knew yoga or meditation or self-hypnosis or something. I'm a wreck!

I'll tell you what's new in school, even though none of it interests me a whole heck of a lot. ALL I CAN THINK ABOUT IS SEEING TODD TOMORROW! It's good to have some distractions, like cheering at the girls' basketball play-offs. Our team is awesome this year, thanks to Shelley Novak, our star forward. She's a great athlete, but I'm telling you, I wouldn't want to be that tall. She's got to be at least six feet. She's cute, but who can notice when they have to crane their necks to see her face? That's really catty of me—I actually feel a little sorry for her. She'll probably get an award at the annual Varsity Club dinner dance that's coming up, but it'll be kind of a bummer to go by herself. She's never had a date, as far as I know.

Twenty-four hours, Diary. Next time I write in here, I'll be describing my reunion with Todd!

Wednesday night

*I saw Todd today!! We met at Secca
Lake at sunset. I think I'm in love, Diary—
for good this time. . . .*

I parked the Fiat at the far end of the Secca
Lake lot, half on the grass under the trees where it
would be hidden by shrubs and shadows. As I
crossed the lot, heading for a path through the
woods, I wondered which car was Todd's rental.
Was he here yet? Was he already waiting for me?

We'd decided to meet on the north side of the
lake, about a half-mile hike from the public beach
and recreation area. A lot of our friends come to
Secca Lake to windsurf and water ski, but the
nature paths are usually deserted.

I strode quickly along the dirt path. My cheeks
were already flushed, and my pulse raced in anticipation. After all these months of secret letters and
phone calls, of deepening long-distance friendship
and intimacy, the moment was finally here. We'd
be together in person. When we talked, I'd be able
to see the expression on Todd's face, to see his eyes
crinkle in a smile, to touch his hand.

A hundred yards from our meeting place I
stopped and took a compact mirror from my shoulder bag to check my hair and lip gloss. There was a
leaf in my hair, and I looked a little wild-eyed. As I

brushed the leaf away I smiled wryly at my reflection. *I shouldn't have bothered wearing makeup,* I thought. *Todd likes my looks—he dated my twin sister, after all!*

I dusted off my Bermuda shorts and straightened the shoulder straps of my turquoise blue tank top. I'd wanted to wear something sexy and romantic, like a dress, but had settled on a more practical outfit since hiking was involved. *I'm ready,* I decided, taking a deep breath. *Here goes!*

I covered the last stretch of path in record time, doing my own version of Olympic race walking. Ahead I saw the path open up into a sunny grove. A boy stood at the edge of the trees, looking out at the lake. For a moment I just drank in the grace of his tall, athletic body, his handsome profile, his curly hair glinting chestnut in the sun. Then I spoke.

"Todd," I said simply.

He turned to me eagerly, his face lighting up. "Jess!" he exclaimed.

For an awkward moment we stood smiling at each other, not sure what to do next. Then Todd strode toward me. I put out my hand, thinking maybe we'd shake, but he threw his arms around me in a hug.

I laughed, breathless from his embrace. "Sorry I kept you waiting, but you know I'm always at least half an hour late," I reminded him.

"That's right." He checked his watch. "Only

twenty minutes today, though. Does that mean something?"

"Yeah, probably." I blushed. "I guess I'm pretty psyched to see you."

"Same here," said Todd. He stepped back, but his warm, strong hands still cupped my shoulders. "It's good to see you," he said quietly. "No, better than good. Incredible."

"I don't look older?" I teased. "It's been a while. I was afraid you wouldn't recognize me."

"Naw. You'll always look the same, Wakefield," he responded. "Gorgeous. How about me? Have I changed?"

"Your hair's a little longer," I observed. "I like it. But I've got to tell you, Wilkins. You've lost your California tan."

"I'm turning into a Yankee," he admitted, chuckling. "Pale as a potato. We just don't get that much sun in northern Vermont—the days are about half as long as they are here."

We strolled over to a flat rock near the water's edge. I thought Todd might hold my hand, but when he didn't, I stuck my hands in my shorts pockets. I was probably sending incredibly mixed signals with my body language. Part of me wanted to tackle him onto the grass and plant a big, wet kiss on his lips, but the other part was shy and uncertain and basically panicked. Todd had come all this way. What did he expect from me? What did I expect from him?

We sat down on the rock. "How was your flight?" I asked.

"Pretty good," said Todd. "A little bumpy over the Rockies."

"Did you get lunch?"

"Yep."

"A movie?"

"Yep."

"That's good," I said. An awkward silence fell over us. Todd cleared his throat but didn't say anything. I fiddled with my gold lavaliere necklace. Then I thought of something he might be interested in. "Hey, the SVH varsity girls' basketball team made it to the play-offs—did I tell you that?"

"Really? That's great," Todd replied. His enthusiasm sounded a little forced. "Shelley Novak and Cathy Ulrich are an unbeatable combination. I bet they both get recruited by Division One college teams."

I couldn't have cared less about Shelley and Cathy's basketball careers. I wanted to talk about the here and now. I wanted to talk about *us*. "It must be weird being back here," I remarked, looking Todd straight in the eye.

He nodded. "I think the last time I was at Secca Lake was . . ."

"When?" I prompted.

He looked away from me, his gaze following a sailboat on the lake's breeze-ruffled surface. "The night before my family moved. With Elizabeth. Saying goodbye," he finished quietly.

I didn't respond—what could I say? My body tensed up, and I could sense Todd stiffening too. It was as if a third person had joined us, sitting right between us on the rock. Elizabeth.

I pushed her away, lecturing her silently. *He doesn't belong to you anymore. That was then. This is now, and he's here for me.*

"That was a long time ago," I said.

"Yes," Todd agreed. "For a while, after I moved and we broke up, I still thought about her a lot—I won't deny it. But lately . . ." He turned back to me, and his coffee brown eyes were glowing. "There's only been one girl on my mind."

He put his hand on mine where it was resting on the rock. Like a fresh wind after a thunderstorm, the air between us cleared—thoughts of Elizabeth were no longer holding us apart. I leaned closer to Todd. "A.J. and I broke up," I said.

I didn't need to tell him why. Our shoulders were touching now, and somehow Todd's arm had found its way around my waist. I looked up at him, and even though I knew his face incredibly well, it was like seeing it for the first time. His deep brown eyes, the strong jawline, the way the hair fell across his broad forehead, his full, firm lips . . .

Both Todd's arms were around me now, crushing me against his chest. For a moment I hesitated. The image of Elizabeth's sorrowful face flickered in front of my eyes. Kissing Todd was like plunging a knife in my sister's back.

But I couldn't resist the passionate warmth of Todd's embrace or the desire simmering in my own body. I lifted my mouth to his. We kissed hungrily, weeks of suppressed emotion bursting into wild flower the instant our lips touched. After the kiss Todd buried his face in my hair. "Oh, Jess," he murmured. "I've been dreaming about this."

"Me too," I whispered.

We kissed again, laughing at our own intensity, clinging to each other like drowning people. We were filled with joy, but at the same time there was something somber in both our hearts.

We'd embarked on an exhilarating, tempestuous, forbidden journey, not knowing—and at that moment not caring—where it would take us and how it would end.

Thursday a.m.

I'm just pausing in the middle of dressing for school . . . and for Todd! We'll meet right after cheerleading practice. Not that I want to wait that long. It kills me thinking that he's so near and I can't be with him every single minute of the day.

When I got home last night, I was sure Elizabeth would guess the truth the minute she laid eyes on me. I felt so incredibly guilty. But she didn't even ask me where I'd been. Obviously it would never occur to her in a million years that I spent the evening in her ex-boyfriend's arms!

My feelings for Todd make what I had with A.J. seem like child's play. This is TRUE LOVE. Jessica Wakefield Wilkins. Or should I hyphenate?

Thursday night

Dear Diary,

I've wished about a thousand times already that Todd had stayed in Burlington and left me in peace. But also about a thousand times I've daydreamed about his kisses, dying for more, counting the seconds until school gets out and I can be with him again. I came really close to playing hooky and cutting classes to be with him, but I exerted some self-control—I don't want to do anything to draw attention to myself. The last thing I need is Elizabeth wondering what I'm up to!

Maybe it was inevitable that at some point we'd get caught. Today was awful. After school I met Todd on a back street a few blocks from SVH, and we drove way up the coast so we wouldn't run into anyone we knew. But guess what? We did

*anyway! I reacted instinctively, doing the
only thing I could. I pretended to be
Elizabeth!*

Todd and I had found a deserted stretch of
beach an hour north of Sweet Valley. I knew we
were safe there—none of my friends would drive
that far on a weekday when we have nice beaches
right in town. So I was completely relaxed, and
having Todd massage suntan lotion on my back
and shoulders didn't hurt any!

Getting out of town had been another story,
however. I'd been shaking in my sneakers as I
walked a few blocks west of the school to the street
corner where Todd was going to pick me up—I
was wearing dark glasses and I had my hair tucked
up in a baseball cap.

When Todd pulled up, he was wearing a baseball cap and sunglasses, too. I'd started giggling,
and I was so nervous I couldn't stop. "I just hope
we don't see any cops," Todd had muttered. "We
look like a couple of crooks about to hold up a convenience store!"

Now I rolled over on the beach blanket to face
Todd, taking the bottle of lotion from him so his
hands were free for me. "This is worth all the
sneaking around, isn't it?" I purred, nuzzling his
neck.

"Yeah," he agreed, smiling. "And it's worth the
burn I'm going to get on my pale Vermont skin."

285

We made out blissfully for another half an hour. Then Todd sat up. "I'll tell you, though," he said, "all this activity's giving me an appetite. I wouldn't mind finding someplace to have dinner."

I sat up next to him, bringing up my knees and wrapping my arms around them. Ahead of us the big orange sun was poised to sink into the sea. "And one of these days we should be getting back home," I said with a sigh. "My parents think I'm at the library researching the extra-credit history report Mr. Fellows is making me do—they'll get suspicious if I stay *too* late!"

"Tell them you went to the mall afterward to give yourself a reward," suggested Todd.

I grinned. "They'll probably assume that anyway."

He hopped to his feet and extended a hand down to me. "Why don't we try out that little hole-in-the-wall café we passed about a mile back?"

"Sounds good," I said, letting him pull me to my feet. I kept my hand in his as we walked back to the rental car.

As Todd pulled the car onto the road I glanced over my shoulder. The sun was about to slip into the ocean. "Here comes the green flash," I told Todd.

There must have been a thin layer of fog at the horizon, though, because the sun disappeared without that last, magical bit of fireworks. "I thought it would put on a special show just for us," I said with a disappointed sigh.

Todd parked the car in front of the Hideaway, a rundown seafood shack perched on the edge of a bluff above the Pacific. Before opening his door, he turned to me. "I don't need any green flash," he said, "to make this day perfect."

I gave him a grateful smile, my eyes unaccountably misty. "Thanks," I whispered.

We walked inside, hand in hand. To my surprise, there were only a couple of empty tables. "It's probably the only place to eat for miles," Todd said by way of explanation.

The hostess seated us at a table by the window. Outside, the sky was fast fading from red and gold to a velvety purple. I opened my menu. "I'm really hungry all of a sudden too," I remarked.

Todd leaned over the table, grinning rakishly. "I'm telling you, it's all that fooling around," he hissed.

I clapped a hand over my mouth to keep from laughing. Just then I heard a piercing—and familiar—voice. "Todd Wilkins!" a girl called loudly. "I don't believe it!"

My blood turned to ice water in my veins. My fingers tightened spasmodically, crumpling the menu. The thing I'd dreaded most had happened: someone had spotted us. And not just anyone: Lila Fowler, the biggest gossip at Sweet Valley High. My best friend.

Todd had a blank look on his face—clearly he was as panicked as me. Neither of us knew what to do, and we didn't have time to strategize—Lila was marching up to our table with a boy I'd never seen before in tow.

"Todd!" she repeated. "And Elizabeth!" She looked right at me and I forced a smile, hoping my best friend wouldn't recognize me. Lila peered at me suspiciously, taking in my outfit: a formfitting, scoop-necked T-shirt and very short shorts. "Wait a minute," she said, arching surprised eyebrows. *"Jessica?"*

There was only one course of action to take. "You were right the first time," I told her, trying to inject a sweet, Elizabeth-like note into my voice. "It's Elizabeth."

"Well!" Lila folded her arms across her chest. "I knew I wasn't the only person who was aware of this place—it looks like a dump on the outside, but it has great food. But I never expected to run into you two. When did you get to town, Todd? How come I wasn't the first to know?" All of a sudden she remembered the guy standing next to her. "Oh, by the way, this is Jordan. He's at the university."

The hostess was tapping Lila impatiently on the shoulder. "Do you want the table or not?" she asked. "There are other people waiting to sit down."

"All right, all right," Lila said with a sniff. Before leaving, however, she jabbed a long red fingernail in my direction. "I want the whole scoop at school tomorrow, Elizabeth!"

Lila and her date were whisked off to the opposite side of the restaurant. "Thank goodness these tables are so small," said Todd with a shaky smile. "I had this nightmare vision of Lila turning this into a double date."

"Of all people." I shook my head. It was so horrible, it was almost funny. "The girl with the biggest mouth on the West Coast."

"What are we going to do?" Todd wondered. "If this gets back to Elizabeth . . ."

"It won't. I'll think of some way to shut Lila up," I promised him.

We sat for a minute in silence. Then Todd placed his menu facedown on the table. "All of a sudden I'm not that hungry," he confessed.

"Me either," I said. "Let's just go."

We scurried out of the restaurant. Lila waved to us, but we pretended not to see her. In the parking lot we leaned against the car to catch our breath. "So much for our perfect day," I grumbled.

Todd put an arm around my shoulders and said ruefully, "This just makes it even more unforgettable."

We headed back toward Sweet Valley, Todd driving well below the speed limit to drag out our time together. We didn't talk much, and I wondered if his thoughts were running along the same lines as mine. *Lila assumed Todd was with Elizabeth. Maybe he* should *have been with Elizabeth.*

When we reached the town line, Todd put a

hand on my knee. "I'd like to take you to Miller's Point," he said, "but I guess I should drop you off at the library. Will you be able to get a ride home?"

I sighed. Miller's Point would have been nice, but there were always SVH couples parked there. Knowing our luck, we'd run into Elizabeth and Jeffrey! "The library's fine. I'll call home and some-one'll come get me."

Todd parked at the curb half a block from the library. Unbuckling his seat belt, he wrapped his arms around me. "I'll see you tomorrow," he said. "Skip cheerleading practice, OK?"

"OK. And you lay low, all right? We don't want any more Todd Wilkins sightings." We kissed, and the passion that had been snuffed out by Lila's arrival came alive again. I decided I wasn't worried. So what if Lila told the whole state? If things got serious between me and Todd, Elizabeth would have to learn the truth sometime.

And things *were* getting serious. I'd taken off my seat belt too, but I was far from ready to get out of the car. Todd and I were locked in a heated embrace, our bodies melting together. I ran my hands up his back under his shirt; his fingers were tangled in my hair. The kiss deepened—if I'd had my way, it would never have ended.

Yes, things were getting serious. The feeling that our letters had given birth to was now intensely physical and real. Todd and I were playing for keeps.

I stayed up until midnight waiting for the phone to ring—I was so sure Lila would call, demanding details about Todd and Elizabeth. I'm nervous, Diary. I told Todd I'd have everything under control tomorrow at school, but I'm still not sure what to say to Lila. And what if I don't get hold of her before she starts yakking?

A couple of hours ago, when I was with Todd, I thought I didn't care if the whole world found out about us. But I do care. It still comes down to one thing: we don't want to hurt Elizabeth.

Friday afternoon

I'm supposed to meet Todd at Moon Beach, but I had to come home and lie down for half an hour. I still haven't recovered from this morning—my brain is absolutely fried. Lila almost blew my cover. Talk about close calls!

Driving to school on Friday morning, I still hadn't figured out what story I was going to give Lila, but I knew something would strike me. It's probably nothing to be proud of, but I'm a good liar when I need to be. Since Elizabeth and Lila don't have any morning classes together, I figured I just had to keep them apart until lunch and then make sure I got to Lila before Lila got to Elizabeth.

"You can have the car this afternoon," Elizabeth said as we walked across the student parking lot toward the school building. "Jeffrey and I are going to a workshop for high-school newspaper staffers at El Carro."

"Great," I responded, casually swinging my shoulder bag by the strap. "I might go to the beach, or maybe do some shopping. And, um, tonight I'm going out for pizza and a movie with . . ." I couldn't say Cara or Amy or Lila, because they might call while I was out with Todd. It had to be a friend, but not a superclose friend. "Uh, with Sandy and Jean."

"Sounds like fun," said Elizabeth.

I glanced at my sister out of the corner of my eye. She looked so cheerful and unsuspecting—a pang of guilt knifed through me. "Yeah," I said lamely.

The homeroom bell would ring in only five minutes, so I was pretty relaxed. Elizabeth intended to stop by the *Oracle* office, which was a safe place—Lila had never set foot in there. We pushed through the door into the lobby of the high school.

"See you later," I said to Elizabeth, heading for my locker.

"So long."

I watched her forge a path through the crowd

of students. Then I blinked in horror. Lila was bull-dozing her way across the lobby too . . . and aiming straight for Elizabeth!

I galloped after my sister, catching up just in time to hear Lila. "Elizabeth, wait up!" Lila shrieked. Elizabeth turned, puzzled. She looked even more surprised when Lila babbled on. "It was *so* wild bumping into you last night. I had *no* idea Todd was visiting. How long is he going to be around? I'd love to throw a big party in his honor. A live band, catering, banners, and balloons." Lila waved her hands dramatically, spelling the words in the air. "Welcome back, Todd!"

Elizabeth stared at Lila as though she had sud-denly started to undress in the middle of the school lobby. "What are you talking about?" she asked.

"Last night at the restaurant. I saw you and Todd!"

"I don't think so," said Elizabeth, her eyebrows furrowed.

Before Lila could say another word, I dove on her, grabbing her arm. "You've really lost it, Fowler," I chided. "She's insane," I informed Elizabeth. "We saw someone who *looked* like Todd, but it definitely wasn't."

"But I talked to—" Lila started to protest. I pinched her arm hard. "Ow!" she yelled.

"Insane," I repeated for Elizabeth's benefit, dragging Lila away from my sister as fast as I could.

I can't even stand to think about how close Todd and I came to exposure and total disaster, Diary. Luckily I can think on my feet, and think fast. I told Lila that Todd had flown all the way from Vermont to see Elizabeth, but Elizabeth didn't want anyone to know because Jeffrey didn't know. Lila loves intrigue, so she agreed to keep the secret. She thinks she has some major-league dirt on Elizabeth! I just hope she doesn't try any wink-wink, I-know-your-secret stuff around Elizabeth.

My life is such a soap opera these days—I forget I'm surrounded by other people living (relatively) normal lives. Believe it or not, the big talk at school these days is about Shelley Novak and Jim Roberts. I know, I know—they don't usually make the headlines in my diary! Jim is a geeky, photography club type—not exactly a stud, though he does have sort of sexy green eyes and this sandy hair that flops all over the place, practically demanding that you run your fingers through it to straighten it out. Not that I personally have ever had the urge!

Anyway, Jim took a bunch of pictures of Shelley at a basketball game recently and he submitted them to a Sweet Valley News photo contest. The pictures are

*really incredible—Shelley actually looks
graceful and beautiful when she's in motion on the court. But for some reason
she's mad at Jim, maybe because he didn't
ask her if it was OK to enter the pictures
in the contest. I understand she's really
shy, but in my opinion she should get over
it and just be flattered. She's the only one
in school who hasn't figured out that Jim
Roberts is nuts about her!*

*Another late-breaking story: Patrick
McLean, the head of a new dance studio in
town, is offering free ballroom dancing lessons as a promotion. Lila thinks we should
sign up so we can polish our social graces.
I know she's trying to distract me from
what she assumes is my post-A.J. depres-
sion. (Meanwhile this is practically the first
time I've thought about him since we broke
up!) I can't think about ballroom dancing
lessons, though, when Todd is flying back
to Vermont in just two days. How will I
live without him?*

Saturday evening

*I'm getting ready for my last night
with Todd. I really don't know what to expect. Last night was a little strange. We
went to the beach for a picnic—gourmet*

food, romantic music on the portable tape player, a skyful of stars twinkling overhead, the whole works. But you know what? The only sparks were in the campfire. In the middle of dinner I remembered how boring Todd can be sometimes. Plus he started asking these roundabout questions about Elizabeth. What's wrong, Diary? I'm not falling out of love with him already . . . am I?

"Do you like the salad?" I asked Todd. "I made it myself."

"It's fantastic," said Todd, taking another bite. "Really delicious."

"I'm glad you like it," I said, pushing my own food around on the paper plate. For some reason I didn't have much of an appetite. "There's lots more."

"I'll just work on this," said Todd. "Thanks."

I put down my plate and reached for the bottle of sparkling cider. As I poured myself another glass I studied Todd surreptitiously. He *looked* the same—gorgeous as always. I couldn't find fault with his hair or his eyes or his smile or his body, or even his clothes, and I'm picky that way. Todd was perfect. So why was I feeling sort of detached and neutral toward him? I wasn't feeling swept away every thirty seconds by the desire to throw myself at him. What was the problem? *It must be me*, I thought, sipping my cider. *What's* my *problem?*

"We've been so carried away the past couple of days," Todd said, reaching across the picnic basket to touch my arm, "I keep forgetting to ask you how school's going these days."

"School?" I looked blank. Not exactly my idea of a romantic topic of conversation! "School's OK. I mean, the building's still standing, as you've probably noticed, although with any luck it'll get knocked down by an earthquake one of these days."

Todd laughed. "So what you're saying is you've become president of the honor society since I moved away."

"I get my body to class more often than not," I told him. "I figure I'm fulfilling my end of the contract."

Todd pointed his fork at me. "But there must be at least one course, one teacher, that gets you fired up. One subject you're passionate about. I mean, what will you major in in college?"

I've always planned to double major in shopping and suntanning—those are subjects I'm passionate about. Basically I can't see worrying about college when I'm only a junior in high school. What's the point? But Todd seemed serious. "Oh, I'll think of something," I replied, stifling a yawn. I lifted the lid on a bakery box. "Cookie?"

Todd shook his head. He gazed at me intently, leaning closer, his eyes glowing in the light of the campfire. *Good,* I thought. *He's going to shut up about school and kiss me already!*

"Things are actually going really well for me academically at my school in Burlington," Todd said. "My grades are even better than they were at SVH. So I got invited to participate in this special program for extra-motivated, fast-track students. Everyone in the program picks a topic that he or she wants to investigate—it can be anything. You work with a faculty adviser at school and do a lot of independent study and research. There's no grade or anything—it's just for fun, for the experience."

For fun? I blinked at him, confused. Was I supposed to say something now? It didn't sound like fun to me. It sounded like a lot of work, and he didn't even get extra credit!

I was about to kid around with him, say something like, "Did you forget who you're talking to? I'm not Elizabeth." But I didn't want to put a damper on our togetherness by saying her name. *Is he starting to wish he were with her instead of me?* I wondered, gnawing my lip. *They have so much more in common. They care about the same things.*

"That's really great," I said with false enthusiasm. "I admire your energy. I hardly ever get around to doing the homework I have to do, much less stuff I don't have to do!"

Todd smiled indulgently. "You have other priorities. That's cool."

Other priorities, I thought. *Right. Like terminating this deadly conversation, pronto!*

I scooted closer to him on the beach blanket. I

knew I looked inviting in my short black skirt and tank top, with the firelight warming my bare arms and legs. "I've always been more into extracurricular activities," I agreed, walking my fingers up his bicep. "Like boys."

Todd wasn't listening, though—he wasn't even looking. His eyes had fixed on some invisible point in the darkness, beyond the fire, beyond the dunes . . . beyond me. "Sweet Valley High should do something like the Burlington program," he remarked casually. "I can think of a lot of people who'd really go for it. Tom McKay, Winston, Robin, Suzanne Hanlon, Penny, Roger . . . Elizabeth."

I sat very still. We'd been carefully avoiding mentioning Elizabeth by name, even though I knew we'd both been thinking about her. What did this mean?

If Todd could talk about Elizabeth, then so could I. "Yeah, Elizabeth would really get into something like that," I agreed. "She'd probably pick some kind of literary project, like re-creating the home life of Emily Dickinson or something. She'd work with Mr. Collins and write hundreds of incredibly boring pages that even he'd have a hard time slogging through."

I couldn't prevent the bite of sarcasm that unexpectedly entered my voice. Todd didn't even seem to notice. "Or maybe she'd do something relating to journalism," he speculated. "Has she written any interesting feature stories for the *Oracle* lately?"

He really sounded like he wanted to know. I stared at him. "Probably," I said with intentional curtness.

He didn't pick up on my tone. Looking away from me, he intently traced a pattern in the sand with a plastic knife. "I guess she's pretty serious about that Jeffrey guy," he mumbled after a while. "I was driving through town yesterday and I saw them together."

Todd hadn't phrased his observation as a question, but there was a questioning note in his voice. *What does he want me to say?* I wondered. *Am I supposed to reassure him that Elizabeth is serious about Jeffrey so he can feel less guilty about seeing me? Or does he want to hear that she's not serious about Jeffrey . . . that she still secretly loves Todd?*

The truth was a little of both, but I decided to keep that to myself. Time to change the subject. "Todd," I said softly, cupping his face in my hands. "We only have two more nights together. Do we really want to waste time talking?"

He looked into my eyes, and I could see what he was thinking. Wasn't that why he'd flown all the way to California, so we could talk? But he didn't speak. Wrapping his strong arms around me, he pulled me onto his lap.

We kissed. As usual, it was great. If the slam books had still been circulating around Sweet Valley High, I'd have had to cross out A.J.'s name under "Best Kisser" and write in Todd's.

Yes, it was a very, very good kiss. But something

was missing that would have made it a fantastic kiss. Were we just going through the motions? Was Todd as distracted as I was?

For a few magical days we'd managed to keep Elizabeth's presence at bay. But now her voice seemed to echo in the sound of the night wind in the dune grass, the ocean waves beating on the sand, the bluesy music drifting from the radio. In my mind I could hear Elizabeth. She'd found out about me and Todd, and she was crying.

I kissed Todd with more passion, trying to focus on him and only him. I could feel the tension in his muscles—he was doing the same thing. But I knew deep down in my heart, it wasn't working for either of us.

Todd leaves tomorrow. We have one more night. What will happen? How is this going to end?

Sunday, noon

What a day! First, at breakfast Elizabeth confided to me that she had a dream about Todd last night. I swear, there really and truly is some kind of freaky psychic link between us, like Elizabeth was right there on the beach blanket last night with me and Todd!

I shuffled down to breakfast at about eleven, a robe loosely belted over my sleep T-shirt. Elizabeth was the only person in the kitchen, sitting at the butcher-block table, flipping through the newspaper.

I slopped some lukewarm coffee into a mug and collapsed into a chair next to her. "Morning," I said, rubbing my bleary eyes.

Elizabeth didn't comment on my bedraggled state because I always look like that first thing in the morning. She sipped her orange juice, skimming an article in the book and movie review section. "Hey," she replied.

There was a plate of blueberry muffins in the middle of the table. I reached for one. It occurred to me that maybe I should just stick the muffin in the pocket of my robe and head out to the patio or back upstairs—I didn't want Elizabeth to ask me about my Saturday night because I'd have to lie and say I went bowling with Amy and Cara, but I'd probably turn red as a lobster because in reality, of course, I spent the whole night in a torrid lip-lock with Todd. Before I could push back my chair, though, Elizabeth looked at me and I saw that *she* was the one blushing.

"I have to tell you something, Jess," she said, talking fast as if she were a little embarrassed. She giggled. "You won't believe the dream I had last night!"

I settled back in my chair, biting into the muffin.

302

"What was it about?" I said, my mouth full.

She giggled again. "You're going to be really shocked. It was *very* racy. Scandalous, in fact!"

I smiled. "Oh, good. May I presume Jeffrey was involved?"

"Actually, no." Her blush deepened. "It was about Todd."

I dropped the rest of the blueberry muffin and it bounced onto the floor, scattering crumbs. I bent over to sweep up the mess with a paper napkin. "Todd?" I squeaked.

"Uh-huh." I heard Elizabeth sigh, and now she sounded almost sad. "It was so real, Jess. I woke up in the middle of the night and I almost started to cry. I thought for sure he was with me, and if I just reached out, he'd be there. But I was alone."

I sat back up and forced myself to meet her eyes, hoping I looked sympathetic and not wildly uncomfortable and guilt-wracked. "Wow, that *is* wild. Todd, huh? Was he here in California or were you in Vermont?"

"He came here to see me. Actually I think he was moving back to Sweet Valley for good. I must secretly hope for that," she said with a wistful smile. "Anyhow, I'll leave out the intimate details. Let's just say we picked up right where we left off and it was . . . wonderful. Fantastic. It felt so right, you know? Like we were meant to be to-gether. I can say this to you because I know you'll keep quiet, but no one's ever kissed me like Todd, and in my dream it was better than ever."

I squirmed uncomfortably in my seat. "What about Jeffrey?" I wondered, hoping to bring my twin back to reality.

"I don't know." Elizabeth wrinkled her forehead. "He just wasn't around. It was like before Jeffrey. And Jess . . ." Tears sparkled in her eyes. "It was better," she whispered. "It's the way I want it to be again. Do you think there's any chance of it ever happening?"

I patted her arm, feeling completely helpless and completely evil. "I suppose so," I mumbled.

"Promise you won't tell anyone." She gripped my fingers tightly, staring me straight in the eye. "I'd hate to hurt Jeffrey's feelings. I really do care about him. We're happy—I'm happy. It's just that . . ." Her shoulders heaved in a shaky sigh. "I guess nobody can ever take the place of your first love."

She rose, heading to the sink with her dirty glass. I slumped in my chair, wishing I could just disappear. As she left the room I thought I heard her murmur something to herself, her voice soft, wistful, resigned. "It was just a dream. It was just a dream."

I felt pretty darned rotten. A cruel traitor to my own flesh and blood. Elizabeth would never look through my diary—she's not a snoop like me! But I'll have to hide it extra carefully for the rest of my life so she doesn't stumble upon it accidentally and succumb to the temptation to read it. Her heart would break in a thousand pieces.

So that was how my day started, and it's not over yet! I'm about to drive to the airport with Todd, then take the bus back. Elizabeth thinks I'm crazy because I said I was going to the library, and I never go to the library on weekends. Plus I've used that lie about ten times this week. Oops!

I don't know how I feel at the moment, Diary. My emotions are all mixed up. I don't want Todd to leave because I don't know what's going to happen next for us, once we're apart again. I don't know what I want to happen. But at the same time the past few days have definitely had their ups and downs, so I'm also a little relieved. No more sneaking around. No more lying to everybody, including—especially—Elizabeth.

Sunday, midnight

He's gone, Diary. Can you feel the emptiness? I've been sitting on my bed for hours, flipping through magazines without really seeing the pages, listening to CDs without really hearing the music or the words. I feel numb, inside and out. I wish I could sleep, but I know if I turn off the *light, I'll just lie there with my eyes wide open in the dark.*

He's gone. And I'm not a hundred percent sure, but I think . . . I think it's over.

We barely spoke on the way to the airport. I have a hunch we were both thinking about Elizabeth, and about how much we love her—I know I was. We returned the rental car and then sat together at the gate until the last possible minute. Our kiss goodbye was bittersweet. After he boarded, I stood at the big plate-glass window and watched the plane taxi to the runway, tears pouring down my face. Right before he got on the plane, we'd talked about when we might see each other again. Todd pretended he really wanted me to come to Vermont, but I knew we were both just going through the motions, saying the kinds of things people are supposed to say at moments like those. It would have been too hard and scary and painful to ask ourselves the real questions, like how much do we really care for each other, and is it worth it to pursue a relationship if it's going to hurt other people?

I do love Todd. But could I ever be with him, openly or in secret, and not think about the pain I was causing Elizabeth? Would my twin's heartbroken sobs always echo in my head?

"This is the final call for flight forty-two to Boston's Logan International Airport," a crisp voice announced over the loudspeaker. "All passengers please board through gate ten."

Todd and I were sitting across the aisle from gate ten, his duffel bag at our feet. We'd been holding hands and talking fast, as if trying to squeeze in a lifetime's conversation in these last few minutes.

"Have fun cheering at the girls' basketball play-offs," Todd said. "And you should sign up for the ballroom dancing lessons—it'll be a riot."

"Say hi to the ski slopes," I told him. "But don't spend all your cash on lift tickets—put some in your piggy bank every now and then." My throat tightened with unshed tears and my voice cracked a little. "Time to start saving for another plane ticket."

Todd looked searchingly into my eyes. "I'd come back to Sweet Valley in a minute, but I don't know if it would be the right thing to do. Maybe *you* should start saving *your* money."

I smiled. "I can't. The mall has a conspiracy against me. As soon as I've saved a few dollars, Lisette's or Bibi's has a sale and I end up spending it all."

Todd stood up, hoisting his duffel. "I guess I should go."

I got to my feet too. "I'll walk you to the gate."

"No." He put his free hand to my face, touching my cheek. "Let's say goodbye here. It's more private."

"Well . . . goodbye, then," I said lamely. I stood on tiptoe and brushed his lips with a quick kiss. I turned away, hiding my tears behind a curtain of hair.

I heard a thud—Todd dropping the duffel to the floor. Then a pair of strong arms wrapped around me. "I'll miss you, Jess," Todd said, his voice hoarse. "Thanks for the last few days. I'll never forget our time together."

I sniffled. "Me either."

We kissed for a long time, our lips salty with tears. Then Todd released me gently. Without speaking again, he picked up his bag and strode across the hall to the gate. He glanced back over his shoulder one last time, and I lifted my hand in a wave. Then he disappeared down the ramp.

Todd was the last passenger to board, and the flight attendant closed the door behind him. Something about that gesture pierced my aching heart like a knife. *I'll never see him again,* I realized, the intuition coming clear and strong. *If I do see him, it won't be the same. We won't be in love—we'll just be friends like in the old days. Friends because of Elizabeth. Always Elizabeth.*

I put my face close to the glass, watching Todd's plane push back from the gate. I wondered if he had a window seat. Was he looking back at the airline terminal, hoping for one last glimpse of me? Or was he already looking ahead to New England, the connecting flight from Boston to Burlington, home?

I'm not the literary type like my sister—I only read when I have to. But at that moment I knew that what I was feeling was exactly like the end of a chapter in a book. Not the last chapter. There was more to come—the story of my life would go on for hundreds of pages, getting more exciting all the time! But I'd reached the end of part of the story. Soon I'd have to turn the page and move on. In the meantime, though, I was locked in the moment. I touched the window with my fingertips, my vision blurring with tears. "Goodbye, Todd," I whispered.

Saturday night

Dear Diary,

We cheered at the finals of the girls' basketball tournament today and SVH won! It was pretty thrilling. Shelley was named Athlete of the Year, so she'll get a big silver cup at the Varsity Club dinner dance. She's pretty cozy with Jim Roberts these days, so I guess they straightened things out, and he'll be her date on awards night.

After the game Elizabeth went with the rest of the gang to the Dairi Burger, but I came home and called Todd. We had a long talk. It's been a week since he flew back to Vermont, so we've both had time to think stuff over. Luckily we came to the same conclusions. We decided we shouldn't talk on the phone anymore or even write letters. I've cherished his letters, and it makes me really sad to think I'll never get another one signed "Love, Todd"—it's like losing my best friend. But we had to face facts. We couldn't enjoy our romance when Elizabeth was always on our minds. When we got right down to it and were absolutely honest with each other, we had to admit that she comes first for both of us. Todd might be crazy about me—naturally!—but he and Elizabeth were soul mates. Maybe someday, if they're not separated by an entire continent, they'll have a second chance at love.

In the meantime, now that both A.J. and Todd are, as they say, history, I've set my sights on Patrick McLean, the dance instructor. Have I told you about him? He's a total heartthrob. Tall, wavy chestnut hair, dark eyes, chiseled features, and the most gorgeous, graceful body. Elegant double-breasted European suits that hang on him perfectly, and he has one pierced ear, which usually doesn't turn me on, but on him it's sexy. He could be a model, and this

310

guy can MOVE. Every day in ballroom dance class there's a huge catfight—all the girls want to be his partner. Amy's managed to elbow her way to the front of the crowd a bunch of times, but I can tell Patrick's singled me out. He demonstrated the tango with me yesterday! I was in a swoon the whole time.

It's kind of fun just having a silly, pointless crush again. I feel like I've been through an emotional blender these last few months. Flirting with Patrick is just a game, and that's the way I want it. It'll be a long, long, LONG time before I fall in love again for real. If ever!

Part 7

Monday night, really late

Dear Diary,

    It's a miracle I'm even writing this. I should be dead—drowned in the Pacific Ocean! Who'd have thought Mr. Russo's extra-credit science trip would end up being so dangerous?

    Needless to say, I didn't want to go in the first place. My whole Sunday was going to be wasted, looking at tidal pools on Anacapa Island and other incredibly boring biology stuff. But I'm really bombing Mr. Russo's course, so he didn't give me much of an alternative. The unbelievable thing is that some people who didn't need the extra credit went on the trip anyway.

Like Elizabeth! Is she a nerd or what?

It was pretty much a nightmare from start to finish. On the boat Mr. Russo paired us up in this stupid buddy system and I got stuck with Winston Egbert, the biggest klutz on the planet. He managed to stomp in our tidal pool, step on all the plants we were supposed to catalog, chase away the wildlife, and basically make everything take about three times as long as it should have. I'd even bet he was responsible for the sudden storm that came up in the afternoon! We packed up early because Captain Marsden heard lousy weather reports on the boat's radio. But I guess we didn't head home early enough. About fifteen minutes into the return trip, the Maverick got swamped by this huge wave and actually started sinking!

Captain Marsden started yelling at us to get on life preservers and climb into lifeboats. It was like a movie or something, except it was real life and terrifying. I probably would have been fine if it weren't for Winston. The minute our lifeboat hit the water, he managed to lose one of the plastic oars. He stood up to try to grab it just as a gigantic wave swelled up under us. I knew we were goners. . . .

313

"Winston, no!" I screeched over the roar of wind and rain. "Stay low or we'll capsize!"

It was too late. Winston lost his balance and toppled into the surging gray surf. I braced myself, but the wave hit the boat broadside and flipped it over, flinging me into the rough, ice-cold sea.

Thanks to my life jacket, I bobbed to the surface immediately. "Winston, where are you?" I hollered. "Elizabeth! Mr. Russo! Captain Marsden! Help!" Had anyone seen us capsize? The captain had told us to stay close to the foundering boat. He'd alerted the Coast Guard and promised we'd be picked up shortly. But now I couldn't see or hear anyone. Elizabeth and Aaron had been in a boat right near Winston's and mine, but they'd disappeared in the fog and driving rain. I'd even have been happy to spot Winston, bobbing in his bright orange life jacket, but he was gone along with our lifeboat. I was alone in the storm-tossed sea. "Help," I cried out again, my voice shrill with fear. A wave doused me, and I felt my life preserver, which I'd foolishly forgotten to buckle, rip from my body. I came up spluttering. "Help!"

I'd been treading water, trying to keep the blood flowing to my chilled limbs. Without the life preserver it was going to get harder and harder to stay afloat. *I've got to swim,* I thought, taking a deep breath and stroking through an oncoming wave. The storm had blotted out the sun, and I couldn't see more than a few yards because of the surf and rain—I didn't know where Anacapa and the other Channel Islands were, or which direction would take me toward the mainland. For all I knew, I was swimming straight out to sea, next stop Hawaii. But I didn't have a choice.

I'm in good shape from cheerleading, tennis, and beach volleyball and I've been comfortable in the water since I was a toddler—that's important when you grow up near the ocean. But I've never been much into swimming laps, and within a few minutes my lungs were burning while the rest of me felt numb and floppy. I switched from crawl to breaststroke and that helped, but not much. For the first time since Winston tipped the lifeboat, it occurred to me that I might actually die. Tears mingled with the rain and salt water on my face. *I'm too young,* I thought, kicking my legs feebly. *I haven't even graduated from high school! I want to have a career. I want to get married, maybe a couple of times. I want to be a movie star and win an Academy Award!*

A sob broke from me, and my mouth filled with water. I coughed, swallowing more water. I could feel myself on the verge of all-out panic, which I knew would be fatal. So for a few seconds I let myself float on the surface as I tried to calm down and catch my breath. That's when I noticed the current.

Even though I wasn't swimming, I was moving through the water at a swift pace. *Of course,* I thought, comprehension penetrating my scared and weary brain. *I'd have gotten tired a lot sooner—I've been swimming with the current!*

Hope flooded my heart, lending new strength to my arms and legs. Maybe the current was pulling me back to Anacapa Island or to the California coast. Or maybe it was pulling me to Japan . . . I refused to consider that possibility. *I bet I'm almost to dry land,* I thought, the wonderful words repeating in my brain like an incantation. *Dry land, dry land, dry land . . .*

I began swimming with renewed vigor. But within minutes my strength was failing again. The cold temperature of the water was taking its toll—I knew I was probably close to succumbing to hypothermia. My wet clothing weighed on me like iron chains. *I'm not going to make it,* I realized.

I was so far gone, I wasn't even scared anymore. As I continued to swim, my arms and legs moving mechanically, pictures flickered across my fuzzy field of vision like scenes from an old silent movie. Elizabeth, my parents, Steven, my cousin Kelly. Our dog, Prince Albert. The cheerleading squad, a big party at Lila's, a bonfire on the beach. The fashion show at Lisette's. Parking at Miller's Point with A.J. Cramming for a test, hanging out at the Dairi Burger, shopping at the mall. Letters from Todd, our first kiss at Secca Lake. My life. My short, wonderful life.

"I'll miss you all," I whispered, my eyes closing.

Suddenly the water felt as warm as a bathtub. I stopped swimming and let myself sink beneath the waves.

I'm definitely the luckiest person ever born, Diary. Just when I was sure I was drowning, and I didn't even care anymore because I was so tired I just wanted to sleep, I felt something solid under my feet. I thought I must be hallucinating, but it was real. I waded up onto the shore of a little deserted island and collapsed.

Here's the incredible part. I was so wiped out, I actually slept for a while, right there on the wet sand. But when I awoke, guess who else washed up? Winston! I've never been so happy to see anybody in my whole life. I know I always say Win is the equivalent of pond scum on the chain of human evolution, but he really came through for me. I would've just sat there feeling sorry for myself, but he got us both busy gathering food and catching fish, building a shelter, sending out SOS signals, and all that jazz. Predictably he got on my nerves, but that was kind of reassuring. It kept me from thinking about how scared I was.

And I was scared, though I'll never admit that to anyone, now that I'm safe at home again. Being a quivering lump of

317

human Jell-O just doesn't fit the Jessica Wakefield image, you know? It's tough sometimes to be me, Diary, I'll tell you. My friends expect me to be full of energy and ideas, to take the lead all the time. I'm always supposed to be bubbly, cheerful, the life of the party. I'm never allowed to get down or depressed, to sit on the sidelines. I wouldn't mind that now and then—a chance to mellow out, have some time to myself, think about the meaning of life and all that. You know, be like Elizabeth. But I have a reputation to uphold. There's only one Jessica Wakefield. What would SVH do without me?

True confessions time. I can't tell this to anyone, even Elizabeth. But on Outermost Island, while we were waiting to be rescued, I found myself seeing Winston in a whole new light. He's really kind of attractive in a skinny, rumpled, goofy kind of way. . . .

We'd been on the island for almost twenty-four hours. It looked like we might be spending another night in our makeshift driftwood shack. A sudden rain shower had sent us scurrying for shelter, but now the late afternoon sun was piercing the clouds with rays of gold. It would set soon, and it would be dark, making it impossible for any kind of rescue boat or plane to see us.

Winston and I sat on a fallen log, idly tracing letters in the rain-pocked sand with a palm frond. "Jessica Wakefield is . . ." Winston scrawled.

"Is what?" I asked.

"A lot of things I never realized before," Winston replied, a smile curving his lips. He wrote "pretty."

I laughed. "Yeah, I look my best with seaweed in my hair and raggy clothes."

He scratched out "pretty" and wrote "brave." I wrinkled my forehead. "You're kidding, Win," I said. "I'm the biggest wimp there is. I'd have bawled my eyes out all last night if I'd been here alone without you to start a fire and feed me and stuff."

Winston shook his head. "You *are* brave," he insisted. "Like this afternoon, when we were picking berries and ran into that bear."

It was true, Winston had been the one to turn tail and run like a deer when we saw the little black bear. I'd thought to throw my berries at the animal, and that seemed to make it happy. "Still," I said.

"OK, if you don't like that . . ." Winston dusted sand over the letters. With the palm frond he wrote "kind."

I looked at the word in surprised silence. I wouldn't describe myself as kind. More often than not I'm the opposite: mean and petty and selfish. Elizabeth is kind, not me.

"Maybe that fruit we ate was poisonous," I suggested. "Something messed up your brain."

"I've never been more lucid," Winston said, looking me straight in the eye.

For some reason I felt myself blushing. To hide my embarrassment, I grabbed the palm frond from Winston. "OK, my turn," I announced, sweeping out Winston's words and writing "Winston Egbert is funny."

He guffawed. "Now, there's an original observation."

I grinned, writing some more. "And sweet."

It was Winston's turn to redden. "Aw, shucks," he mumbled.

I was on a roll. "And generous," I continued.

A shy, pleased smile crossed his face. "You think so?" he said.

"Definitely. I was being a total pill yesterday when we first washed up here, blaming you for everything. I would've told me to take a hike, but you shared your food with me anyway."

"I wanted to stay on your good side in case we ran out of food and you started to entertain cannibalistic thoughts," Winston joked.

I laughed. "Thanks anyway, but I'll stick to kelp sandwiches." I was about to toss the palm frond aside—it was time to start jumping up and down and waving our arms in case any planes passed overhead. First I wrote one last word in the sand. "Cute."

Winston cleared his throat. He was redder than a tomato now. "Ahem," he choked out. "I think you're the one losing your marbles, Wakefield."

"No way, Egbert," I countered. "If we had a mirror, I'd show you. You look kind of sexy and disheveled. Being shipwrecked really becomes you!"

I smiled at Winston and he smiled back. For the first time I noticed that he had really beautiful eyes, with long curly lashes. He had a nice straight nose and a strong chin. His lips weren't bad either. I found myself wondering. What would it be like to kiss him? Would I burst out laughing right in the middle of a smooch, remembering all the stupid tricks Winston had played on me in the past? Knowing Winston, even at a moment like this he'd have some kind of gag ready. A whoopee cushion or a palm buzzer or a squirting lapel pin. Then again . . .

I leaned my shoulder against his. Winston slipped an arm around me. When he spoke, his voice was husky. "Jessica," he began.

"Umm?" I looked up at him, batting my eyelashes invitingly. My hair was snarled and my lips were a little on the dry side, but I was still the best-looking girl Winston was going to bump into on Outermost Island.

He brought his face down to mine. He's tall, so it took a few seconds. We were just about to kiss when a buzzing sound filled the air. Winston shoved me aside and leapt to his feet. I almost toppled from the log. "A helicopter!" Winston shouted, dashing out to the shore.

I galloped after him, jumping up and down and screaming at the top of my lungs. "Here we are! Here we are!"

The helicopter looped around. This time it came

even closer to our little beach—we could feel the wind. And see the pilot—he saluted. He'd seen us!

Winston threw his arms around me and we danced in a dizzy circle. "We're saved!" we shouted.

There was no room to land on the beach, so the helicopter buzzed back over the water, probably to notify a rescue boat. My heart was as light as a feather. Our ordeal was over—we were going home.

Winston and I stood side by side, gazing eagerly out to the sea. Soon a boat appeared on the horizon, growing bigger as it raced toward us, a wide white wake spreading out behind it. Winston took my hand, giving it a squeeze. I knew that already both our thoughts were leaping ahead, to tonight, to tomorrow. Away from our experience on the island and back to our families, our houses, our friends, school.

Our almost-kiss was already forgotten.

Maybe I will kiss Winston someday. I wonder how serious he and Maria really are?

Tuesday morning

I just woke up and read what I wrote in here last night. I must have had salt water clogging my brain. Winston Egghead Egbert? Right, I might get together with him in some reverse parallel universe where geeks turn into studs! If anyone finds out I

322

even thought for five seconds about kissing him, I'll never be able to hold my head up in this town again! Maybe I should rip that page out of my diary!

Tuesday afternoon

Dear Diary,

   My first day back at school since being stranded. I'm the absolute center of attention, which is driving Lila nuts. I LOVE IT! But I wouldn't go through that experience again for all the fame in the world. Sure, it was great being interviewed by dozens of newspaper and TV reporters when we got back to the mainland. I'll never complain about having my face on the front page of the Sweet Valley News. *And everyone's treating me like a queen. My family's falling all over themselves trying to do nice things for me, especially Elizabeth. They were pretty traumatized by how close they came to losing me, and it made them realize how much they love me.*

   But that's just it. Almost dying made ME realize how much I love them too. How much I love my crazy, unpredictable, sometimes boring, sometimes fabulous life. My family means the world to me—I am just so incredibly lucky to be a Wakefield.

Especially to be a Wakefield twin! I missed Elizabeth the most when I was stranded on Outermost Island. I kept thinking about how worried she must be, but I also knew that her twin intuition had to be telling her that I was OK. I never really doubted I'd get rescued because I knew Elizabeth and Mom and Dad and Steven would do everything humanly possible to find me. All I had to do was wait.

Elizabeth really is the best sister in the world, Diary. More precious to me than anything (even my custom-designed Nadine wardrobe!). I can't believe I ever seriously considered getting involved with Todd. It must have been temporary insanity. I'd never do anything to hurt Elizabeth, not for a million bucks and not in a million years. When Winston was scribbling in the sand on the island, he should have written JESSICA WAKEFIELD IS LOYAL. And also, THANKFUL.

It's good to be back where I belong, Diary.

Epilogue

I closed the spiral notebook and lowered it to my lap, looking with tear-filled eyes toward my bedroom window. The sun was just coming up—rays of soft pink light filtered through the curtains. Unbelievably, I'd stayed up all night reading my diary.

Sniffling, I wiped my damp cheek on the sleeve of my robe. I felt exhausted and drained from reliving the emotions I'd recorded in my journal: love, jealousy, insecurity, doubt, guilt, fear, compassion, sorrow, joy.

When I started reading my diary, I didn't know what to expect from it. What would it teach me? Now, in the morning light, the lesson seemed crystal clear. As I'd read the passages about Todd, my memories of that time had confirmed what I already knew deep in my heart. *I have a special feeling for Todd,* I thought, fingering the tattered cardboard cover of the notebook, *and I always will. But it's nothing like the feeling he shares with Elizabeth.*

There was a very good reason he and I had ended our secret relationship before, and it was the same reason that would prevent us from resuming that relationship now or ever. I could never betray Elizabeth. And I had a hunch that with a night to think things over, Todd would wake up missing Elizabeth. He had turned to me in the heat of the moment, but now that the moment had passed, he'd realize that he owed it to himself to straighten things out with her. She's the one he really loves. Their relationship has survived so much: him moving to Vermont, her dating Jeffrey, Todd's secret romance with me. Through it all, they've always shared a once-in-a-lifetime passion and commitment.

"And that's OK with me," I whispered. I crawled back into bed, a tired smile on my face.

I'd call Todd later and talk some sense into him. Things would work out for all of us. Peace stole into my soul and I closed my eyes, dropping instantly to sleep.

I woke with a start a few hours later. *What time is it?* I wondered, rolling over and squinting at the clock on my night table. Twelve noon. "I definitely need more sleep," I mumbled into my pillow, pulling the covers back over my head.

I was starting to drift off again when I heard a sound—maybe the same sound that had woken me up in the first place. I sat up in bed, listening more carefully. There it was again. Voices. *Elizabeth*, I realized. *And Todd!*

I bolted over to the open window and pushed the filmy curtain aside. Sure enough, my sister and Todd were down below, outside on the patio. There was a pitcher of juice on the table, and a box of doughnuts and a bouquet of flowers as well. But Elizabeth and Todd were too busy for brunch. They were squeezed onto the same chaise lounge, looking a lot like a human pretzel. Todd said something and Elizabeth giggled. Then she whispered in his ear and he kissed her on the nose.

Snatches of their conversation drifted up to me. "I don't know why I flipped out like that," Todd was saying. "I guess sometimes I worry because you're so independent. You don't seem to need me."

"I need you tons," Elizabeth assured him. "But I think you're right about one thing. Every now and then we get too busy doing our own things, and we don't make enough time for us. We stop being in tune with each other and we get out of sync. That's when it's easy to have a misunderstanding."

"Let's not take each other for granted, ever," Todd said.

They kissed again and I turned away from the

window, smiling sleepily. What had Lila said yesterday? Trouble in paradise for the perfect couple? It certainly looked as if they'd made up. Elizabeth and Todd were in heaven again.

I took a quick shower and threw on a bathing suit and cover-up. Trotting downstairs, I grabbed a peach from the fruit bowl on the kitchen counter and sauntered out to the pool.

Elizabeth and Todd were still in a tight clinch and didn't see or hear me. "Don't bother getting up," I drawled, dropping into a chair and chomping into my peach.

They sprang apart, sheepish looks on their faces. As Elizabeth tried to smooth her rumpled hair and clothes, I gave Todd a secret thumbs-up sign. He smiled, the message in his dark brown eyes clear as the midday sky. *Thanks for understanding.*

"Morning, Jess," he said. "Or should I say, afternoon?"

"I would've slept until dinnertime if you guys hadn't been yakking so loud." I yawned widely. "I didn't sleep too well last night."

"Me either," Todd said. "I had this really bad dream."

There was the tiniest hint of a question in his voice. I nodded, assuring him that I'd reached the exact same conclusion. If he broke up with Elizabeth to go out with me, it really would be a nightmare! "What a coincidence," I replied. "So did I."

Elizabeth laughed. "You two are on the same wavelength. Maybe you should be going out," she kidded.

Todd raised his eyebrows in surprise. I blinked. If she only knew how close she was to the truth!

Recovering quickly, we both groaned, exaggerated expressions of distaste on our faces. "No way!" we shouted together, and then all three of us broke into laughter.

Bantam Books in the Sweet Valley High series
Ask your bookseller for the books you have missed

SIGN UP FOR THE SWEET VALLEY HIGH® FAN CLUB!

Hey, girls! Get all the gossip on Sweet Valley High's® most popular teenagers when you join our fantastic Fan Club! As a member, you'll get all of this really cool stuff:

- Membership Card with your own personal Fan Club ID number
- A Sweet Valley High® Secret Treasure Box
- Sweet Valley High® Stationery
- Official Fan Club Pencil (for secret note writing!)
- Three Bookmarks
- A "Members Only" Door Hanger
- Two Skeins of J. & P. Coats® Embroidery Floss with flower barrette instruction leaflet
- Two editions of *The Oracle* newsletter
- Plus exclusive Sweet Valley High® product offers, special savings, contests, and much more!

Be the first to find out what Jessica & Elizabeth Wakefield are up to by joining the Sweet Valley High® Fan Club for the one-year membership fee of only $6.25 each for U.S. residents, $8.25 for Canadian residents (U.S. currency). Includes shipping & handling.

Send a check or money order (do not send cash) made payable to "Sweet Valley High® Fan Club" along with this form to:

SWEET VALLEY HIGH® FAN CLUB, BOX 3919-B, SCHAUMBURG, IL 60168-3919

NAME _____
(Please print clearly)

ADDRESS _____

CITY_____ STATE _____ ZIP_____
(Required)

AGE _____ BIRTHDAY_____ / _____ / _____

Offer good while supplies last. Allow 6-8 weeks after check clearance for delivery. Addresses without ZIP codes cannot be honored. Offer good in USA & Canada only. Void where prohibited by law.
©1993 by Francine Pascal   LCI-1383-123